*L²⁰*

***The woman was full of contrasts, Cameron thought. Fire and ice. Sweet and wary.***

Haley's arms slid up his shoulders, glided around his neck, and he reveled in the abandonment with which she finally let go.

He wondered if she would do the same while making love.

The thought brought him up short. He preferred the slow, lazy route to getting a woman into bed. He liked the chase and the control. But right now, he didn't feel so leisurely, or in control. Haley had done funny things to his head, as if he'd had too much wine. He wanted to toss her onto the bed and bury himself in her.

Yet she was lying to him, hiding something, and he knew it. He badly wanted to believe in her, but he couldn't.

What if this woman he wanted so badly was a criminal on the run…?

Dear Reader,

It's autumn. There's a nip in the air, the light has a special quality it only takes on at this time of year, and soon witches and warlocks (most of them under three feet tall!) will be walking the streets of towns everywhere. And along with them will come vampires, perhaps the most dangerously alluring of all romantic heroes. (The six-foot-tall variety, anyway!) So in honor of the season, this month we're bringing you *Brides of the Night,* a two-in-one collection featuring vampire heroes who are (dare I say it?) to die for. Maggie Shayne continues her wonderful WINGS IN THE NIGHT miniseries with *Twilight Vows,* while Marilyn Tracy lures you in with *Married by Dawn.* Let them wrap you in magic.

We've got more great miniseries going on this month, too. With *Harvard's Education,* Suzanne Brockmann continues her top-selling TALL, DARK AND DANGEROUS miniseries. Readers have been asking for Harvard's story, and now this quintessential tough guy is rewarded with a romance of his own. Then follow our writers out west, as Carla Cassidy begins the saga of MUSTANG, MONTANA, with *Her Counterfeit Husband,* and Margaret Watson returns to CAMERON, UTAH, in *For the Children.* Jill Shalvis, an experienced author making her first appearance here, also knows how great a cowboy hero can be, as she demonstrates in our WAY OUT WEST title, *Hiding Out at the Circle C.* Finally, welcome Hilary Byrnes. This brand-new author is Intimate Moments' WOMAN TO WATCH. And after you read her powerful debut, *Motive, Means...and Marriage?* you *will* be watching—for her next book!

Enjoy! And come back again next month, when we bring you six more of the best and most exciting romance novels around—right here in Silhouette Intimate Moments.

Leslie J. Wainger
Executive Senior Editor

Please address questions and book requests to:
Silhouette Reader Service
U.S.: 3010 Walden Ave., P.O. Box 1325, Buffalo, NY 14269
Canadian: P.O. Box 609, Fort Erie, Ont. L2A 5X3

*Lee/1*

# HIDING OUT AT
# THE CIRCLE C

## JILL SHALVIS

INTIMATE™MOMENTS®

Published by Silhouette Books
**America's Publisher of Contemporary Romance**

SILHOUETTE BOOKS

ISBN 0-373-07887-0

HIDING OUT AT THE CIRCLE C

## *JILL SHALVIS*

When pressed for an answer on why she writes romance, Jill Shalvis just smiles and says she didn't realize there was anything else. She's written over a dozen novels so far and doesn't plan on stopping. She lives in California, in a house filled with young children, too many animals and her hero/husband. You can write to her at P.O. Box 1280, Chino, CA 91708-1280.

For the laughs, the companionship,
the acceptance, the fun. For all the love in our life.
Forever to David.

# *Prologue*

She had to hurry. Her very life could depend on it. Sprinting up the stairs to the tiny flat she and the other geologists stayed in during their stint with EVS—Earthquake/Volcano Studies—in South America, Haley came to a skidding halt.

Blood stained the open door. Just inside lay two very still bodies. Oh, God. Danyella and Frederick. Her colleagues. *Her friends.*

Haley backed up, feeling faint and stiff with terror. But for the grace of God, it could have been *her* lying dead on the floor. She slapped a hand over her mouth to stifle her panicked breathing and whirled, running as fast as she could back down the stairs.

The sharp pain in her abdomen told her that she needed the ulcer medicine in her purse, badly, but she couldn't stop. If she did, they'd find her, and Haley doubted she'd ever need her medicine again.

*Think, think.* She had to think, but it was all she could do not to scream in frustration and fear. Last week, she'd made *the* discovery. The one she'd worked on for so long. She'd created a system that would take some of the mystery out of earthquakes and volcanoes. But something had gone wrong—terribly wrong. Earlier today, she'd found EVS's office building destroyed by a bomb. And now she'd made the grisly discovery that two of her five-member team had been murdered. If what she suspected was true, Haley had no doubt she'd be next. The team would be systematically wiped out, one by one, because of greed.

It was simple. She believed her system priceless because of the lives that could be saved. But someone else cared more about the quick money to be made. With a strength she didn't know she possessed, Haley calmed herself and hailed a taxi, holding her breath in the oppressive heat as the insane driver sped into traffic, dodging through throngs of people, bikes and cars.

The taxi screeched to a halt at the international airport in Peru, and so did her heart. She had no family who would help, and nowhere to go except...home. The United States.

Watching her back, feeling desperate and more frightened than she'd ever been, she got on the first plane she could—to Los Angeles. She had little cash, but stopping at the bank just didn't seem plausible at the moment, so she used a credit card.

Haley had come to this continent with other brilliant geologists, to study earth movement. It had been Japan before that, and before that, Europe. Anywhere plagued by volcanoes and earthquakes. She'd been the youngest on the team, but wasn't she always? Having finished her doctorate by her middle teens, Dr. Haley Whitfield had been quickly accepted into the elite group at EVS. Their goal: to predict earthquakes and volcanoes in order to save and preserve lives. She'd done her part—developed an undersea computerized system that would help anticipate those events—but she'd never in her wildest dreams thought it would be used to cause them. Yet, that's what someone had done. Used her ideas to *create* earth movement. To kill.

She knew this without a doubt. Knew that yesterday's tragic earthquake several hundred miles to the south, on an unknown and totally uncharted fault, hadn't been natural. Thousands had died—because of her system.

Motivated by adrenaline and fear, she rushed toward her departure gate, numb with shock. Work was her life, and everything—absolutely everything she'd worked for—she was leaving behind. The pain in her stomach twisted like a knife. Who knew where Bob and Alda, the other two geologists were, or if they were even alive? Or if Lloyd Branson, head of EVS, had escaped the bomb? Had the sweet, quiet, unassuming man been murdered, too? Her heart ached for those she'd known as her only friends, and she prayed they were safe, that they were right this minute fleeing as she was.

Somehow she made it through the flight to L.A. The minute she got off the plane, the pager on her hip vibrated to life, nearly scaring her right out of her skin. With shaking hands, ignoring the crowd jostling around her, she lifted EVS's high-tech, compact pager and saw she had two messages. The heavy turbulence on the plane must have masked the vibration.

The first printed message renewed her terror.

It was from a South American number, and signed "Alda." "Haley, I hope you've gone. They think you're responsible! Run, Haley. If you haven't already, run!"

Haley swallowed hard. So she wasn't the only one left alive, thank God!

But the second message had her staggering to a chair, mindless of the crowd around her. It, too, was from South America, from another number she didn't recognize.

"Come back or you're next."

She was next.

What now? The U.S. government had its own program going at the United States Geological Survey, the nation's center for earthquake research. Studying plate tectonics and shifts in the earth's crust, they also searched for methods of prediction. The geologists there were also developing a way to reduce the effects of earthquakes, utilizing a method that would eventually approximate the system that Haley had already created. But the

USGS believed they were the brightest and the best. They'd never accept the fact that she'd developed a superior system—only to lose it.

Haley firmly turned off her pager, but couldn't bring herself to throw it away. Somehow, sick as it seemed, the thing was her only link to that insane world. She shivered and closed her eyes, willing herself not to cry. She could be thankful for one thing—that without her or the other geologists to recreate it, the system couldn't be used again. And without the notes and records destroyed in the bomb blast, she couldn't produce another system like it in less than a year.

So here she was, running for her life, a suspect in the bombing and the murders. Those were crimes for which, if extradited back to South America, she'd be executed swiftly. What to do?

Well, if she didn't want to die, she had to completely disappear.

Suddenly Haley felt three times her twenty-five years. Yet she was alive, wasn't she? So what if all she had was the twenty dollars in her purse and the clothes on her back? She was alive, she reminded herself again as she swallowed two pills for her ulcer. For however long, *she was alive*.

She blinked back tears and forced herself to remember that was a *good* thing.

# Chapter 1

When the plane from Los Angeles finally arrived in Colorado Springs, everyone waiting in the terminal moved and shifted in anticipation. Everyone, that is, except Cameron Reeves.

He leaned negligently against the wall, as far away from the hustle and bustle as possible. While waiting for the aircraft to unload, he amused himself by watching the people rush around like busy little ants. Nellie, his sister-in-law, was no different. She burst off the plane with her usual sense of urgency and he found himself grinning at the sight of her, bulging with pregnancy. He saw her turn her head to a woman walking next to her, whisper something, then squeeze the woman's hand before coming toward him.

"Cam!" She stopped short, her seven-and-a-half-months-pregnant belly taking up the entire aisle. Hands on her hips, she gave him the once-over, ignoring the poor people struggling to get around her. "Where's Jason?"

"I came instead."

"Why?" she demanded. "What's the matter?"

"Now there, Nellie—" he started, ready to soothe. In the two weeks she'd been visiting her mother in Los Angeles, she'd ballooned. She looked ready to pop.

Her pretty green eyes narrowed and Cam wondered if all women, no matter how even-tempered, turned psychotic while pregnant. "Don't tell me," she insisted, holding up a hand. "I'm sure I don't want to know."

"It's not serious, Nellie. Jason just..." Cam hesitated, watching with fascination as people managed to push and shove their way around this huge woman who, just last spring, had been the tiniest thing he'd ever seen.

"He just what, Cameron?"

He winced at the use of his full name. Well, his brother had warned him she'd be ticked. "Okay, he fell off the barn roof—"

*"What?"*

"But it's only a sprained wrist. I swear it."

They looked at each other, brother and sister-in-law, and despite their equal concern for Jason, smiled. Then laughed. Jason was undoubtedly the clumsiest, most wonderful man alive. And they both loved him.

"How come Zach didn't come?"

Cameron grinned at that. His other brother had vowed to stay as far away from either Jason or Nellie as much as humanly possible. "He's afraid that growth you've got going there is contagious." He reached out to rub her belly fondly, taking it as a good sign when she didn't snap his hand off.

"Poor Jas. Only a sprain, huh?" Nellie sighed, relented, and finally moved to hug Cam. Her stomach hit him first, and he staggered slightly, before adjusting himself to accept her weight.

"Nice visit with your mother?" Cam pulled her to his side and they started to walk.

"*Yeah, right.* Cam, wait." Nellie slanted him a indecipherable look. "Actually, this works out better that Jas stayed home. You'll handle this better than he would, anyway."

"Handle what?"

Nellie glanced over her shoulder, then looked at him. "We're still looking for a housekeeper, right?"

She knew they were. They lived in an isolated area, the Circle C Ranch somewhere between too big to be small, and too small to be big. Even though both his brothers loved ranching, they struggled with the work. It didn't help that since the last housekeeper had left about six months ago, Nellie had been killing them all slowly and painfully with her horrid cooking and experimental casseroles. Or that no one wanted to clean the ranch house regularly because they all were exhausted from the long, hard days outside. Not to mention the house's sheer size. Now, with Nellie pregnant, Jason worried about her working too hard.

"Don't tell me," Cam said cautiously. "You decided to take cooking lessons."

"No, something better." She pulled away from him and took his hands. "I've hired a housekeeper. I don't know how long she'll stay, but—"

"You hired us a housekeeper on the plane from Los Angeles?"

"I met her in LAX. My plane was late, and I'd gotten hungry—"

"There's a surprise— Oof." Cam rubbed his gut, which Nellie had just elbowed. "Go on."

"My arms were full. A million people were pushing and shoving and this woman was the only one who stopped to help me." Her eyes filled with sorrow. "Oh, Cam. You should have seen her, poor thing. She can't be any older than me, and she's so scared. I think she's running from someone, and I—"

"And you just wanted to help."

"Yes."

Cam understood perfectly. He and Nellie shared what the rest of the family called the "bleeding-heart syndrome." Both had a deep, burning desire to right wrongs, fix other people's lives and bring home strays. Cam lifted his head, shifting his gaze over the remaining passengers. He found her immediately. She stood rock still and apart, her shoulders squared, head high. He didn't see anything but her pale, proud, tear-ravaged face. She looked at him—*straight* at him—and when their eyes met, he felt a jolt.

Her eyes were electric blue. And even from far away, they were the widest, deepest eyes he'd ever seen. For the first time in too long, he felt a stirring of something he couldn't name. He swallowed hard against it.

"She's alone?" he asked in a low voice.

"All alone. And nowhere to go. Her name's Haley and all I know is she flew in from South America, but she's from the States. Somewhere."

As collectors of the needy, he knew neither he nor Nellie could care less if the young woman could cook or clean. All that mattered was that she needed them. But both of them knew from past experience that Zach and Jason weren't easy sells.

"She's wonderful," Nellie said quickly. "We bonded immediately."

Which, given Nellie's current temperament, said a lot. Besides, Cam trusted her instincts implicitly. "All right," he said, his gaze still locked on the woman.

"All right? Oh, Cam, just like that?" Impulsively, Nellie hugged him again, laughing in delight. "Sometimes I think I married the wrong Reeves."

"You know you did." He grinned.

She still held him close, the baby between them like a basketball. She batted her eyelashes at him. "Will you tell Jason about her?"

He laughed and shook her off. "No way."

*"Please?"*

Still looking at the woman, because strangely enough, he couldn't tear his eyes away, he asked, "You promise not to cook anymore?"

"I promise."

"Deal, then." He couldn't ask for more. "I'll tell Jason."

"And Zach," she clarified.

"Yeah, and Zach. But it's going to cost you." There would be hell to pay for this, he knew. Just last month, when he'd brought home the abused puppy, the one that even Jason couldn't doctor up, they'd spent three hundred dollars on surgery and veterinarian fees. Zach and Jason both had extracted a promise from him not to bring home anything else, but Cam would worry about that later.

With Nellie in tow, he threaded his way through the waning crowd and stopped before the woman.

"Hello." Cam flashed a quick, self-deprecating smile that hopefully signaled he was harmless. A tad too thin, he decided. He usually liked long hair on a woman, but her dark, short cut swung gently to her chin, suiting her narrow features. She had a pale, elegant face that at this moment was staring at him as if *he* were the one being interviewed. "I hear you'd like a job," he said to her.

She nodded—regally, he thought—giving him a queen-to-peasant look that had his smile spreading. Spunk. He liked that, too.

"You live on a ranch, far from town?" she asked, a flicker of a frown crossing her face.

"Pretty far from Colorado Springs," he admitted, sensing her unease, and again giving her that smile that said he couldn't hurt a fly. "The Circle C is north and slightly east, at the base of the mountains. It's an hour from here."

"Isolated?"

He grinned. "Isolated enough that Nellie has to talk to herself for company."

Nellie rolled her eyes. "There are some small towns out that way," she told Haley. "But nothing close to the size of Colorado Springs."

"Good." She straightened her already impossibly straight shoulders. "Yes, Mr. Reeves, I'd like a job."

He had absolutely no idea what he was going to do with a hoity-toity housekeeper, except enjoy looking at her. "My name's Cameron. Cam, if you'd like. That's what my friends call me."

"Thank you." She nodded, and though she was a good foot

shorter than him, she managed to tilt her nose down at him.
"Cameron. My name is Haley W-Williams."

God, he loved that voice instantly, all deep and husky as if
she'd just woken up. A man could lose himself in a voice like
that. But while her vocal cords screamed sex, nothing else about
this woman did. Her shadowed eyes barely hid her exhaustion
and something else that might have been fear. She hugged her
purse close to her, and for the first time, he noticed that she
didn't seem to be dressed properly for autumn in the Rockies.
Her thin blouse tucked into trim-but-also-thin slacks wouldn't
protect her once they went outside the terminal.

And since when did a homeless, down-on-her-luck housekeeper wear clothes that looked like they came from Saks Fifth
Avenue?

"Let's go get our luggage," Nellie said.

"I have none," Haley said quietly, though her eyes were
anything but calm.

Cam watched a hardness come into that electric-blue gaze.
His mild curiosity leaped to avid stage. "Well, then," he said
lightly, giving Nellie a look when she opened her mouth to
express sympathy he instinctively knew Haley wouldn't appreciate, "we'll just get Nellie's then. Ladies? Shall we go?" He
offered them each an arm, amused when Haley refused to take
it. When he had Nellie's suitcase, he directed the women toward
the exit.

"Wait," she said. "This position... It's for room and board?"

The position offered whatever she needed, but he didn't say
that. "Yes."

"I'd have my own room?"

She needed a place to stay, that much was obvious. As well,
she'd need some more clothes and personal things. But at the
moment, he was more concerned with soothing her obvious mistrust of him, and wariness of any implied "duties," than anything else. "Yes, of course. Our ranch house is large, but we
also have a guesthouse. It'll be all yours, if you want it. You'd

eat with us since you'll be cooking. And we can come up with an agreeable salary, I'm sure.''

She'd gone from fragile and frail to downright beautiful as pride and anger sparked color into her pale cheeks.

''I won't do any...*anything* except cook and clean.'' She lifted her chin.

Damn, but her dignity had his blood humming. And her haughty indignation tickled him, though he struggled not to show it. He appreciated the glory of a woman's temper, but didn't like to cause it. No, that was something he steered clear of—except for Nellie because it was so much fun to goad her. And because *he* didn't have to sleep with her at night; Jason did. ''I wouldn't expect anything else from you.''

Haley stared at him, weighing his words for honesty.

Nellie smiled gently at her. ''Believe me, Haley, no one will bother you. You'll be safe.''

Haley turned away, needing to think for a moment. Running for her life, she realized this job was her only choice. Her credit cards were useless. She could be traced as far as L.A., she knew that. That was why she'd used a cash machine at LAX to withdraw money for the flight with Nellie. From L.A. International she could have gone anywhere, and since she hadn't used her real name when buying her ticket, there would be no way to figure out her location—unless she used her cards or withdrew more cash.

Thank God Nellie had come along when she did. After her brief spell of panic and self-pity on arriving at LAX, Haley had turned her pager on again out of morbid curiosity. She'd immediately gotten another grim message from South America.

''You can run, but you can't hide. I'll find you.''

That was when she'd met Nellie. Haley chose to believe it had been fate, for she'd needed to get safely away and think. She *could* have tried to find her mother. Last she knew, Isabella Whitfield had been in Manhattan, but Haley knew she'd have been far from welcome there. And wouldn't this mess she'd gotten herself into just prove to her mother once and for all what a failure she was?

But to go with this stranger and his wife simply because she'd liked the woman on sight? Because she'd looked into Nellie's eyes and felt a kinship she couldn't explain?

"Haley? You ready?" Nellie asked.

It seemed too easy. Too good to be true. To just disappear for a while in the Colorado Rockies and pretend to be a house-keeper. Suspicion was second nature to her. "That's it? Let's go? Just like that, you're going to take me to your home?"

Cam looked at the kind, warm Nellie, exchanged an indecipherable glance, then turned back to Haley with an easy shrug. "Yep."

The man wasn't harmless, despite his light and easy manner and smooth, charming voice. No man with eyes that full of blatant sexuality could be harmless. And Haley didn't need a seismograph to register that smile as ground-shaking. "Aren't you going to ask me for my references?" she questioned, expecting it all to be a trick, or a trap. "Or if I can even *cook* for God's sake?"

His smile was slow, wide and devastating. "Darlin', if you don't burn water, you can cook better than Nellie, here. And we'll be mighty grateful for that, believe me." He chuckled when Nellie jammed an elbow into his stomach. He rubbed the spot with his hand.

"What if I'm a mass murderer, or on the run?" Perverse of her to push her luck, she knew, but she couldn't help it.

"Are you?" he asked, his thumbs hooked through his belt loops. He didn't look overly concerned.

"No. Not a mass murderer, that is." She gave an involuntary shudder as the bloody image of her team flashed through her mind. God, would she ever be able to forget? Or sleep again? At that moment, she doubted it, but the first and foremost thing had become survival. Even a couple of hours ago, she'd been ready to give up, to let them catch her. But no longer.

She wanted to live.

*She* wanted to catch *them.*

Cameron looked at her, and though he could have no idea what was going on in her head, she saw a rush of compassion in his eyes.

"As long as you're not wanted by the law," he said easily, "I don't have a problem. Nellie doesn't, either."

Well, she *was* wanted, but evasion of that statement came shamefully easy. Anything would have, to protect her neck. Literally. "You trust your wife's judgment, then."

He nearly choked with laughter and her eyes narrowed as she took a step backward. With a small giggle, Nellie hurried to explain. "No, Haley, this isn't the husband I told you about. Cam's my brother-in-law. Jason couldn't come. He...well, he fell off a roof," she finished lamely, watching as Haley took another step away. "It's really not as crazy as you think."

"No, it's not," Cameron said, that insufferable grin in place. "Besides, everyone knows Zach is the crazy one, not me or Jason."

"Cam!" Nellie sighed and shook her head as she took Haley's hand, pulling her forward. "Please, don't misunderstand. We all live together on the ranch, and we need a housekeeper, just like I told you. Desperately."

What were her choices? She couldn't call the police, not while she was the main suspect in the EVS bombing. They'd send her back and she'd face trial— The thought made her stomach flop. She needed a place to hide, a place where she'd be safe until she could figure out what to do without getting herself killed. "Why me?"

"Because I like you," Nellie said, lightly squeezing her hand.

Just that easy gesture nearly undid Haley. When was the last time she'd been offered unconditional friendship? Affection? Been accepted for a reason other than her brain?

Nellie, still holding her hand, added, "And because I'm living in a houseful of men who don't know squat about what it's like to be female. Something between us clicked from that first moment, Haley. I felt it, and I know you did, too, or you wouldn't even be considering this. If you don't come, I'll worry about you. You don't want that.''

"You don't even know me." How in the world could these people be so trusting? Didn't they know what kind of world they lived in? Of course not, they lived in Colorado. On some little ranch where nothing penetrated. It sounded...lovely, irresistible. Safe. And when it came right down to it, what other choices did she have? None. "Okay," she breathed.

"Okay?" Nellie repeated, rubbing her belly, looking tired. "You'll come, then?"

"I'll come."

Nellie laughed once, then hugged her tightly. Feeling awkward, uncertain, Haley patted her back, meeting Cam's eyes over Nellie's shoulder. They were warm, easy and friendly. Relieved. Haley didn't want to think about that—how a complete stranger could care so much. She pulled away from the unaccustomed contact and shoved her hands into her pockets. It was easy to be nice to Nellie because she liked her. It wouldn't be so easy, however, to be nice to Cameron Reeves. She most definitely didn't *want* to like him. She couldn't afford to.

It didn't matter; she wouldn't be staying long.

"I'm so glad you'll come," Nellie whispered, grabbing her hand. They walked then, in companionable silence, weeding their way through the hordes of people, and Haley was thankful for the few moments of quiet.

No one could have followed her. Maybe whoever was terrorizing her would assume she'd been killed in the explosion. Relief at that thought made her giddy. Until she remembered her messages.

They stopped at the exit. Cold air blasted through the opening. She glanced up in surprise as Cam stripped off his denim jacket. He held it out, going still when she backed from him. She'd accept his job offer because she didn't have a choice, but she wouldn't accept his charity.

"Take the jacket," he said easily. "It's not going to bite."

No, but *he* might.

"It's cold out," Nellie added, belting her own sweater high over the bulge of baby.

It had been hot in South America. Haley hadn't thought of this. "I'll be all right." She felt the flood of heat fill her face as they both looked at her. Cam's features were purposely inscrutable, but she felt sure he hid pity—and she hated that.

Nellie didn't manage to hide a thing and she looked at her, worry and concern evident.

"Take the jacket, Haley," Cam said. "She'll hound you about it, otherwise. It's easier this way." Then, without waiting for a response, he wrapped it around her shoulders, holding it while she slid her arms into the sleeves. She felt surrounded by warmth, softness and an unfamiliar-yet-heavenly scent.

Cam pushed her gently out the swinging glass doors. The sky loomed dark, and Haley realized she had absolutely no sense of time.

They headed across the street to the parking structure, Cam attentively holding on to Nellie, who seemed tired. "Not too much farther, Nel," he murmured, craning his neck to check for cars.

Nearly across the street, all three of them stopped in surprised shock when, with a loud squealing of tires, a taxi gunned its way directly toward them.

Haley froze, capable of only one thought—*They found me and now they're going to kill two innocent people to get me!*

Cam muttered a ripe oath as the taxi swerved recklessly away, spraying them with gravel. Immediately he pushed back Nellie's hair to see her face. "You okay, Nel?"

"Fine. Idiot!" Nellie shook her head. "He's going to kill someone, or at least give them heart failure."

Haley stood still, shaking, as both Nellie and Cameron shrugged it off.

"Haley?"

She blinked, realizing that Cam had taken her shoulders. Her heart slammed in her chest. "It was just a taxi," she said dazedly.

"Yes," he said, concern deepening his voice.

One warm hand slid up to cup the back of her neck and she knew by the tightening of his jaw that he could feel her trembling like a frightened rabbit. She struggled for control, but found herself babbling helplessly. "Just a stupid taxi driver in a hurry."

"That's right," he said in a low, soothing voice. "Just a guy trying to make a buck. And he's gone. He can't hurt you."

Because his kind voice threatened to release the emotions she held so tight and deep inside, Haley shoved his hand away. "I'm okay."

His lips curved, as if he was undisturbed by her abruptness, approved of her toughness.

"Come on," Nellie said, still shaking her head. "Let's get out of the middle of the street."

Haley let them pull her along, but she wasn't so far gone that she missed the single, worried look exchanged between brother and sister-in-law.

At Cam's truck, a brown-and-white puppy with ears bigger than his body jumped up in the window, wiggling and barking happily.

"This is Max," Cam told her, gently pushing the animal aside, after letting it lick his face. "Hey, Max, calm down, would ya?" He bent low to the puppy and whispered conspiratorially, "I've told you before, never let a female see how eager you are." Fondly, he rubbed the dog's ears.

Nellie petted the puppy, too, enduring more of the happy, ecstatic kisses, then crawled into the back seat, claiming exhaustion. "I'm going to take a little nap," she said, yawning and rubbing her stomach. "Cam, just carry me in when we get there."

"But Nel, I'll break my back."

"Oh, shut up," she muttered good-naturedly.

Haley hesitated, her gaze frozen on the bouncing dog.

"He won't bite," Cam assured her.

"What kind is he?"

"A purebred mutt." He grinned. "Just stick out your hand so he can sniff it."

At the moment, her fear of what she'd just left behind overruled her fear of Max. There'd definitely not been much time in her life for dogs—if any. She cautiously held out a hand. The little guy wriggled hopefully, then nailed her with his large, puppy-dog eyes. They were the warmest, biggest eyes she'd ever seen. Something inside her softened. "Hi there," she said, reaching for him. She jumped when his warm, wet tongue licked her fingers. "Max seems an ostentatious name for such a little thing."

"It's a nickname for Maximum-Amount-of-Money-Ever-Spent-on-a-Dog," Cameron said wryly. "Vet bills. Lots of them. Don't ask." He held open the door for her and she climbed into the front. Max settled in the back, on top of the already groggy Nellie.

"Find your own spot, buddy," she mumbled. But she let the puppy stretch out on her.

Cameron started the truck, maneuvering out of the lot while Haley waited tensely for him to bombard her with questions.

They left the city and the lights far behind as they headed down a narrow highway toward the black mountains in the distance. In the back seat Nellie's breathing evened out. So did Max's. Cam adjusted the heater to nice and low, aimed at Haley's feet, which were icy cold in her meager flats. With a flick of his wrist, the interior of the truck was filled with soft, country blues.

She was in a strange place, in a stranger's truck, heading toward some unknown ranch house in the middle of nowhere. Panic filled her for a moment as the realization hit her. *She must be insane!*

No, not insane, just desperate. And no matter what happened, it would be better than what *would* happen to her if she gave up. Again, her gut twisted painfully at the thought of her lifelong work—all destroyed, gone forever.

She was going to a place where no one knew her past, or

what she'd done. She could just be Haley Williams for a while—whoever *she* was—and that was a surprising relief.

She nearly hit her head on the roof of the truck, when after ten full minutes of silence, Cam said, "You can relax a little bit, Haley. You'll snap in two if you pull yourself any tighter than you are."

It was true. She gazed out the window. The mountains were getting closer. "I'm fine."

"Are you?" He shot her a look. "You don't look fine. Are you in pain?"

Oh, great. So the man could read minds as well as look sexy as sin. "No," she lied; slowly, surreptitiously, bringing her hands from her lap to her stomach to press away the nagging ache. "Of course not."

His eyes slid over the movement, but he didn't comment, just drove with that quiet confidence that could slowly drive her crazy. Why didn't he ask her questions? Demand answers? She would. *Anyone* would. Finally, when she couldn't stand it any longer, she exclaimed, "Go ahead! Just get it over with. Ask me!"

His eyes didn't leave the dark, narrow road, but his lips twitched. "I'm not going to ask you anything."

She wasn't the crazy one, she decided. *He was.* "Humph."

He smiled. "What sorts of things should I be asking you?"

"*Lots* of things." She looked at him. "Like where I came from. What I do for a living."

He went quiet for a moment. "Do you really want me to ask you those things?"

"No!" she snapped. "Oh, just forget it." She sighed, shifted, and tried not to notice how wonderfully warm his jacket felt, how good it smelled.

"Why would it matter to me what you've done for a living, as long as you can take care of cooking and cleaning my house?" he asked curiously.

She'd been taught manners at an incredibly young age so she managed to catch herself before she sputtered at his ridiculous question. "Because you've hired me. You *should* care what I've done."

His eyes met hers then, and for the first time she realized how dark and melting their brown depths were. "What if I trust you?" he asked.

Haley thought of how the system she'd created had allowed someone to kill innocent people instead of save them. Thought of the pager that sat in her purse, ready to terrify her again at a moment's notice. The truth was, she hadn't deserved to get away alive. Yet, this man sitting next to her, this *stranger,* trusted her. "You should be more careful with that trust," she said carefully. "You could get hurt."

Something flickered in his eyes, then was gone. "Not me."

But he *had* been hurt, she realized with sudden insight. At some point, he'd been badly hurt. And no matter how casual he appeared, he would only let her get away with so much. He was not stupid—not by a long shot. "You don't even know if I can cook."

"I'll take my chances."

She muttered under her breath about the lackadaisical attitude of Midwestern cowboys, but he ignored the verbal attack and seemed amused.

"Why, darlin', you sound like you care what happens to me," he drawled.

"Of course, I do. You're writing the paycheck."

He laughed and shook his head. And drove on into the night, never once bothering her about her past.

Hands propped behind his head, Cam stared at the ceiling. Having trouble sleeping hadn't been a problem in a long time, but it was late and here he lay, still trying to drift off.

Both Jason and Zach had accepted Haley easily. Especially since, he'd noted with amusement, she'd managed to charm both of them without trying. He found it vastly interesting that she didn't use that same charm on him. In fact, she did everything in her power to make sure he *didn't* notice her.

It wasn't working.

Oh, he knew he had no business hiring her for the sort of work he needed done without knowing if she was even fully capable. Cooking the hearty meals necessary for him and his brothers would be a challenge. So would keeping up the big house. But something about the wary, vulnerable-looking Haley Williams had appealed to his soft spot, which was never far beneath the surface.

Maybe it had been the pride and intelligence—two of his favorite qualities—he'd seen shimmering in her eyes. It didn't matter what her past was, she needed help in some way or other, and he could provide it.

That was all. It had nothing to do with her being a woman.

Oh, he loved women—all kinds. But it didn't mean he could be serious about them. He had done that once and would *never* do it again.

Never.

There was more to life than pain, stress and hard work. *Much more*. He liked to take things easy now. Enjoy and Savor—that was his motto. That was why he tinkered with making furniture instead of working in Denver at the stock brokerage, as he had for years. It was why he let his brothers run the ranch that was his. Some considered it a lazy way of life for a man just short of his thirty-second birthday, but not Cam. Thanks to a lesson learned the hard way, he knew just how precious life could be— and he intended to get the most out of it this time around.

Which meant all he wanted was to help Haley in any way he could, and enjoy her hopefully excellent cooking.

*Nothing else.*

But the truth of it was, he couldn't forget the wariness in her eyes after she'd gotten off the plane, or her terror during the taxi incident. Or how gallantly she'd tried to shrug them off. She might think she'd fooled him, but beneath her rough-and-tough exterior, she was scared.

And he wanted to know why. Just to protect his family, of

course. For no way would he allow himself to become *personally* involved.

Haley lay in her bed, far from the main house in a tiny, but lovely cottage, hopelessly wide-awake in spite of her exhaustion. Max was sprawled on her feet—a warm little bundle of fur. He'd insisted on coming with her, though she didn't know why. She hadn't encouraged him in any way, yet he'd followed her out of the truck. Nellie had asked if she minded, and what could she say? Then Nellie told her that Max had been found abused and abandoned, and that he still wasn't entirely comfortable around men. He also didn't like to sleep alone.

Well, that made two of them, on both counts. Haley had never been comfortable with men, either. Or dogs. Mostly because she'd never been around them much. Her mother had loved the male species, but had thought dogs nasty beasts—not that either attitude would have affected Haley much at boarding school. Dogs—and men—hadn't been allowed.

She lifted her head and peeked at the sleeping Max. The little guy seemed harmless enough. He was even sort of cute, in a puppy sort of way.

Her stomach felt like fire, as a combination of nerves and acid burned the already painful ulcer. Hugging a pillow to soften the pain, she rolled onto her side and stared out the window into the night.

Colorado was the most incredible, magnificent place she'd ever seen—and she'd seen plenty. The rolling hills, the tall, noisy trees she knew to be aspens, the vast black sky, the isolation...it all appealed to her. Amazingly enough, just looking at it seemed to lesson the ache in her stomach.

She could simply get up, take her medicine and a sleeping pill as usual, and be fine until morning. But she didn't want to do that; she wanted to be fine without help.

Sighing, she closed her eyes. Then jerked them open again as the macabre memories of blood and death flashed across her lids.

"Okay, okay," she murmured to herself until her breathing slowed and her heart thudded dully. *You're okay. Alive.*

But Dani and Frederick weren't. And she had no way of knowing about poor Lloyd Branson, her kind boss. Or Bob. Alda seemed okay, but was she safe?

Haley froze.

Could one of them have been responsible? No. *No.* She refused to think about them in the same thought as betrayal. They wouldn't. Couldn't.

But who else knew of the now destroyed system and how much it was worth?

Sitting up, she threw the pillow across the small room. The violent gesture cheered her considerably as she gave herself a tough talk, reminding herself it was past time to shelve the self-pity—and the ulcer—and get on with it.

Max whined softly and looked at her. "It's all right," she said quietly, feeling badly for having scared the little fellow. He looked worried, so serious with that wrinkled forehead. She petted him, then even smiled when he became a boneless, wriggling mass of happiness.

How tempting this life suddenly was. No pressure.

Here she wasn't just a brain. Here she was a real person, with real feelings. Here, for the first time in her entire life, she had a true friend. One who liked her not for her IQ, but for just who she was.

Pulling the beautiful homemade quilt to her chin, Haley inhaled the fragrance of the dried flowers on the lovely oak dresser and allowed herself a smile when Max again settled on her feet with a little grunt. "You like it here, too, huh?" She couldn't blame him. The main house was a dream come true, huge and airy, and decorated with a homey, welcoming charm.

The people inside were the same. She liked Nellie's husband, Jason. Liked the way he absolutely doted on Nellie. Zach seemed quiet and reserved, but had a smile nearly as devastating as... Haley's own soft smile faded as she thought of the *other* brother. Cameron Reeves.

She could list his obvious faults in her head: overtly charming—a fault because she didn't trust "charming"; far too gorgeous for his own good; eyes melting with sensuality—okay, not a fault, but close enough; and a heart of gold. This last she considered a fault only because it made one vulnerable. But he also had another side. There was an edge there; a hard, dangerous side she didn't understand. Didn't want to. She had her own problems.

She liked cool, calm and collected, and she wanted those around her to be the same. But she suspected Cameron was none of those things. No. He was a man who felt, and felt deeply, and didn't mind it a bit. She'd seen the proof of that when he'd allowed Nellie to take her home simply because she had nowhere else to go. Thankful as she was, that just seemed plain crazy.

Or did it? Were there really people in this world who cared so much about the welfare of others?

Haley hadn't missed how Cam had looked at her, and just the remembering had her stomach doing a slow roll. He wasn't simply kind and gentle. He had much more depth than that. He had a rough, sensual facet that scared her. No man had ever looked at her as he did. Actually, men rarely looked at her at all.

And if this was what it did to one's insides, she simply couldn't handle it. She'd have to tell him...what? *Stop looking at me with those sexy eyes that make me think with my hormones?* She snickered at herself, disgusted.

She'd needed to disappear to save her life—and she had. But good Lord, at what cost?

# *Chapter 2*

**S**urprisingly enough, once Haley fell asleep, she didn't budge again until a light knock sounded on her door. Instantly, she came awake, and moaning at the sunlight streaming through her window, she leaped guiltily out of bed.

She'd overslept on her first morning of work.

She ran across the bedroom, mentally berating herself for screwing things up so soon, then nearly killed herself *and* Max, when they got tangled together on their race to the door.

Skidding to a stop, she looked down in dismay. She wore only a chemise and her panties, having had nothing else to sleep in. "Uh...who is it?" she called out, running an agitated hand through her mop of short hair.

"It's Nellie."

The warm cheerful voice went a long way in relieving both Haley and Max. He started a happy whine, but still, Haley hesitated. Surely if everyone was annoyed she'd messed up already, Nellie wouldn't sound so friendly.

"Haley? Are you there? I thought you might want to— Oh, *hell*." Haley could hear Nellie's frustrated sigh through the door. "Haley, there's no polite way to say this, and I don't want to hurt your feelings—"

"I'm fired," Haley said flatly, her stomach tightening. She leaned her forehead against the door. She'd been an idiot to think she could handle this, even for a short time.

"No! No, that's not it at all. Haley, honey, do you think you could open the door?"

Haley glanced around and picked up the light quilt thrown over the back of a chair. She wrapped it around her, and with a fatalistic shrug, opened the door. "I'm so sorry—"

"No, wait," Nellie implored, her hands full of what looked like stacks of clothes. "I just brought you some things. I thought you might need..." She trailed off, looking sheepish as Max barked joyously, obviously thrilled to find two of his favorite people together. "I scared you, I didn't mean to. I know you need something to wear. Max, *please,* be quiet a minute."

Haley pulled the quilt tighter, thinking if she'd ever been more mortified, she couldn't remember. "I'll be fine. I don't need—"

"No. No, don't get embarrassed, please," Nellie said quickly, her eyes full of compassion and nothing that even closely resembled pity, thank God. "I don't want that. Max!" she warned the yipping, wriggling puppy. "Put a lid on it."

"I don't want to take your clothes." It was hard to remain dignified wearing nothing more than a borrowed quilt, but Haley had to try. It was all she had left. "Please, try to understand. This is very difficult for me. I'm not used to needing—"

"Just let me do this." Nellie dropped the clothes onto the couch and sighed as she stretched her back. Ruefully, she glanced down. "I'm wearing maternity clothes now, anyway, so you might as well have these. I know I'm pushing this on you, and it's not because I feel sorry for you." She laughed lightly as she straightened. "It's because I feel sorry for *me.* I want a friend here, Haley. I love my husband and his brothers dearly, but sometimes...I get lonely."

Haley could understand that. Yes, she'd led a team of five

for long months in tight quarters. But she was young, always so much younger than everyone she worked with. The gap between her and the others could bridge the Grand Canyon. Even she and Alda, the only other American female, hadn't become more than casual acquaintances. Lloyd, a quiet, unpretentious man, had taken her under his wing, but Haley didn't fool herself; he'd needed her brain. She couldn't remember how long it had been since she'd made a *real* friend to share personal things with. One who had nothing to do with work.

And suddenly, she wanted that more than anything.

"Please, take these clothes from me," Nellie begged softly, stooping for the wildly excited puppy, nuzzling him close. "And know it's just me pushing our friendship, not me dishing out pity."

"I don't know what to say," Haley said slowly, unbearably touched. She pulled the quilt tighter around her.

Nellie let Max go and folded her hands beneath her bulging belly. Her eyes were wide and earnest; her smile, shy and needy. An inexplicable urge to cry overcame Haley. She'd been on her own for so long, she could hardly remember what it was like to have someone think of her, but she didn't remember it having been this nice. "Thank you," she said softly, then found she could laugh, after all. "You saved me from cooking breakfast in my underwear."

"Now that's a sight that would have had the guys silent for a change," Nellie said, with a matching laugh. The tension left her face. "I'm glad you're here. And I'm glad I didn't insult you."

Haley eyed Nellie's nicely curved hips and full bust that even pregnancy couldn't hide. "What's insulting is that I won't be able to fill out these clothes as well as you."

Nellie laughed again. "At least *you* can see your feet." She let the puppy go, then swiped her hands down her jeans-covered thighs nervously. "Uh, Haley?"

"Yeah?"

"You *can* cook, can't you?"

Haley smiled. "Now's a fine time to ask."

Nellie smiled back. "I mean, I don't really care whether you can or not—I want you here anyway—but the guys are going to wake up in about twenty minutes, starving as usual."

"They'll be fed," Haley vowed. From the moment the two women had met in the crowded airport, something had clicked. Nellie had somehow seen past Haley's distant, calm exterior to the real person inside. Maybe because she had no idea who Haley was and what she was capable of, but it didn't matter. Haley had a real friend—and she didn't intend to blow it.

Which didn't change the fact that she hadn't the foggiest idea how to cook. From a very young age, she'd been squirreled away in schools for child prodigies; then she'd been busy studying for her various degrees before she'd settled down four years ago, at the age of twenty-one, to study earth movement. In South America, as in all the other places, there had always been a local paid to work as their live-in, since the geologists' long, exhausting hours didn't allow much time for cooking or cleaning.

In all those years, Haley had never spent more than five minutes in a kitchen, but she had no doubt she could tackle it. After all, she decided with forced confidence, like anything else, it was simply a matter of mastering the technique. She was good at that.

Though she hoped to God she found a cookbook in that kitchen.

A few minutes later, garbed in a pair of jeans and a sweater, both of which were slightly too big in all the wrong places, Haley found herself in the kitchen of the main house.

Nellie looked at her expectantly.

Haley smiled, hopefully reassuringly. "Go. Go do...whatever it is you do. I'll be fine."

"Are you sure?" Obviously, Nellie was less than certain about Haley's abilities. She rubbed her lower back as if it ached. "Let me help you this first time."

"I'm the housekeeper," Haley said firmly. "And I'm ordering you out of my kitchen." She needed to be alone for this. Especially if she was going to make a fool of herself.

"Okay," Nellie said, drawing out the word. She moved reluctantly to the door. "Well, I'll be with the horses. Everyone tends to gather here about seven for food. That gives you some time yet." Still, she hesitated by the door. "Haley, are you sure you don't want me to help you? It's really okay to tell me."

"I'll be fine," she repeated, trying to remain calm. God, the kitchen was huge. Despite the coolness of the morning, sweat pooled at the base of her spine. She watched Nellie reluctantly leave and she bit her lip. *Could she really do this?*

She *had* to. With no money and nowhere else to go, what choice did she have? She couldn't come out of hiding, not until she figured out what to do. She couldn't withdraw money without fear of being traced. And for now she couldn't even call for help, not until she had some hint of who was involved, or until she could clear herself. No doubt, she was in a mess.

With a firm sigh of resolution, Haley searched the kitchen, familiarizing herself. Humming with triumph, she pounced on the shelf of cookbooks she found and buried herself in her new work with the same focus and single-mindedness she tackled everything.

That was exactly how Cameron found her, twenty minutes later—bent over two pans, both steaming from the heat, her brow crinkled in such fierce concentration, she might have been studying Latin instead of cooking. He took a minute to admire how perfectly adorable she looked in jeans. And how perfectly behaved his precocious puppy seemed, sitting at her feet.

"Do you always frown when you cook?"

She jumped in surprise, then made him smile when she shooed him off with a hand. "Go away," she said rudely, turning back to whatever she was stirring. "It's not ready yet."

He would have liked to oblige her, but something smelled so absolutely delicious, his mouth started to water. He moved closer, but whether to satisfy his belly or his strange need to be near her, he didn't know. "I'm starving. What's cooking?"

She spared him a quick, frustrated look. "I need a few more minutes."

"Eggs?" he asked hopefully, trying to catch a glimpse over her shoulder.

The woman actually tried to muscle him out of the way so he couldn't see. "Come on," he cajoled. "Let me look. Mmm. Is that an omelet?"

Her blue-eyed gaze flew to his and he wondered at the surprise he saw there. "Is that what it looks like?" she asked hopefully.

"Yeah, and it looks scrumptious." He leaned over, his body brushing up against hers. She moved away instantly. Max didn't, and yelped when his tail got stepped on.

"I said go away," she mumbled again. "Don't you cowboys hear?"

He smiled. Damned if he didn't like her. "You should know, such sweet talk turns me on." He sniffed appreciatively over her shoulder. As always, he was famished. "God almighty, so does that smell. What is it?"

"It's soap. I don't wear perfume." She swatted at him.

He grinned. "I was talking about the food, sugar. But you smell good, too." Moving in closer, he sniffed in exaggeration at her ear, earning a smack in the chest that had him laughing out loud.

"You fool," she exclaimed, never taking her eyes off whatever smelled so good, but a reluctant quirk of her lips softened her words. Encouraged, he nudged even closer, hoping to talk her into a spoonful, and discovered—perfume or not—she *did* smell as good as the food.

"Back off," she warned, rolling a shoulder into his chest when he crowded her again.

He did back off, but only because he'd felt her stiffen when he'd touched her, and that quick flicker of something that might have been fear in her eyes bothered him. When her shoulders slumped imperceptibly in relief, he slipped his hands into his pockets and studied her thoughtfully. She wasn't easy around friendly teasing, or maybe just men, and even now she stood there trying to ignore the fact that he watched her. It might be a while before she felt comfortable with the rambunctious bantering he was used to. But he figured, being the patient man he was, he could wait.

Besides, the waiting was half the fun. So he backed off and winked at Max, who lolled his tongue as if to say, *I was here first, buddy. Wait in line.*

"Food!" Jason exclaimed, staggering into the kitchen, adjusting his arm sling. "Is that really—dare I ask—*real* food you're cooking?"

"Thank God," Zach said reverently as he moved into the kitchen, as well. He caught a plate in midair when Jason tossed it to him from the cabinet. "It sure smells real."

Cam watched as Haley smiled at his brothers, and damn her if it wasn't an easy, carefree smile.

"It all depends on what you call *real* food," she said.

Zach moved in close to look, as Cam had done only a moment before. He, too, sniffed in appreciation. Cam waited gleefully. He was going to enjoy watching Haley set down his brother, who in Cam's opinion could use it.

Nothing happened. Except Haley actually moved *out* of his brother's way to let him see.

*Okay,* Cameron thought, eyeing his older brother speculatively. Cam knew he and Zach looked alike, with their sun-streaked light brown hair, brown eyes, tall and rangy bodies—but that was where the resemblance ended. Somehow he hadn't thought Zach's quiet, reserved nature would appeal to Haley.

Or maybe he'd just hoped.

Haley laughed at something Jason said; the sweet, musical sound ringing in his ears. Cameron seriously considered hurting his brother, but it would take too much energy. Besides, he was damn hungry.

Zach inhaled deeply, smiled gently at Haley and grabbed a

fork. Smiling back, Haley dished out a heaping helping for him. Jason pushed his way in, grinned at Haley from ear to ear, and also earned himself a full plate.

"I'm starving, too," Cam said, muscling his way back to her and grabbing his own plate. But when he held it out to Haley, she just looked at him blankly. "Smells great," he added, with his most charming, gotta-love-me smile. He gestured with his very empty plate, watching out of the corner of his eye as Zach and Jason dug in with gusto.

Haley put her hands on her hips and stared at him. "Serve yourself."

Jason laughed, then choked it back into a cough at the murderous look Cam sent him. Ducking his head, he shoveled food into his mouth, unable to contain his knowing grin. "Tough luck, brother," Jason said around a mouthful. "It's terrific, Haley."

"Thanks," she said sweetly, then scowled at Cam. "You're in my way."

*She was crazy about him,* Cam decided, scooping his own food. Now all he had to do was get her to admit it.

Cooking had been as easy as following the given formula. Or in this case, the recipe. Haley was still riding on the high of that as she contemplated the big, silent, and very messy house.

She didn't *have* to work, she knew that. She could keep running. Or better yet, make a decision on what to do. But for so many years, she'd been thinking *so* hard, always pushing herself. For now, just for now, she needed a break.

Nellie had gone into Colorado Springs to have her nails done, claiming she knew exactly how vain it was, but didn't care. If she had to be fat, she'd said with a good-natured laugh, she wanted to at least have good nails.

The guys were off doing whatever ranch people did. Haley had no idea what that was, exactly, but assumed it had something to do with the heavy beating of horse hooves and shouts she'd heard leave not too long ago.

Cleaning was truly a whole new ball game for her. The physical aspect of it felt good, she discovered immediately. Digging out a bucket of cleaning supplies that looked as if it hadn't been used in a while, she attacked the kitchen first. The instructions on the pine-scented cleaner claimed it cleaned tile to a perfect shine.

So why, after running the mop over the tile, didn't it look clean, much less shiny? Frustrated, Haley read the directions again. Then she started over.

No luck. Still no shine. With a sigh, she tossed the container over her shoulder and got down on her hands and knees to scrub harder, convinced she was seriously lacking if she couldn't handle even this basic chore. Finally, an hour and many sore muscles later, she could see a slight improvement. The directions had conveniently neglected to mention the elbow grease required.

Pausing to stretch her already aching back, Haley had to laugh at herself. While the physical exertion helped ease her mind, she would never have pictured herself performing such a mundane chore as mopping.

Blowing her hair from her face, she scrubbed more, spending long moments with her mind blessedly free. Free of the haunting memories she knew she'd carry with her forever.

*Bam, bam, bam.*

Haley jerked upright at the exploding sound. Gunshots. Oh, God! She leaped to her feet and ran to the window, but she could see nothing.

Cursing her stupidity and her lax attitude, she sprinted to the living room, tripping over Max who'd fallen asleep in the entrance. *This was it, they'd found her.* Whoever had destroyed her team, her work, had found her.

Heart slamming against her ribs, she scooped up the confused pup and ran to the big window at the front of the house, peeking out the long, flowing, tieback curtains.

Still, nothing.

She held her breath, wondering what to do. The blood roared

in her ears so loudly she could hardly think, but she had to. If they'd found her, she had to figure out a way to keep everyone else safe. Thank God Nellie wasn't home, but where were the men?

Max yawned and stared at her, completely unconcerned. If there was someone out there, the puppy could care less. "Some watchdog," she hissed furiously at him. He just nuzzled her hand.

How could she have done this? How could she have put more innocent people in danger?

Off to the right of the main house she could see two large barns. Her heart nearly stopped when Cam stepped out of one, scooped something up and headed back inside.

She had to warn him.

Watching carefully, she slipped out the front door and dashed across to the barn, knowing that she could be shot down any second.

It didn't matter. She had to make sure no one else got hurt. That no one else would die because of her.

Cam looked up, the surprise evident on his face when she tore into the barn. Ignoring him, she whirled and shoved first one door closed, then the other—not an easy feat since the doors were twice her height and heavy.

"What—"

"Shh!" she demanded over her shoulder, struggling with the large bolt. "Do you have a gun?"

"A *what?*"

"A gun!" she fairly screamed, slamming the lock home.

"God, no." He shuddered with distaste. "Haley, what are you doing?"

She turned back to him, panting and leaning against the closed doors. Without sunlight streaming through, the barn seemed dim...and huge. "Is there a back door?"

"Yeah." He cocked a hip against a long worktable and looked at her, amused. "Should I go lock it?"

"Yes! And hurry." Breathless, she moved toward him, scanning the walls for windows. She knew the bolt on the door wouldn't hold and with some crazy notion of pushing one of his benches in front of the doors, she started clearing one of them off, shoving some things to the floor. "Where're Zach and Jason?"

Cam raised those golden eyebrows of his until they disappeared into the lock of hair that had fallen across his forehead. "Riding. They'll be gone awhile yet if there's any justice."

"Good," Haley said in relief, struggling with a rage and a grief so great she could hardly contain it. She would not be the cause of any more deaths. Especially not these people, the first to care about her in too long to remember. Moving closer, she hoped Cam knew how to shoot, since she had no idea how herself. But he was a cowboy, and all cowboys knew how to shoot—didn't they?

"We have to hurry," she told him, surprised when he laughed and didn't move.

"Darlin', I *never* hurry. But I suppose, you being a lady and all, I could try to oblige you."

The sensual, husky laziness his voice had taken on would have warned a more sophisticated, experienced woman, but not Haley. "Okay, good," she said quickly. "I have something to tell you, Cameron. This isn't going to be easy."

"Well, I have to admit, it's been a while since I— Since my barn days," he finished tactfully, his meaning completely escaping her. He glanced at the bench she'd just cleared. "Uh, it's pretty dirty in here, Haley."

She narrowed her eyes and, for the first time, really looked at him. In his gaze, which had landed unerringly on her, was a mixture of hopeful speculation and amused disbelief. And yes, the heavy-lidded look of arousal. She realized with horror that they were absolutely *not* talking about the same thing.

But then something else—something even worse—occurred to her. "What is that?" she demanded, pointing at the thing in his hand.

He held up the tool. It looked suspiciously like a...gun. *Oh, no.*

"It's my nail gun," he said. He bent over his table to a long piece of smooth wood and pulled the trigger.

*Bam, bam, bam.*

The ache in her stomach escalated into a dull pain.

"See?" He lifted his head and smiled. "I'm making shelves."

"I see," she managed to say, weakly. She leaned on the bench she'd just cleared. "I've...gotta go now." She turned back toward the barn doors. There was no gunman, no one after her. And she'd just made an ass of herself in front of the one man who could alter her pulse.

"Haley?"

She didn't, or rather, *couldn't,* answer. She heard him drop his tool belt and head for her, so she sped up. But he still stopped her before she could open the bolt. She refused to look at him until he gently turned her to him and lifted her chin.

His gaze searched her face. "Obviously you weren't just seducing me in my barn."

She shook her head, and now her heart raced again, but for a different reason entirely. "No."

His smile was wry and self-deprecating. "I have to say, it was the most appealing almost-offer I've ever had. I'll never look at that table in quite the same way again."

She tried to step back and encountered the barn door. She didn't know much about these things, but his disappointment was palpable. Wasn't there a rule against turning a man on and then trying to withdraw?

He moved back, his smile still easy and charming, and Haley breathed a sigh of relief. He wouldn't push.

"So what did you barrel in here about, if it wasn't to toss me down on my workbench and have your merry way with me?"

He was teasing her—she could tell by his sparkling dark eyes—and she didn't know how to handle that. "I—" It seemed so stupid now. *I thought someone was trying to kill you.* "Nothing."

His gaze shuttered, cooled so fast it startled her. He didn't believe her, that was clear. She didn't blame him for finally showing suspicion. But that he'd waited until she'd obviously lied disturbed her. He'd been willing to give her the benefit of the doubt—that is, until she'd proved she wasn't worthy of it.

She forced a smile. "I just wondered what you do out here."

"I make furniture."

She glanced around, realizing that while they stood inside what was once a barn, it had been converted into a studio of sorts. Long workbenches ran the length of the place, each scattered with tools, wood and partially put-together projects, including the shelving unit he'd been working on when she'd burst in.

"I thought you were a rancher."

"My brothers are." His voice, so warm and friendly only a minute before, seemed brusque now. He shifted away and moved back to his bench, running a loving hand along the wood that even her untrained eye could see was beautiful, bare oak. He gave the wood a gentle pat that conveyed his feelings better than words ever could. "Ranching seems like too much work for me."

"Too much work?"

He shrugged. "I'd rather do this. It's...easier. More fun."

This was something Haley couldn't understand. She'd been bred to work, and had loved it with a passion she could hardly explain—especially to a man such as this. But she'd never thought of anything she'd done as remotely "fun." "So you let your brothers work the ranch?"

If he sensed her disapproval, he didn't show it. Or no longer cared. "They love it."

She asked him the question that had flitted about in her mind since she'd arrived. "You all live together. Why?"

"We're family," he said simply. Though he remained alert,

he again relaxed. "The house and the land are mine legally, but that doesn't mean anything. We work it together."

"You mean, *they* work it. You—" She gestured around her. "You do what's easier."

Still smiling, he leaned against the nearest bench, crossing his booted feet. "Whatever," he drawled.

That cavalier attitude annoyed her, especially since she had a feeling he was putting it on for her benefit. Had her lie annoyed him or the interruption of his work? She had a feeling it was the former. "Do you do that on purpose?"

"Do what?"

"Put on that good-old-boy act."

"How do you know it's an act?"

Oh, yeah. She'd annoyed him. He was watching her intently now. She frowned and dropped her gaze from his. There was only one problem with that. Her eyes then settled on other parts of him; like those strong, broad shoulders stretching his flannel shirt in interesting ways across his chest, or those snug, faded jeans that fit his long, lean legs so nicely. Her frown deepened when she raised her gaze back to his and realized she'd been blatantly staring, and that he was fully enjoying the fact.

Which didn't explain the funny way her breath had caught in her throat. She couldn't be... No. There was absolutely *no* way that she was experiencing lust.

At the thought, a pain erupted in her belly so fast and so sharp, she couldn't contain her small gasp. Cam straightened immediately and was by her side before she could blink.

"What is it?"

Just as quickly, the pain passed. She wouldn't have felt it at all, except that she hadn't taken her pills last night or this morning. "Nothing." She pulled her shoulders back and yanked on the door. "Just nothing."

He reached around her to help. "It's something," he insisted.

"I'm fine, just fine. Really. And I've got work." She walked out into the bright, crisp October day. The blue, open Colorado sky loomed overhead, blending into a picture-perfect hilly landscape. In the distance, Aspen trees tossed in the wind, their round, flat leaves creating a unique rustling sound.

He waited until she'd gotten a few steps away. "Don't work too hard."

She stopped and turned. "That's an unusual thing for an employer to say to an employee."

"Things are different here than wherever you came from."

"That's the truth." How surprised he'd be to know she'd headed a team of five of the world's most brilliant geologists, some twice her age, leading them to the exciting discovery of a system of volcano-and-earthquake prediction and prevention. How shocked he'd be to know that at least two of them were dead because of that discovery. Not to mention the thousands who had been killed in the earthquake that had been purposely created as a test.

"Maybe someday you'll tell me about it," he said seriously.

Haley thought about how good it would feel to tell someone about the horror her life had become. But trust didn't come easily for her in the best of times, and certainly not now.

"Haley?" He took one step toward her. "I'm a good listener."

She shook her head and found herself, for the second time that day, inexplicably close to tears. Far too close, she realized, as her next breath shuddered through her. "I've got work" was all she could manage as she turned and ran the entire way to the big house.

Cam watched her go, standing there for a long moment before turning back to the barn. That had been the strangest interaction he'd ever had. She'd slammed into his studio, and, for a moment, he couldn't believe his luck. It had been so long since he'd let a woman get to him, it had taken him a minute or two to see the terror in her eyes.

And when he had, it had stirred something deep within. Standing there now, with the light wind sliding over him, he had to admit that those feelings had been fiercely protective.

Yes, he always felt that way about anyone or anything in pain or in need, but this had been different.

Then she'd lied and everything inside him had gone cold. He knew nothing about Haley, and he'd do well to remember that. All he felt for her was empathy. No different from when he'd given that old cowboy, Joe, a job for the winter because he had nowhere else to go. No different from when he'd taken Max in. No different at all.

He smirked. *Right.*

"Whatcha staring at?"

Cam let the unaccustomed tension drain out of him and faced his oldest brother. "Our new housekeeper."

"Oh, yeah?" Zach turned, watched as Haley ran the rest of the way into the house. "She's nice," he said cautiously. "And she can cook breakfast."

"But?" Cam asked, looking at him. "There's always a but when you talk in that attorney voice."

"You like her."

At Zach's flat statement, Cam sighed, never having gotten used to his brother's unerring ability to sense things others couldn't. "I like a lot of people."

"She's different," he countered.

"No," Cam denied, but caught his brother's long, solemn look and relented. "I've only known her for a day, Zach."

"Yeah, but you've got that look in your eye. That 'protect the victim' look with a whole helluva lot of lust added in."

"Don't you have to go feed your cattle or something?" So he was a sucker for a victim, he couldn't help it. Having Zach point it out only annoyed him.

"I don't want to see you hurt."

Cam wanted, quite badly, to laugh his brother off, but he couldn't quite manage it. "I'm a big boy now, you know."

"It's been a long time since Lorraine died."

Cam let the air whoosh out of him as his good humor completely faded, to be replaced by that sense of...unbalance that had plagued him for what seemed like years now. "And you think I'm looking for another wife?"

"No, of course not."

"Haley Williams is our housekeeper, and that's it," Cam said firmly. "Stop worrying. You sound like Mom used to."

"Do I?" Zach asked evenly, pulling off his hat and swiping his forehead with his sleeve. "Lorraine was bad for you."

"She's dead, Zach."

"She lied to you, hurt you."

Unreasonable temper surged. "Back off."

"There was no Haley Williams on board Nellie's plane yesterday."

Tension seized him instantly. "What do you mean?"

"I checked."

"Why?"

They stared at each other for a long moment before Zach relented.

"I'm an ex-cop," Zach said with an apologetic shrug. "Bad habit."

At the clear concern in Zach's gaze, Cam closed his eyes. But all he saw was the image of Haley in the barn, clearly terrified, also clearly willing to lie to cover that fact. *Not again. Please, God, not another liar.* "What did you find out?"

Slowly, Zach put his hat back on, slid his thumbs into his back pockets and studied the sky. "She did come from South America. But no Haley from Los Angeles to here. She must have paid cash and used a different name."

"You haven't even passed the bar, and already you're acting like a lawyer." Cam sighed. *Dammit.* "Okay, you're not going to let it alone, so let's hear it."

"Either she wanted someone to think she stayed in L.A., or she's not who she says." Zach looked at him. "I could have dug further, but it didn't feel right. Do you want me to?"

"No." That wasn't what he wanted. What he *did* want no longer surprised him. He wanted Haley to tell him the truth herself, wanted her to take away this terrible wariness and suspicion. He'd been down this road before and couldn't face it again.

"What do you suppose is going on?"

"I don't know." Cam rubbed his chest, not understanding the ache that had settled there. Why did he care?

"You've been there, done that," Zach warned. "Another woman who can't be honest."

"Which is your kind way of saying she's a liar."

Zach raised a brow. "Are we talking about Haley or Lorraine?"

"I'm not in the mood for this, Zach."

Zach lifted his hands in a gesture of surrender.

"I can't explain it, but she's all right," Cam insisted. "I just know." *He hoped.*

"Which leaves only one thing."

They looked at each other.

"She's running," Zach said.

"Yeah." But from what?

Haley ran directly into Cam's den, closed and locked the door and lifted her shirt. There against her hip, attached to her jeans, was the pager, vibrating with a chilly evilness.

With shaking hands, she lifted it, pressed the button to get her message. Again from an unknown number in South America. Fear sucked the oxygen right out of her lungs at the printed words.

"Haley, I'll find you."

Suddenly the pager went off yet again, this time from Alda.

"Haley, where are you? Who's done this to us?" The typed words continued across the screen. "Lloyd's dead. He died in the explosion. That's what the police said, and now they're looking for you. Bob's missing. Haley, where are you?"

Haley stared at the pager as a possible betrayal whipped the heels of her fear. Everyone gone or missing except Alda. Was it possible? It *had* been Alda who insisted that the team and EVS *not* go public with their discovery. Haley had always believed Lloyd and EVS would sell it to the U.S. government so that the USGS could continue the study. But Lloyd had agreed with Alda to wait, to keep the public ignorant, until after the final test. Those tests had never taken place.

*And now they were looking for her.* Haley could only hope they wouldn't find her—at least not until the real killer made a mistake and showed himself.

# *Chapter 3*

Haley kept busy for the rest of the day because she had to. If she didn't, the humiliation of the barn scene would kill her. And if that didn't, then the horror of what she'd learned would.

Lloyd dead. Only three of them left now, assuming Bob was indeed still alive. The pain in her gut made her decide not to think about it.

It seemed all her life there had been things from her past she'd needed to avoid thinking about. Losing her father before she'd known him. Being shunned by a high-society mother who couldn't handle the burden of raising a ''special'' child. Being responsible for the deaths of too many people to count, when all she'd ever wanted was to make the world a safer place.

She needed to forget, just for a little while, or she'd self-destruct. Besides, she'd been bred to work, and without it, she felt useless.

The big house was lovely but, as she quickly discovered, clean only on the surface. She found someone's stiff, dirty socks under a cushion on the couch, a stack of long-forgotten mail behind a potted plant in desperate need of water, and a half-eaten tortilla, crisp with age, in a far corner of the patio. She cleaned it all, and shocked herself by how much she actually enjoyed doing it.

But even with the peace and solitude, there was the knowledge that all this was temporary. Soon, she'd have to come up with a better plan. Such as how to get help without getting herself extradited to South America.

Even sooner, she'd have to figure out what she could manage for dinner; but one worry at a time. She took a stack of rugs outside to shake out the dirt, and spotted the wooden-rail fence in the side yard. She decided to throw the rugs over it so she could shake the dust loose with her broom.

Laying out the rugs with great concentration allowed room for no other thoughts to intrude. Not the raw grief from seeing the bodies of two of her team members scattered in their own blood, not the bitter disappointment of the destruction of her earth-movement system, and certainly not the fact that she owed her existence at this moment to a big, fat lie.

The rugs took up the entire length of the fence. She couldn't see the other side, but she'd stopped jumping at every little noise. No one knew where she was or they would have come for her by now. Momentarily sidetracked by the wide, open sky and vast expanse of land around her, Haley took a deep breath of fresh and blessedly cool air. Something settled inside her.

She hadn't been back in the States for so long, she almost didn't recognize the content feeling for what it was. And she didn't realize she wasn't alone until she glanced up and saw the huge bovine head—as wide as her body and nearly half as long—hanging over the fence like one of her rugs, its face inches from her own.

With a muffled scream, she stepped back and tripped over her broom to land gracelessly on her bottom in the dust.

"Moooooo," the cow offered, gazing at her with a curious-but-blank stare.

Rich male laughter rang out and Haley closed her eyes and gritted her teeth. Why, of all the people living in this house, did it have to be *him* to witness her second most embarrassing moment of the day?

She opened her eyes to find Cameron squatted in front of her, proffering a hand. Childish as it was, she couldn't resist, and before he could so much as blink—or make the comment she could see he was itching to make—she'd grabbed his hand and pulled him down into the dirt beside her.

Haley didn't know what she expected—anger, indignation, bafflement? Anything but more laughter. On his butt, there in the dirt, Cam tipped his hat back and roared.

She waited, simmering, until he subsided. When he did, she pushed to her feet, brushed the dust off her jeans and shot him a look that would have withered anyone else.

He just grinned. "What a hot temper you've got, Haley Williams. And a hell of a right arm, too."

She turned from him and nearly stumbled again. The cow still stared at her from less than a foot away. Haley's startled curse earned her another laugh from Cameron.

"Margaret won't hurt you. Her only thought is *Where's my food?*" He stood and patted the cow on the head affectionately. "She's sweet, but not too bright."

"Margaret? You *name* your cows?"

He shrugged and gave her that harmless, I'm-so-innocent smile. As if he'd ever been innocent. "Why not?"

Haley looked at the cow and suddenly couldn't help herself. Never having been within miles of a cow before, she wanted to touch it. Tentatively, she reached out a hand, then whipped it back when Margaret shifted her huge head to gaze balefully at her with those big brown eyes.

"She doesn't see too well," Cam said. "But you can touch her. Go on, she won't bite." He took her wrist, drawing her hand close until she could smooth it over the cow's soft, warm forehead.

She couldn't contain her small smile.

Cam watched her. "Never touched one before, huh?"

"No," she admitted.

"Well, for a city girl you're doing okay, then."

The funny—and sad—thing was, she was no more a city girl than a country one. She truly belonged nowhere. Her entire life had been spent studying, observing and scrutinizing. Locked away from reality, Haley hadn't realized until that very moment that she didn't seem to fit into any one, specific setting.

She didn't belong anywhere. Or to anyone.

Forcing the thought away, she reached again for the cow and just managed not to flinch when Margaret snorted very wetly and noisily. With one last look at Cameron and Haley, the cow slowly lumbered away in search of more grass. Or whatever cows went in search of.

Cameron's eyes sparkled, and she knew he wanted to laugh at her. She liked to think he didn't dare. "I've got work," she said with as much dignity as she could manage.

His lips twitched. "So you've said." He rocked back on his heels and looked at the perfect sky marred only by a few streaks of white cloud. "Storm's brewing. We'll have rain tonight."

She wrinkled her nose, squinting at the sky. "There're no rain clouds."

"I can feel it," he said simply. "I love the rain."

She did, too. No matter where she'd lived, whether the rain had beaten against wide, frothy fronds of palm trees, whipped at the desert floor, or streamed down mountainsides, she'd loved it. To find this unlikely common ground set her further off-balance. Purposefully, she picked up her broom and went to move away, but he reached out and took her hand.

"Do you like it here, Haley?"

She glanced down at their joined hands pointedly, hoping he'd take the hint and let go. He didn't, so she pulled free. "I haven't been here very long. Only a day."

"All right, then. *Could* you be happy here?"

The big house stood behind him; wide, open and inviting. She'd never had a home—or a real one, anyway. Boarding schools had been her haven as a child, since her mother had never sent for her and had visited only occasionally. After that had come college. Then her work, which had her either closeted away in a laboratory, or traveling all over the globe. She'd always dreamed of a permanent place to belong...but what would she do with one?

"Haley?" Cam stepped closer, ducking his face to look into hers.

"I don't know," she said quite honestly. "I've never really had a place like this to stay before."

"Where's your home?" His voice, with its low, rich quality, almost lulled her into answering more truthfully than she intended.

"I don't have one."

He tipped his head, considering. "Everyone comes from somewhere."

"Not me."

His smile faded. "You're full of secrets, aren't you?"

"Yes," she said honestly. "I'm sorry."

He let out a long, frustrated breath, once again showing that slightly rough, earth edge she'd sensed earlier. "It's my problem, not yours." Taking the broom from her hand, he stepped up to the first rug she'd hung and smacked it. Dust swirled and he shook his head. "I never noticed how dirty these were," he said a little apologetically. When dust had stopped rising from the rug, he moved to the second.

"Wait! That's my job."

He twisted to glance at her over his shoulder. "I'll do it. You look tired."

*She looked tired.* "I'm the housekeeper."

"It's okay, Haley." *Smack! Smack!*

She wrestled the broom from him and blew the hair from her face. "*It's my job.* Now go away and leave me to it."

"Can I watch?" As her eyes narrowed dangerously, he backed up, raising his hands in surrender. "Wow. You should see how blue your eyes get when you're riled. They're something."

She thought about wielding the broom as a weapon and

bounced it in her hands. "You've got to have work to do. Go
do it. Go ranch."

"My brothers are doing that."

"Then go...do something. Make another shelf."

He grinned in his usual easygoing way as she turned the
broom in her hands, holding it like a baseball bat. "I don't feel
like it."

*God save her from lazy cowboys.* "Well, go feel like something. You're in my way."

The grin spread. "You like me."

She rolled her eyes and turned her back to him, listening to
him whistle as he sauntered away.

"Oh, and Haley?" he called out. She refused to look at him,
but that didn't stop him from yelling, "Don't scare any more
cows. It's not good for milk production."

His laughter rang out in the cool, afternoon air.


That night, standing in the kitchen, at a total loss over what
to make for dinner, Haley began to panic.

Zach came in. "Hey, Haley. How's it going?"

"Fine," she said politely, thankful *this* brother didn't seem
as innately curious as his younger one.

"The house looks great," he said, proceeding past her to the
refrigerator. "It hasn't been so clean since... Well, ever."

He stuffed an apple into his mouth, grabbed two armfuls of
chilled food, and dumped it all on the counter, kicking the door
closed with his foot. He smiled around the apple when he noticed her staring, then began to open an assortment of containers.

"What are you doing?"

He pulled the apple from his mouth, taking a huge bite. "I'm
making a sandwich. I'm hungry."

She moved to his side to protest. "But I'm going to cook
dinner for you."

"Oh, don't bother for me, thanks. I'm studying." Another
bite, and the apple had nearly disappeared.

"Well, at least let me make whatever it is you're going to make for yourself."

He shot her a smile. "You worked hard today, take a break."

"Dinner's my job," she protested, watching him make short work of a piece of chicken he found in some foil. Where, she wondered, eyeing his tall, lean body, did he put all that food?

"Nellie and Jason are going out to dinner to be *alone*," he said, rolling his eyes. "Take advantage."

Nellie's absence explained why Max had been trailing her for the past hour. But it didn't rid Haley of guilt. She had to work. She owed these people everything.

"Cam's in his studio," Zach continued, starting on the second piece of chicken. "He'll be there all night."

She tried not to wonder why the mention of his brother's name made her stomach tingle. "All night?"

"Yeah." He pulled out a huge roll that surely one person couldn't eat by himself, especially one who'd already eaten an apple and two pieces of chicken. "He's in the mood to work, for a change."

She saw that he spoke without rancor or bitterness. Just plain acceptance...and love. "What is it he does, exactly?"

Zach laughed softly as if she'd told a joke, but in truth, she had no idea what was so funny. "It's amazing, isn't it? People from three states over clamor for his furniture, not even minding that he won't give them a finish date. He'll just get to it when he gets to it, he says, and they agree. I still don't understand it."

Haley watched as he stacked cheese and meat four inches thick on the huge roll, wondering how he would get his mouth around it. "Is he any good?"

"The best," Zach said simply.

"What are you studying?" she asked, fascinated by his appetite.

"For the bar exam."

"An attorney. That's impressive."

"For a cowboy, you mean?" He smiled and piled three-quarters of a new bag of chips on the plate. Then, as an after-thought, he dumped the rest onto the plate, too. "Don't be too impressed," he said wryly. "I seem to collect occupations. I was a cop once. A bartender, too." He balanced the plate and three cans of soda easily in those long gangly arms and made his way to the door before he paused. "It's nice to have you here, Haley," he said sincerely. "It's nice to be looked after."

She nearly laughed. "But you're not letting me look after you at all."

"We don't want to take advantage."

"But you're paying me to do this."

He grinned. "No, not me. Cam is. He'll get his money's worth, believe me. He always does." His color drained and he looked as if he wanted to hit himself. "Wait. That didn't come out right."

She'd taken an involuntary step backward, but common sense prevailed. Last night, her safety had taken a back seat to escape. Going home with strangers had been infinitely preferable to the alternative of being dead. But after a night and a day with these people, she sensed she was safe. Especially after the barn fiasco when she'd unintentionally thrown herself at her new boss and he'd acted with gentlemanly restraint, if not a great deal of humor.

Even so, she wanted to clarify things. In her profession, where she was required to carefully observe and study, she'd found it the best method. "I'm a housekeeper," she said firmly. "Nothing more."

"We know that," Zach said quickly, sincerely. He shrugged his wide shoulders in emphasis, since his hands were completely full of food. "And no one expects more. In fact, if either of my brothers even looks at you cross-eyed, I'll sue them for you—I promise."

She smiled at that, as he'd intended. "I thought brothers tended to wrestle and fight, not sue."

"When we were younger, but not anymore," he vowed. "I may be the oldest, but Cam's the strongest. Neither of us messes with him now. Besides, suing him hurts where it counts the most—his wallet.''

Haley had a hard time picturing Cameron expending enough energy to worry about anything, much less his financial situation. ''He doesn't seem to care about money much.''

''No.'' Zach sighed dramatically. ''He doesn't.'' And then he eyed her strangely. ''Haley, I meant what I said. You're safe here. If there's ever anything you want us to know, or if you need any help, you could just tell us. We'd be there.''

''Okay,'' she said slowly, trying to read between the lines. Did he know something, suspect something? When he only stood there, looking at her expectantly, she lifted a shoulder self-consciously. ''What?''

Disappointment crossed his features. ''Nothing. Have a good night.''

She watched him go, once again marveling at how much food he was going to consume, then turned to the empty kitchen. She should have been relieved at her miraculous respite, but she felt oddly...unsettled.

It was quiet, almost too much so. She went out the back door and saw little Max, fast asleep on his padded bed. Standing on the porch, listening to him snore softly, she watched the daylight fade into night. A gigantic cloud hung where the sun was making its lazy descent behind the shadowed mountains. A fat, black cloud that, as Cameron had told her earlier, promised rain.

Rain would suit her mood.

She stood there in the very cool air, her arms wrapped around her middle, wondering at the strange and unexpected turn her life had taken. What had really happened there in South America? Someone—Alda? Bob?—had gotten greedy. Someone had decided they wanted the system for themselves. Who? The system was destroyed now; did they think they could re-create it? She didn't *want* to blame either of them, but no one else alive knew what they'd created. Where were they now? Were they hiding, as she was? Both were American, and both had worked previously for the United States Geological Survey. If she called the USGS, would they know what had happened? Would they even believe her? She knew she had to try.

It was time to stop burying her head in the sand. Because of the time difference between Los Angeles and Colorado, it was too late today. But first thing in the morning, she'd call the USGS base in California. It might give her peace of mind.

They'd probably want her to come work for them, tell them what she knew. She didn't want to go back to being a geologist. It was ironic that she'd lost the taste for it, since once upon a time, it had been all she'd ever wanted. But she wouldn't reproduce that system, no matter what. With the knowledge in the wrong hands, anything could happen. Terrorists could blackmail governments for billions with the threat of a massive earthquake or volcano.

The implications were terrifying. Good Lord, no wonder someone wanted her dead.

Darkness had fallen while she stood there and she'd never seen such a complete and utterly still black night. There were no sounds as a huge, ominous cloud stretched across the entire yawning sky. She couldn't even see her little house, only fifty yards away. Little Max snored on.

Never in her life had Haley felt so alone, so isolated.

Suddenly lightning bolted, and she nearly leaped off the porch. She braced for the thunder, but still wasn't prepared for the resounding boom that had Max jumping up with a cry, straight into her arms. She pulled him close, her heart pounding, and at the next crack, whirled toward the door with every intention of turning on each and every light in the entire house.

"Don't go."

She swallowed her scream as the next brilliant flash lit the Colorado night like day, highlighting the planes and hollows of Cameron's rugged face from where he stood on the porch steps.

"Lightning storm," he said simply, moving up the few steps to stand before her. "You haven't lived until you've seen the entire show. Come on." Taking the whining puppy in the crook of one arm, he grabbed her hand.

"It's going to rain," she said inanely, her heart still thundering in tune to the storm.

"Oh, yeah. It's going to rain." He tugged at her hand gently, murmuring quietly to Max. He led them to a beautiful, wide wooden bench on the far end of the veranda.

"I...should go in."

"Sit down a sec." He did, and pulled her down next to him. Max huddled pathetically in his lap while Cam ran a large soothing hand over his quivering back. Then he pointed off into the far distance where the entire sky had rippled with jagged streaks of blue light. "Watch," he said, his voice filled with awe. The air split with the crash of thunder.

"I thought you were working."

"The work'll wait."

"But—"

"Shh. Just listen, it's beautiful."

It seemed decadent. Wasting precious moments sitting on a bench, with a man she didn't really know, watching nothing but time go by. Haley hadn't spent much time in leisure, if any. Her time had never been her own. But the wild sky, churning and venting violence like a casual whim, had caught her. She couldn't look away.

"You'll be hungry," she said during a brief lull, feeling as if she had to say something.

"No." His face was turned upward, raptly watching as flash after flash of lightning exploded like a fireworks display, streaking the sky with jagged lines of light.

"I really should go—"

For a man who looked so at ease, lounging back against the bench, he sure could move fast, reaching for her with a hand corded with strength. "Come on, Ms. Restless, just sit a minute. Can't you do that?" His eyes sparkled with amusement.

"Just sit and watch the rain?"

"Just sit and watch the rain. You don't always have to be doing something. Or do you?"

His eyes were as dark as the night, and surprisingly, as full of secrets, but not necessarily happy ones. His scent floated on the wind; an intriguing mix of horses, wood and pure man. On her chilled arm, the warmth of his hand soaked into her, and even as she thought it, his fingers loosened to run along the length of her skin, causing a strange sort of shiver.

"You're cold."

Goodness, he was dangerous to her pulse. "I'm fine."

He shook his head. "You're stubborn, is what you are." He moved the now sleeping Max off his lap to the bench and slid closer to her until his body brushed against hers. She didn't want to think about how deliciously warm he felt. "Now watch. The rain's coming."

Another surprise—somewhere over the past few minutes, her loneliness had vanished, along with her nervousness about the dark night. She didn't want to think about the reasons for that, but she had to laugh when he casually stretched his long arm over the back of her shoulders.

"What?" he asked, blinking innocently.

She stared pointedly at his work-roughened fingers, settled inches from her shoulder, then turned to him. "Your move. It wasn't very subtle."

He sighed. "Just like a woman, you can't be quiet for five seconds."

Her eyes narrowed and she opened her mouth to retort.

"Shh." He squeezed her shoulder gently, then pointed. "Look."

The first drop fell, then another. Within a split second, the sky had simply opened itself up, dumping upon the dry and crusted earth below. Each individual, fat drop bounced off the ground with a little ping. More lightning. More thunder. *Ping, ping, ping.* Fascinated by the unexpected concert of nature, she sat mesmerized.

They stayed there in silence, simply enjoying the night. She found that since she'd made the decision to call the USGS in the morning, she felt better. So she sat, content.

Even when she shivered again, she didn't want to move, for

the lightning came at regular intervals, marring the black sky and riveting her gaze. She'd seen storms before—hundreds— but never anything like this.

She hadn't forgotten about Cameron; that would have been impossible. He filled her senses. She felt him, watched him, could almost taste him. He pulled her closer, and she realized she was shaking with cold. "I'd give you my jacket," he drawled in her ear with a husky voice that invoked its own shiver. "But I already did."

And she hadn't returned it. Remorse hit her and she started to rise. "I'm sorry—"

He held her close. "Don't be. Just make sure you don't wash it before you give it back."

"Why?" She made the mistake of looking at him. His dark, heavy-lidded eyes smoldered.

"I want it to smell like you." He leaned close, laughing a little when she flinched at the drum of thunder.

She pulled her head back and stumbled over her words. "The storm was beautiful, thanks, but I've got to go."

"You ought to do that more," he said, letting her go this time when she pulled away.

She reached the back door. "Do what?"

"Relax." Standing, he stretched lazily, then came toward her with that same long-legged easy grace she'd admired in Zach. Only this time, in Cameron, it didn't seem quite so harmless.

As for Cam, he wished he didn't invoke that particular expression on her face—the one that clearly stated how uneasy she felt around him, how wary she still was. Wanting to delay her, he said, "It's early yet. Want to sit some more?"

Haley hesitated, her hand on the door as if ready to bolt at the slightest movement from him. "What for?"

He laughed. "Just because. We could watch the storm again, or just talk."

She shook her head slowly. "I don't think so. I really have—"

"I know," he said, shaking his head. "You have stuff to do. Well, it's my stuff and it can wait."

She sighed and looked away. "You don't put a very high priority on work, do you?"

"The work will always be there." He moved closer. "But fun... That's another thing entirely. You have to grab it when you can."

"Hmm."

"Now take today...." She tensed and he knew she expected him to grill her about the barn incident, but he didn't work that way. "When you caught your first glimpse of Margaret—" he grinned wide "—that was fun."

"I see." One brow rose haughtily, her chin lifted.

Despite his good intentions to remain distant and wary, he liked her. Especially when she used that prim, annoyed tone as a defense. He pictured her as a teacher, and not for the first time, wondered exactly what it was she'd done before. "Fun is easy, Haley. Everyone likes fun."

"It has its time and place," she admitted. "But there are other things."

Her blue eyes were full of mysteries he could only guess at as she watched the rain fall. "Like what?"

"Like responsibility."

"Something I'd guess you'd be very good at." Because he couldn't resist touching her, he tucked a wayward strand of silky dark hair behind her ear. "What is it you really do, Haley?"

She licked her lips when he stepped closer, but didn't move away or object. "I told you, I'm a housekeeper."

"Now, maybe."

"You don't think I've done this before?"

Nellie had told him she'd caught Haley sitting on the kitchen floor, avidly reading the directions on a bottle of pine-scented cleaner, muttering to herself. She'd thought it cute and meticulous, but to Cam, it told him much more than that. It told him she wasn't used to using it. "You're avoiding my question."

"And you said you weren't going to ask me any," she reminded him.

He smiled, though it was a struggle. He wanted her to open up, to tell him she wasn't normally a person who hid things, who lied. That she had a really, really good reason for doing so now. Fool that he was, he'd probably believe her. "I said I wouldn't push you about where you'd come from and what you'd done. And I won't. This was just a harmless question, part of our casual conversations. You know, from one person to another."

"And therefore," she concluded, lifting a brow, "a different matter entirely, right?"

"That's right." Yeah, he really liked the way she got all huffy and pompous. It suited her. And stirred his juices. "So, are you going to tell me?"

"No." She glanced over at the next sharp flash of lightning while he tensed. The thunder rumbled. The rain still fell, dripping off the patio, creating an intimate aura. She turned her head back to his and once again, their faces were only inches apart. Slyly, he slipped an arm around her waist.

"Kind of clichéd, isn't it, Cameron? Using a storm as a scene of seduction?"

"Only if it works," he said, laughing, loosening up again. "Is it?"

"Not a chance."

"Ouch," he said good-naturedly, experienced enough not to back away. Yet. He was pleased that her breathing didn't seem so even, because his had all but stopped. Her skin glowed softly in the soft light from the kitchen window. The cold had added a touch of color to her pale cheeks. Nellie's sweater, a little too big for Haley's thin shoulders, kept slipping down, giving him tantalizing glimpses of more creamy skin that he ached to touch. The burst of arousal didn't surprise him so much as experiencing it here, now, with her. She was someone he wanted to help. *That was it.*

But already, she'd become far more.

Tread carefully, he told himself. *This one had thorns.* Well, so did he. "I know it's not all men because I've seen you smile at Zach and Jason, so why me?"

"Why you what?"

Their bodies didn't touch except where his arm curled around her waist, but the electrical current running between them made it feel as if they were. He could almost feel her soft curves resting against him. "Why are you so wary of me?"

"I'm not," she replied, dropping her gaze. But she raised her hands and pushed him back a foot or so.

He went willingly. "I don't bite. I'd like to, but I won't."

Her lips twitched and that sparkle he liked to see so much in her eyes came back. "I'd bite back."

Laughing, he dared to step toward her again. "Want to play?"

She shook her head, her eyes still smiling.

"Don't suppose you'll invite me to walk you back to the guesthouse?"

"With a man who's already threatened to bite?"

He sighed. "Guess we'll have to do it here."

Alarm flashed across her face. "Do *what?*"

Slowly, very slowly, he drew her against him, keeping his gaze locked on hers. "Dance in the rain."

"There's no music," she said, sounding breathless. Her hands were fisted tight against his chest, her entire body rigid.

"Of course there is, darlin'." He slid his hands around her waist, realizing just how tiny she was. "Listen to it," he whispered, then fell silent, willing her to relax, to hear the incredible beat of the storm that crashed all around them.

He twirled her around the porch to the rain and thunder, until she relaxed slightly, then even more. When he dipped her, she clutched at him, startled, then smiled in genuine pleasure. He did it again—to see that smile, to feel her hold him, appreciating the little laugh she gave when he bent her low over his arm.

More rain, more thunder, and still they danced. Haley settled against him, holding on to his shoulders and moving easily. The fluid way she swayed against him had him pulling her closer, nuzzling his face in her hair. "Fun?" he murmured.

"Well...maybe, yes, a little."

He whirled and twirled them slowly about the wooden patio in tune with the falling rain, enjoying how perfect she felt in his arms, the heat of her skin beneath the sweater.

Contrasts, he thought. The woman was full of them. Fire and ice. Sweet and wary. Her arms slid up his shoulders, glided around his neck. He rubbed his cheek against hers, reveling in the abandonment with which she finally let go.

He wondered if she'd do the same when making love.

The thought brought him up short. He didn't deny a definite sexual pull, but since Lorraine had nearly destroyed him, he'd preferred the slow, lazy route of getting a woman to bed. He liked the chase, and the control. But right now, he didn't feel so leisurely, or in control, and he didn't think this was a good thing. Haley had done funny things to his head, as if he'd had too much wine. He wanted to run with her through the rain, toss her onto the cottage bed and bury himself in deep.

Yet she was lying, hiding. He badly wanted to believe that she was just another unfortunate victim in a cruel world, but he couldn't be sure. Was there a violent ex? Or something far more sinister, such as she'd committed a crime?

No, he wouldn't picture that. Couldn't.

*Sucker*, claimed the cynical little voice inside his head.

"I hear the music," she whispered.

"Me, too, darlin'." Her thighs bumped against his. He could smell the storm in her hair, feel the silkiness of her skin and he was going crazy. "You feel good, Haley. Real good." Finding his lips near her ear, he sank his teeth into the soft lobe, smiling when she shivered. He knew exactly what was happening to her because it was happening to him, too. He dipped her again, but she didn't laugh this time. And he saw that her eyes were closed, her mouth open a little as if she needed to force air into her lungs. Good Lord, but she did something to his insides. It startled him, for she hadn't been honest, and ever since Lorraine, honesty had been a major criterion for him.

He couldn't seem to help himself.

He brought Haley upright, cruising his lips along her jaw-bone, making his way toward that delicious-looking mouth. He was hard just thinking about the things he was going to do to those lips, but before he got there, she slapped a hand against his chest, drew a ragged breath and leaned back.

"Wait."

He blinked, and Haley watched warily as those brown, glazed eyes focused in on her. "Wait?"

She shook her head, unable to believe how she'd lost herself in that dance. "Don't kiss me."

He stared at her for a minute. Her heart slammed against her chest as his hands made one last sweep down her spine before he released her and took a step back.

"Don't kiss you," he repeated.

She managed a quick smile. "You sound like a parrot."

"Sorry." He winced, ran a hand through his hair. "That was some dance, Haley. We'll have to do this again sometime."

No chance of that, she silently promised herself. The man was simply too smooth. Far too smooth. She considered herself as unsensuous as they came, but even she had nearly melted into a little pool of longing at his feet when he'd run his hands over her back. "I don't think so."

"Now that's a challenge," he said, leaning back against the railing. "But you look beat, so it *will* have to wait for another time." The rain had stopped. He took her hand, tucked Max in his other, and walked them to her little house. At her front door, he set down the puppy and smiled. "You're okay when you let go, Haley. And a great dance partner."

"Flattery won't get you a kiss." She had no intention of encouraging him.

"Ah." He sighed. "And you say such nice things."

Laughter bubbled, but she didn't dare vent it. He'd just take it as an invitation.

"It's good to have you here." His eyes were unusually serious. "Are you going to stay?"

She went from amused to instantly wary. "What makes you think I'm not?"

"Do you really want to get into that?" he asked softly.

She had an image of death and mayhem. "No," she managed, though the weak woman in her wanted to throw herself down and weep out her troubles. "No," she repeated, more firmly. "But...I'm not sure how long I'll stay." Maybe only as long as tomorrow, she thought with a burst of sadness, if the USGS thought they could help her.

Cameron looked as if he wanted to say more, but he didn't. His sharp eyes shuttered again, but still she saw a flash of temper, reminding her this man could be much more than a handsome cowboy. His expression was carefully blank now, and very distant, which for some reason, made her want to cry. "I've...never danced in the rain before," she admitted in a conciliatory voice.

He looked at her with those mesmerizing eyes for a long moment. "No? Well, then, I'm glad it was me the first time." He bent and she stiffened, but all he did was kiss her cheek lightly. "You haven't had much time for frivolous things, have you?"

She shook her head, resisting the urge to touch where he'd just kissed.

"Maybe you'll make time now."

Being with him tonight had been exciting in a way she hadn't expected, but as fun and as frivolous as it had been, she couldn't repeat it. "I don't think so."

"Ah, another challenge. But I figure you've had a rough few days so we'll save it." He ran a finger over her jaw. "Sleep good, Haley. Dream of me."

His touch had her stomach all aflutter. "I'd rather not."

He laughed. His thumb skimmed her lower lip. "But you will."

Then he sauntered away, and only when he'd disappeared into

the night, did she allow her weak knees a break, sinking to the
step with a long, shaky breath. Max crawled into her lap, and
she nuzzled him close.

"I won't dream of him," she whispered to the puppy.

But damn him, she did.

# Chapter 4

Haley tossed and turned a good part of the night, then awoke in a bad mood. For hours, she'd been locked in the conflicting and disturbing memories of South America, then of the sweet, comforting feel of a man's warm, hard body against hers. *Cameron's* body.

She showered and yanked on Nellie's clothes, wishing she could buy her own things. She had money. Lots of it, actually. Lloyd had been a generous man and she'd rarely spent a dime. But the simple truth was, she was afraid to be found. It was far safer to remain a pauper for now.

Breakfast was fairly easy. All she had to do was repeat yesterday's magical performance. God help her when they tired of eggs, because she had absolutely no idea how to cook anything else.

But even knowing what she was doing, she went about the omelet and potatoes slowly and meticulously, whispering each step to herself to ensure success. Turning away from the stove, a pan of eggs in one hand, a spatula in the other, she stopped short, startled.

At the table sat Jason, Zach and Cameron, each waiting with a smiling, expectant face. Max sat on the floor, his little tail going a mile a minute. She had to laugh in embarrassed amazement. "I didn't even hear you guys come in."

"That's because you concentrate so hard," Jason said, watching as she put down the pan to fill plates up. She dropped bread into the toaster. "Jeez, I've never seen anyone cook so intently before."

She must have looked startled because Zach hurried to say, "Not that we care how you do it, Haley. Just that it tastes as good as yesterday."

Jason nodded, looking hopeful. Haley turned to glance at Cameron, who sat perfectly still with his hands in his lap. She raised her eyebrows, waiting for his comment, but he just grinned.

"Following your strict orders from yesterday morning, ma'am," he said with an exaggerated drawl, saluting her with his fork. "I'm not saying a word. I'm just hoping for a handout, is all."

She was busy trying to hide her laugh when Nellie waddled in, holding her back. Jason jumped up to pull out her chair, giving her a quick, smacking kiss. "Hey, Nel, just in time."

"Ahh." She sighed loudly as she sat. "No, Haley, honey, you don't have to serve me," she protested as Haley hurried to bring her some orange juice. "We'll get our own plates. I just want to sit a minute."

"I'll get it," Haley insisted as she took down another plate, worried about Nellie's pallor. "Stay. You look beat already."

"I am."

"Well, if you'd keep your hands off me, baby, you wouldn't be so tired," Jason joked.

"You guys are going to have to move that bed away from the wall," Cam said with a straight face. "It squeaks."

Nellie giggled guiltily and Jason leaned in for a long, passionate kiss. Haley hovered between being embarrassed and touched, but Zach just appeared disgusted.

"Oh, *please*," Zach said, pushing away his plate. "Not at the table."

Cam laughed and slathered his toast with butter. "Zach, if you'd just ask Thea out, you could get it whenever you wanted, too. Has anyone seen how she looks at him?"

"With stars in her eyes," Jason quipped, lifting his lips from his wife's. "That poor woman, Zach. She wants you bad."

Zach closed his eyes and bore the moment. "She's the librarian."

Jason grinned. "Ask her out, man. Then she wouldn't have to drive all the way out here on the pretense of retrieving your library books."

"'Oh, Zach!'" Cam squealed in a falsetto. "'You owe me twenty-five cents, Zach.'"

Zach growled and stood. Cam blinked at him, the picture of innocence.

Jason hooted. "Do us all a favor, Zach. Just kill him."

A wrestle would have ensued then, but Nellie shut them all up when she gasped and held her stomach, grimacing.

Utter silence, then everyone spoke at once.

"Nel? What's the matter, baby?" Jason leaped to her side. Cam stood too, then moved behind her to rub her shoulders, his face tense and worried. Zach reached for the phone, swearing up a storm.

"Stop," Nellie said quietly, raising a hand. She let out a slow, controlled breath. "I'm fine, really. Just a twinge." Then she laughed a little, as they all stared at her with wide, terrified eyes. "Stop it, I'm fine."

With a collective sigh, the men sat back down. From where she stood by the sink, Haley glanced at Nellie, sick with worry. Nellie winked, and Haley stared at her, flabbergasted. *She'd faked that contraction.* Just to make peace. And in the process, she'd tamed three huge beasts. Struggling with a huge smile, Haley turned away. But her humor faded quickly enough.

Breakfast, or any meal with these people, was far more than just the sharing of food. And they were much more than merely related by blood. Zach's quiet voice telling a story everyone listened to, Jason and Cam's merciless teasing of Nellie, Nellie getting them all back with a mere batting of her eyelashes. They fought, they laughed, they loved. And dammit, just watching them caused a lump in her throat that couldn't be swallowed away.

Haley shoved dirty pans into the sink, and stared at the greasy water. What was it like to belong with people like this? People who accepted you just for who you were. Nothing more, nothing less. For years, the only meals she'd bothered with had been wolfed down between long periods of quiet study and work. As a child, she'd been forced into silence at a table full of other, equally bright, and equally terrified children, watched over by hard, ungiving caretakers. Meals had been stifling and lifeless, nothing like the lively exchange that even at this moment was going on behind her.

She made herself get over it and moved back to the table, juggling three full plates. She placed one before Nellie and Jason, then Zach.

Cam looked at her.

She held his gaze evenly.

With a sigh, he pushed back his chair to get his own plate. He'd just started to rise when she plopped down yet another full plate in front of him, biting back her smile.

A heavenly scent wafted up from it, mixing with the rising steam. Cam took a second to appreciate that, then smiled, slow and wide. *She'd served him.* He looked up. Haley's straight, unwavering gaze had an instant liquid warmth swimming through him.

"Thanks," he said.

She nodded, and when she turned away her arm brushed against his shoulder. He physically jolted as if she'd cattle-prodded him, and it was the strangest thing. If he closed his eyes, he'd feel her slight body in his arms, just like last night. But he didn't close his eyes because they were glued to the soft swaying of her hips as she walked gracefully back to the sink. She had the most squeezable little—

"Cam?"

He scowled and looked at Jason. "Yeah?"

"Take a picture, it lasts longer."

Zach choked on his toast. Nellie smacked Zach on the back, then elbowed Jason, while shooting Cam a dirty look.

Haley glanced over her shoulder, frowning. "What's going on?"

"Nothing," Cam said quickly.

"Then why," she slowly asked, putting her hands on her hips and looking at each of them in turn, "is everyone staring at me?"

Cam looked to the others at the table for support, but he shouldn't have bothered. Immediately, three pairs of eyes lowered and food was shoved into three very busy mouths. So much for "thick and thin" and all that crap. His family had bailed ship. "Because you're so pretty?" Cam smiled innocently at Haley, laying on the charm.

Haley's eyes narrowed suspiciously, but she moved back to the counter.

"Aren't you going to eat?" he asked when he realized she had no intention of sitting with them.

"No," she said, not looking at him, her hands busy with dishes. "I'm fine, thanks."

"Haley," Nellie said around a full bite, "please, come sit with us. We don't expect you to serve us like this. It's not right. We want you to eat with us, as part of the family."

"But I'm not," she said softly. "Excuse me." She left the room.

Haley went directly into the den, where she'd set her purse down earlier as she'd come inside to cook breakfast. Her beeper was vibrating and this time there was no message, just a phone number that she knew to be South American. Not only South American, but for her old apartment.

Where the murders had taken place.

She stared long and hard at Cam's desk. On it was a cellular phone that Nellie's mother in L.A. had insisted her daughter take home with her to that "wild place." A cell phone, based and billed out of L.A., in a different name from whose house she was in, couldn't be easily traced, could it? God, she didn't know, but she had to take the chance.

She dialed the number on the pager and stood rooted when she recognized Alda's cool, calm voice giving a greeting.

"Alda?"

"Haley! My God. Where are you?"

Suspicion gripped Haley, though she couldn't explain it. How long did it take for a trace to take hold and locate her? Was Alda capable of such a thing? She had no idea, and was taking no chances. "Alda, what is happening?" she asked quickly, watching the clock on the desk. She'd stay on for a maximum of sixty seconds.

"Exactly what it looks like!" Alda drew in a sharp breath. "We need help, Haley. Who have you told about the system?"

"Wait." She tried to think. Why would Alda care? "Are the authorities looking for me?"

"Yes. Where—"

"Am I the only suspect? Are they questioning you?"

Alda hesitated. "What are you saying?" Her voice had chilled.

"Where's Bob?" Haley asked, ignoring Alda's question and giving in to a terrible foreboding. "Alda, where's Bob?"

When Alda hesitated again, Haley lowered the phone and gently disconnected. Her head was spinning, her heart heavy with grief, betrayal. *Fear.*

She had to risk another call on the cell phone, to the USGS. She set her purse on the desk and called Information.

Then, with shaky fingers, she dialed. But she'd no sooner heard the greeting on the line, when Cam strode into the room.

He smiled at her and she felt herself freeze, phone in hand. She knew enough about him to know he'd *never* sit idly back and let her deal with this alone. Nope, dammit. The cowboy would get himself killed.

"Hello," he said easily, just as the USGS receptionist repeated her greeting a little impatiently. Cam walked over to the desk, moving papers around, obviously looking for something. He didn't seem to be in a hurry to leave, or to notice that Haley desperately wanted him to.

Damn it.

Carefully, she lowered the phone from her ear and flipped it off, disconnecting the now annoyed receptionist. "I'm sorry, I know I should have asked to use this phone first—"

"Don't be silly, Nellie won't mind. And don't hang up on my account," he said, glancing at her with a soft smile. "I'll be out in a sec."

Did his smile have to be so devastating? "No matter," she said lamely. "It's...not important."

He dropped his papers to the desk. His eyes never left hers as he came around to stand before her, but they went cold. "Not important? Then why are you chewing your nails?"

She dropped her hand from her mouth with a small oath and turned from him. Why did he have to probe so deeply? Why did he have to look at her like it mattered?

She glanced down at the phone, desperate to make the call. To get this nightmare over with so she could go on with her life.

She felt Cam's hands on her hips, gently turning her to face him. In his usual unhurried and graceful manner, he slid those hands around her waist, slowly drawing her close. She had a terrific urge to plunge her hands into his hair, and surprised herself when she gave in to it. She knew she shouldn't have, but it felt so good to be held, wanted. To be alive.

"You've avoided me," he said in a deep, husky voice, leaning forward to bring his lips to her hair.

How could she explain? "I've been busy." Against her better judgment, she tipped her head back, allowing him access to her neck, then nearly moaned as his mouth moved over her skin. "Very busy," she repeated weakly.

"Mmm, I've noticed. The house looks great." He teased her ear with flirty little passes of his tongue, and her knees went weak. "Make your call, Haley. I'll wait."

Her eyes fluttered closed. "I don't have to make a call."

Feeling him stiffen, she pulled back and opened her eyes. He dropped his arms and his pleasant smile, and stared at something on his desk. With his jaw tight, he picked up the little piece of paper she'd scribbled USGS's phone number on. "This is the number you were calling?"

"Yes," she said, misunderstanding his cause for concern. "I know, it's long-distance. I'll pay—"

"If you're going to offer to reimburse me, you'd better stop right there, or you'll really make me mad." He turned on her, his brows knitted tightly together. "USGS?"

"United States Geological Survey. I...have connections there."

"Connections?"

"I'm sort of..." Damn. "I'm a geologist."

"I'm paying a geologist to keep my house?" He perched a hip on the desk, crossed his arms over his chest and looked at her. "Why don't you tell me the rest, Haley?"

She had to tread carefully, she reminded herself as her temper flared. Very carefully. This man might move slowly and not have much drive when it came to worldly ambition, but he had a mind as sharp as a tack, and right now it was aimed directly at her.

If she was in danger, though, so was he. For his own protection, she had to make it good. *Very good.* "I was just calling to check on a friend."

"Actually, I'm still stuck on the fact you're a geologist."

"It's no big deal."

Turning her head away so he couldn't read the self-disgust in her face, she moved toward the door. She had to be alone. God, she'd lied with an ease that made her sick. Since when had she gotten so good at that?

*Since her life, and that of everyone she cared about, was on the line.*

"Haley, wait." He cursed when she didn't. "Just—" He swore again, and at the sound of a thump, Haley turned. She'd forgotten her purse, and Cam had just inadvertently dumped it to the floor, scattering its contents.

"I'm sorry," he said, lithely dropping down to pick up the loose items.

From the door, she could see what would happen, and was powerless to stop it. Her heart slammed against her ribs as Cam's hand stilled in midair.

On the floor lay her two bottles of pills. Eyes narrowed, he lifted them and scanned the labels.

Haley stood there, feeling stripped bare as he touched everything personal she owned. Finding her feet, and her voice, she squatted beside him and yanked up the purse. She extended her hand for the bottles, but he held them out of reach and looked at her.

"What are these?"

She almost didn't recognize his voice, it sounded so low and gravelly...and urgent. "They're mine," she said.

"This one is for ulcers," he said, sounding horrified. "And this other...sleeping pills? My God, Haley."

Her throat burned, her face flamed with humiliation. She knew what her failings were, but to have him know, too, was worse than she could have imagined. Snatching the bottles from his hand, she put them in her purse, keeping her head averted. "Get away from me."

Still kneeling next to her on the floor, she heard him make a wordless sound of regret and concern. With a gentleness she couldn't face, he took her shoulders in his hands, turning her toward him. "You're sick."

"No." She dropped her gaze and noticed the T-shirt he wore had slightly frayed sleeves where they stretched over his biceps.

His chest seemed impossibly wide. It should be illegal, she thought a little wildly, for a man to look so good in an old shirt.

"You said you wouldn't lie," he accused, almost roughly, his fingers digging in to her. "But you keep on doing it, dammit."

"I'm not sick now," she said carefully. She sat back on her heels. "I haven't taken any of those pills since I got here."

"But your stomach has hurt." He waited a beat. "That's what the problem is, isn't it? You have an ulcer."

*Ulcers,* she almost corrected.

"And you can't sleep. What's the insomnia from, Haley? South America?" He leaned close to see her face. "You won't tell me," he said softly, his eyes hard and glittering. "Or you'll make up more lies. Won't you, Haley?"

"I don't know," she answered as honestly as she could, with one hundred and eighty pounds of male frustration staring at her. "It's complicated."

His mouth tightened at that. "Your passport is there." He nodded toward the things she'd shifted back to her purse. "Do I have to steal it so you won't run?"

"You promised me that first night, remember, Cam?" There was no controlling the catch in her voice. "No questions."

His fingers tightened on her. "That was before I realized you were going to turn out to be a liar."

"I can't tell you more!" she cried, wishing she could explain.

"You mean you *won't.*"

"It's—"

"Complicated?" he offered with mock patience.

"Yes! Damn it, yes. It's complicated. It's—" She choked it off before she added *and dangerous.* Deadly. Fear for him and the others made her speak harshly. "Stay out of it, Cameron. You've got to stay out of it."

"What if I won't?"

"I'll leave." The thought was enough to make her heart drop slowly to the floor, but she knew she would. She'd have to.

A veil came down over his eyes. "You know, I just realized

something." He stood. "I'm nagging at you." He stretched his shoulders as if his neck ached, and even Haley, who was completely inexperienced in such things, could read the hurt he barely managed to mask.

He moved toward the door. "Use the phone, Haley. I won't bother you again."

"You're not bothering me."

He stopped with one hand on the door. The look he gave her didn't bear close analysis. "You want to be real sure about that, Haley."

"Of course I am." Couldn't he see how difficult this was? She didn't want to keep secrets, she *had* to. "I—I like being with you, Cam."

"How do I know I can believe that?"

"It's the truth."

"Is it? Then promise me one thing. Don't lie to me anymore. It turns me into someone I don't like very much." He shut the door quietly behind him before she could soothe his feelings, or even make that promise.

Which was just as well. She'd be lying again.

Without giving herself a moment to think, she dialed the USGS again, silently apologizing to Nellie's mother, who would no doubt get this bill.

She didn't use her real name, and she didn't state the purpose of her call. Since both Bob and Alda had once worked there, Haley simply asked for them, using their full names, as if she expected them to be there.

The answer she received had her sinking to the floor in shock.

Dr. Bob Herntz couldn't be reached because two days ago he'd been killed in an unfortunate car bombing in South America. Then she got her answer on Alda, and a new grief mingled with her rage. Dr. Alda Jones, also known to the USGS because she was not only Bob's significant other, but because she'd written numerous textbooks on geology, could not be reached, either.

She'd disappeared.

Dear God. Could it be true? Could it be Alda?

Sometime later, when Haley had immersed herself in chores, her pager vibrated again. Without looking, still horrified, she reached for her hip and shut it off.

She didn't want to know.

Haley was attacking the upstairs with a vacuum cleaner when Cam found her the next morning. She didn't hear him coming, which gave him a minute to watch as she stared sightlessly ahead, obviously troubled.

It reminded him how little he knew about her, which bothered him. Doubt and suspicion had spread like a disease the day before, driving him crazy all night. Damn, but his past had a nasty way of keeping up with him. Firmly, he pushed the unhappy memories away. The truth was, he'd come down hard on Haley, after promising not to, and he felt badly. "Haley?"

She just kept vacuuming, her eyes glazed with such emotion that for a moment he could only stand there, overwhelmed. What was going on inside her pretty head?

"Haley." He touched her shoulder and she jerked back, eyes wide, until she saw him. The way she sucked in her fear both fascinated and infuriated him. He reached over and switched off the vacuum. "You never ate breakfast," he said inanely. *Never ate?* Who was he, her mother?

"I'm not hungry." Leaning forward, she reached again for the vacuum, but he stopped her.

"It's hard to talk with that on."

Without a sign of the smile he'd hoped for, she said, "I know."

"Are you all right?"

"Of course." But she avoided his gaze as they wrestled over the vacuum. "Why wouldn't I be?"

"I don't know, but I wish you could tell me." She chewed her lip, silent, and he tried another tactic. "I'm going into town. Come with me?"

"I have work."

"It'll wait."

"I don't think so," she said quietly. "Thanks."

So polite, so distant. So hurt. He turned her toward him, aching a little at the turmoil he sensed just beneath her surface. Surprised at the surge of tenderness and protectiveness she somehow invoked, he found he couldn't let go of her. "Haley, we need to talk."

She'd stiffened at his touch. "About?"

Start slow, he warned himself. *Real slow.* "Your salary and hours, for one. We never discussed it."

"It doesn't matter."

"It should. What you're doing here is important to us, and we want to make sure you get compensated. And I don't want you working all hours of the day."

She looked at him then. "What I meant was, I'd work here for free."

Touched, he reached up and caressed her jaw. "We're that great, huh?"

She shook her head, a little noise of wordless amazement escaping her. "You have no idea what you have here, do you?"

"What do you mean?" His hand slid to her lovely neck.

"Your family," she said, closing her eyes when his thumb played with the sensitive spot at the base of her neck. Her pulse fluttered wildly, flattering him. "You take them for granted," she whispered. "You shouldn't. They're...wonderful."

"Yes, they are." Because he couldn't help himself, he bent his head to the spot he'd touched and tasted her. Her hands came up to grip his shoulders hard, but she didn't push him away. He took his time, cruising his mouth over her jaw. When he looked at her again, those incredibly blue eyes had turned cloudy with confusion, and with what he hoped was arousal.

"You're a part of this family now," he said, meaning it. "We want you to be."

"You don't even know me."

"I know," he admitted, sliding his lips softly across hers once. The touch electrified him, and her, too, if that husky catch of breath was any indication. "But I want to. Let me know you, Haley. Trust me."

She shook her head but still didn't draw back. "I'm not ready for that. Please..."

"Please what?" He kissed her softly again, biting back his moan at her incredible sweetness.

"I think," she said shakily, stepping away, "we should go to town now."

He smiled past the ache of her inability to trust him, relieved she'd agreed to come. "On the way you can tell me how much you want in wages."

She looked uncomfortable. "I told you, I don't care about that. You're already giving me room and board."

"You must need money, Haley," he said gently. "Come on, you can think about it while I drive."

"Fine. But I'm only going with you because there're some things I need," she warned. "So don't get any ideas." She pushed him aside lightly.

"What kind of ideas?" he asked, all sorts of wicked ones dancing in his head before he could stop himself.

She blushed. "Oh, just forget it."

They were in his truck before she spoke again. "Since you insist on paying me," she said in that haughty, sexy voice he loved, "I think you should know—I don't come cheap."

He threw back his head and laughed. "I never thought so, Ms. Williams. I never thought so."

After that, he let her sit quietly, as she seemed to want to do, on the long drive into Colorado Springs. Once there, she refused to accept his company, insisting that he drop her off at a mini-mall while he went on to the lumber store. Though it roused his suspicions again, he really had no choice. She was entitled to her privacy and distance.

He needed *his* distance, as well. He had no idea what was happening to him, but it had to stop. There could be nothing between him and Haley. Nothing. At least not until he knew what she was hiding.

* * *

Haley glanced longingly at the cash machine outside the grocery store, wishing she could get the money she needed. But fear was a heavy motivation.

It would lead them—Alda?—straight to her.

*Alda.* Haley struggled to remember a sane world, and the kind, caring woman Alda had always seemed. But that led to worry about what she should do next, and since she hadn't a clue, she gave up. She had to stay hidden or she'd find herself as dead as Bob. Or worse, rotting away in a South American jail cell. If she could just stay safe until Alda made a mistake. If only she hadn't panicked on the USGS call, she might have learned more. If, if, if.

With a heavy sigh, Haley turned around, trying to decide how far the twenty dollars she had would take her. There were some things she needed she just couldn't bring herself to ask Nellie for. As she moved toward the automatic doors of the store, her wandering gaze collided abruptly with a medium-build, dark-haired man who stood across the way. He leaned against a pole, staring at her.

*No big deal.* Just a curious stranger. Absolutely nothing to worry about. But he watched her intently, and her heart pumped triple time. *This is ridiculous,* she told herself, even as she dashed into the store and ducked behind one of the newspaper stands, shaking. *Ridiculous,* she repeated to herself. But she made herself walk down two long aisles before venturing back out again.

The man had disappeared.

Breathing a sigh of relief, Haley studied the minimall carefully and spotted a bakery. Surely she deserved a doughnut after that scare. Heading down the walk toward the bakery, she stopped to admire the delicious, flaky-looking croissants in the display case. She was hungry. And she'd forgotten to eat, again. No wonder her head and stomach hurt. Yep, she was going to splurge and buy herself—

A shadow fell across her, blocking out the sun.

Reflected in the window, and standing directly behind her, was the same stranger.

With a strangled gasp, Haley moved quickly, racing down the walk and slamming into the first store she came to.

A video store.

Haley dashed down an aisle of videos. Trembling behind a life-size cardboard cutout of Tom Cruise, she looked around. What should she do? What if he came in here and grabbed her? She'd scream like hell, that was what!

No one came. Huddled behind the huge poster, she began to feel relieved. Then incredibly foolish. Of course, no one came— *because no one was after her.*

She had to stop these panic attacks. They did nothing but annoy her ulcer and make her head ache. Her fear was totally unfounded. She'd left no clue, no trace. And who could possibly guess that Dr. Haley Whitfield, head of EVS's team of geologists, was now doing duty as a housekeeper on some ranch in Colorado? No one. Encouraged by that, she straightened and left the store. The man had disappeared.

Eager to be on her way, Haley slipped into the bakery, almost desperate now for food. Her head throbbed, her stomach grumbled and hurt. Nothing like panic to stir an appetite.

"I'll have one of those croissants," she said politely, bending over the display and pointing.

"Sure thing, ma'am."

Haley raised her gaze and froze. Behind the counter was her stranger. The man who'd been following her. Their eyes met— his, cold, hard and knowing—and she whirled.

Running, blinded by fear, Haley expected to be grabbed any moment. Or shot. Her skin crawled. Her breath escaped her in sobs as she fumbled with the door, and for a second, she thought she couldn't get out, that he'd caught up with her and was holding it shut. As she fought and clawed at the handle, her heart slammed each beat, but finally the door opened. Without looking back, she took off. The prickly feeling at the base of her neck increased.

She was being followed. Oh, God. Her feet pounded the cement walk, and as she got to the front of the grocery store, she chanced a glance over her shoulder, still running full speed.

Then, with a sickening thud, she crashed into something as hard and ungiving as a steel pole, and it knocked the sense right out of her.

Cam's first thought from flat on his back, with Haley stretched out over him, was *Ouch!* But he tightened his grip on her as she began to struggle, wincing when he got a knee uncomfortably close to his groin. "Lie still a minute, Haley."

She reared back, her eyes wide, her face so pale it looked translucent. "Cameron? Oh, God, he's right behind me."

Cam managed to pull his wits together after the bone-shaking collision to look over Haley's shoulder, but both the walkway and the parking lot were empty. He held her arms. "Who?"

Haley glanced around, but when she saw no one, she sagged over him. "He's gone. Again." Then she threw her arms around his neck and buried her face in his chest.

Concerned, he sat up, cradling her in his lap right there on the sidewalk. "Haley?" He pushed the hair from her face, but she only shook her head and burrowed tighter against him. Her arms, still clamped around his neck, trembled, and his alarm grew. "What happened?"

She shivered.

He looked around them, prepared for anything. An older woman got out of a station wagon, went into the dry cleaners. A teenager came out of the grocery store. Somewhere, a truck started and rumbled away.

Nothing out of the ordinary. "Haley?" He stroked her chilled arms. "*Who's* gone?" She just held him, so he sighed and pulled her closer. "I'm here now," he whispered in her ear, soothing her as best he could. If anyone thought it strange to see a man and a woman embracing on the sidewalk, no one said a word. "Come on," he said after a minute. "Let's get you back to the truck."

"I'm okay." Her voice, muffled against his shirt, sounded

embarrassed. But she pushed out of his arms, sniffled once, and avoided his gaze.

He knelt before her. "Haley, can you tell me—" He stopped abruptly as she went even paler, and her pupils shrank into twin pinpoints of shock. Swearing, he pushed her head between her knees. "Take a deep breath," he demanded, sick with worry. "There you go. No, damn it, don't try to get up yet. You'll faint. Come on now, another one. That's the way, darlin', do it again."

When she'd done as he said, and when her color looked slightly better, he yanked her back into his arms. Too skinny, he thought, rocking her slowly. Too damn skinny. He hadn't seen her eat enough to sustain a bird, and he cursed himself now, noticing how light and fragile she felt in his arms.

"Haley, tell me what frightened you."

After a hesitation, she shook her head. "Nothing. I'm sorry. It was nothing."

The slow anger he'd kept buried for years surfaced. *Another liar,* his brain screamed. But this fabrication wasn't over an outrageous credit-card bill. Or whom she'd lunched with. No, this was much more serious. Cupping the back of Haley's head, Cam looked into her eyes. They darted nervously from his. The rage built, but strangely enough, not at her. Someone had indeed frightened her, and he didn't like it. "Haley—"

"Please," she begged softly. "Let it go."

Memories assaulted him, of another woman. Dammit. He wouldn't push yet another to trust him. He wouldn't. "No. I won't let it go."

"I'm fine," she repeated. "Really."

"Right." Cam stood, and just managed not to groan at his aches and pain from having been slammed to the concrete. He reached down and, despite her protests, scooped her up, then marched to the truck.

"I can walk!"

She might not weigh enough, but she did feel good against his chest. "Humor me."

Huffing a little, she settled against him. "This isn't a movie, Cameron. You're not some cowboy hero."

Without a word, he settled her in his truck, removing his hands from her with some reluctance, which only annoyed him all the more. "When was the last time you ate?"

She looked away, a habit that was quickly becoming irritating. "Haley, dammit."

She scowled. "I don't know. Yesterday. I think."

He swore ripely, the temper he rarely acknowledged simmering a slow burn. "You little fool." He slammed her door, then leaned down to look at her through the open window. "I'm going to the bakery to get you something to eat. *Don't move.*"

"No! Not in there," she said quickly.

"Why not?" He glanced back over his shoulder, saw nothing. But when he looked at her again, she'd collected herself, even if she was as pale as a ghost. At this point, he refused to speculate, just reacted with the fear she'd instilled in him. "One more time. What in the hell's going on?"

"Nothing."

He took a deep breath. Resting his elbows against the door, he gave her a long look. "Haley, darlin', you were running like hell when I found you."

Again, she looked away. He brought her face back, keeping his voice low with difficulty. "You jumped me."

Still no answer.

"Oh, I know," he said conversationally, his eyes sharp on her, waiting for a reaction. "You missed me." He watched the emotions war within her; the humiliation of having misled him to think she missed him, against her need to keep her reasons to herself.

"Yes, I missed you," she eventually agreed, the words coming from between clenched teeth. "Hope I didn't hurt you in my excitement."

She still didn't trust him enough to let him help her, and that got to him good. Her pallor hadn't changed. The realization that she was convinced whoever she'd run from would, and could, come get her, sobered him. The urge to protect was amazingly strong, made all the more difficult for him because he was still furious with her. Changing his mind about the bakery, he straightened, walked around to get back into his truck.

"What are you doing?" she asked.

"We're going to a drive-through." He thrust the truck in gear. "And while we're doing it, you can explain things to me." He quickly pulled into the first fast-food place he came to and ordered just about everything on the menu. Then he looked at her, only to find her staring at him as if he'd lost his mind. "What? Did I forget something?"

"You ordered enough food for ten people."

*Nerves,* he wanted to tell her. And he hadn't felt them in a good long time.

"Why did you come back so soon?"

"I missed you, too, darlin'." Pulling forward, he paid the lady in the bird hat at window two and took the food.

"You couldn't have gotten your lumber so soon."

"Observant as well as intelligent," he murmured, feeling a little nasty and more than willing to take it out on her. *"Eat."*

She pulled out a chicken sandwich and took a token bite. Then she shoved that aside, searching through the bag past the salad, past the bread, past the corn on the cob. With a faint smile, she took out the french fries and dug in with gusto.

Cam watched in amazement. "That's the least healthy thing in there."

"I know." She ate another. And another. Then poured catsup all over them and dug in again. Her color came back.

"Eat the other stuff," he protested. "Something good for you."

"I like this," she said stubbornly. "Now tell me why you really came back."

She was stalling, but at least she didn't have that trapped-doe look in her eyes anymore. "I realized that I hadn't given you any money—"

She tensed, then wiped her fingers and shoved the food away. "I don't need your money."

The woman had enough pride to fill his gas tank. "You can't be done eating already." Her scowl deepened and he realized something horrifying—*he was nagging again,* just like his mother would have. "I just wanted to give you what I owed you for the work you've done."

"I never did get to the store," she said softly.

He pulled back into the lot of the minimall and turned off the engine. "Eat first, while it's hot."

When she had, he came around for her and took her hand as she alighted. He tugged gently until she looked at him. "We're going to talk, Haley. When you're done in here."

"I don't feel much like talking."

"Tough." He nodded toward the store, struggling to rein in all he was feeling. "Let's go."

"You can wait here."

"No way," he said, rubbing his sore and bruised backside. "I can't take another tackle to the pavement."

Heat flooded her face. "I don't need a guard."

He stopped her with a hand on her shoulder. "*Something* scared you here, you can't deny that." He put a finger to her lips when she would have done just that. "Maybe I forgot to tell you I really dislike being lied to. And I'm not leaving you alone, so forget it."

She sighed and entered the automated doors, not looking to see if he followed.

Since it seemed to be so important to her, he pretended not to notice what she threw into the shopping cart, knowing by the lovely shade of pink on her cheeks that she was embarrassed. Halfway down one aisle, he caught her giving the lipsticks a longing glance.

She protested when he stopped. "Come on, I'm done," she said, trying to tug him along.

"Hmm." He touched a fire-engine-red lipstick. "Nice color."

She rolled her eyes.

"Much as I'd love to see this on you, I don't want to have to fight off Zach."

"Don't," she mumbled, still trying to pull him away. "Just forget it."

But he was locked on the image of her in the red lipstick, with matching fingernails and toenails to boot. He caught her horrified gaze and laughed. "Okay, maybe not. But this would be pretty." He held out a light rose-colored gloss. "And I bet it tastes good, too."

At his suggestive leer, she let out a little laugh, making him realize she didn't make that pretty sound nearly often enough.

"Fine." She capitulated, grabbing it from him and tossing it in the cart. "But don't think *you're* ever going to taste it."

"Uh-oh." He pushed the cart toward the checkout. "Another challenge."

She just shook her head, some of the haunted look fading from her eyes.

Cam bided his time, waiting until they were back in the truck before turning to her. "I'm going to ask you again, Haley. What happened to you today?"

She fiddled with her purse, put on her seat belt, and looked everywhere but at him. "I thought someone was following me, but I was wrong. I panicked over nothing."

One of his hands was on the headrest above her. He touched her cheek softly with his other until she looked at him. *God, those eyes,* he thought. So clear, so absolutely full of mysteries. "*Is* someone following you?"

Her mouth tightened. "I don't think so. No. No one's following me."

"But it's a possibility?" he prompted.

She dragged her lip across her teeth and dropped her gaze. "Okay, look. I had trouble on my last job. One of my...co-workers sort of lost it."

"Lost it?"

"You know...went crazy."

His throat closed. His anger drained instantly to be replaced with concern. "Did he hurt you, Haley?"

"N-n-no." Again she bit her lip. "And it's a she. But either way, I don't think that's a problem because no one knows where I am. I just panicked there for a second. I'm sorry."

"Didn't you tell your boss? What kind of job was this?"

"My boss...couldn't do anything about it. Complicated policies, I guess."

Could she be more vague? "You can't be too safe. Let's call the cops."

"No!" She lowered her voice instantly. "It's not necessary. Really. She can't find me here."

He wished she'd look at him, because every instinct he had was screaming. *Another damn lie.* And yet...he still wanted her. Her hand rested on her thigh. He reached for it, frowning at its iciness. Bringing it up to his mouth, he ran his lips over her knuckles.

"You shouldn't do that." Her voice sounded light, whispery. And he knew how she felt because his own throat had gone dry.

"I shouldn't do a lot of things," he said, unhooking her seat belt and drawing her stiff body close. His fingers slid into her short, silky hair. "You have a way, darlin', of knotting me up inside." He bent to kiss her cheek, her jaw. And then because she smelled so good, tasted so delicious, he kissed her ear, her neck, then her jaw again.

She shivered when he skimmed his lips over hers, but kept her hands at her sides. "You really shouldn't...do that."

He smiled against her neck. "Why? You like it." Her hands moved then, to his shoulders, and he expected to be pushed away.

"I think we should go now," she whispered instead, still holding him.

"You think too much." But he gave her one last quick hug. "You'd feel better if you talked about it. Maybe your head and stomach wouldn't hurt so much."

She ducked her face as if the pain was a weakness to be embarrassed about.

"I don't like to think of you in pain."

"I'm—"

"I know," he said with a little laugh directed at himself. *Idiot.* "You're fine." He wanted to kiss her, *had* to kiss her. Watching her, being this close, he felt the urgency grow inside him until he was tense with the need of it. He wanted to plunder, dive in until neither of them knew their name, but the gentleness so deeply ingrained in him wouldn't allow it. So he glided his arms around her again and started with her chin, nipping it between his teeth, gradually moving along her face, leisurely drawing out their pleasure. He was rewarded when her body softened and leaned against his.

Her first sigh, the glorious feeling of her arms slipping around him in feminine surrender, stirred his blood. Taming the need was worth it, he decided in hazy delight, and with tormenting slowness he brought his lips back to hers. This time they parted immediately beneath his. Her shy tongue met his, and his last coherent thought was that this kiss wasn't going to be enough. He felt her clinging to him, heard her helpless moan...and he craved more.

A kiss wasn't supposed to devastate, he thought in confusion; it was supposed to satisfy. A kiss wasn't supposed to make the blood roar in his ears, or make his head swim; it should bring simple pleasure. But there was nothing simple about this. Oh, the pleasure seeped through him, but he sure as hell wasn't supposed to tremble just because she sighed his name in that low, sexy voice.

Being with a woman should be easy. Not rip a hole through his heart and leave him bleeding, helpless and needy. Carefully, purposefully, he drew away and stared at her, his world rocked by that one "simple" kiss.

Haley's eyes fluttered open, glazed and cloudy. "I think," she said on a very shaky breath, scooting back a little, "it would be best if we didn't do that often."

"I was thinking the opposite." Her lips were wet and swollen and he wanted to taste them again.

She straightened and tucked her legs beneath her in a defensive gesture that stopped him from reaching for her. "Things are mixed up enough, Cam. I..." She looked out the window and sighed. "Too mixed up to add this complication."

He wondered if she realized it was the first time she'd used his nickname. "That was some kiss, Haley. You should know. It left me wanting more."

"I can't give you more." Desperation crept into her voice.

He struggled with the patience that usually came so naturally, and didn't find it. "Why? Dammit, why?"

"Because I'm trouble, Cam. With a capital *T*."

For two days, Haley cringed at the memory of that day. She'd never forget the almost-comic, stunned surprise on Cam's face as she'd plowed him to the ground. She'd never tackled a boss before. Nor, she thought a little ruefully, had she ever kissed one.

She'd avoided him, but he'd done the same right back, even as he made sure that someone was always near enough that she never felt alone. She knew her lies and innate wariness had gotten to him, but she didn't know what to do. She couldn't tell him the truth—could she?

Sometimes she thought she should; then she remembered how many had died and decided against it.

She stood in the large living room of the ranch house, dusting. She'd discovered the Crock-Pot the day before, and the large recipe book inside it, so dinner should be a snap.

She hoped.

She'd dropped potatoes and carrots into it exactly according to the recipe. Then a large roast. She expected to need a miracle, but to her utter surprise, when she'd checked the pot an hour ago, a delicious aroma had arisen. And it actually looked good, though personally, she'd prefer a greasy burger and fries.

Cameron had left strict instructions. She could cook breakfast and dinner, but everyone had to fix their own lunch. Yet something strange had happened to Haley—something unexpected. She found she enjoyed the kitchen activities so much, she'd actually connived to be in there when everyone wandered in around noon. So it became natural for her to make the sandwiches—which even *she* could do well.

Haley didn't like to think about how attached to everyone she'd become. Or how much Nellie seemed to enjoy having her. Or how much she enjoyed bantering like old friends with Zach and Jason.

Then there was Cameron.

She'd never danced in the rain before. She'd never shared a laugh over a cow. And she'd certainly never been kissed by a man the way he'd kissed her.

Well aware that such a thing could go nowhere, she couldn't keep her heart from giving a little leap whenever she saw him. For two long nights now, she'd lain awake, torn between fear for her uncertain future, and a longing so fierce she couldn't ease the ache.

She longed—oh, how she longed—yet she couldn't put a name to it. Her life had been pathetically short on romance, and most of that was by choice. Men didn't understand her, and most seemed intimidated by her. It would be laughable if she'd had a friend to laugh with. But she'd been pathetic in that department, too. Maybe because she'd always been around people much older than herself, maybe because while her brain was overly developed, she'd ignored her social skills... She didn't know.

But she'd read plenty, and her deepest, most secret fantasy was to have a romance. A real, true romance, just like in the books she loved. Last night, with nothing to read, she'd actually started a journal. She'd kept a record of her life before, plenty of times. But those had always been careful notes of her studies or projects, never anything personal. This time, and for the first time, she'd outlined her feelings in detail, purposely steering away from anything technical. Just feelings. And she'd been shocked by what she'd discovered.

She was infatuated with her new boss.

Confused and a little frightened by the depth of her unexpected feelings, she put a little too much "oomph" into dusting the top of the mantel, and two picture frames slid down. Reaching for the first one, she slid her rag over the dusty top of it, then went still.

The snapshot showed Cameron, maybe several years ago, dressed in a suit and tie. But the surprising elegance of his dress wasn't what shocked her, or even how good he looked—it was the possessive way his arm was wrapped around a tall, beautiful and very pregnant woman.

"That was my wife," he said quietly, from behind her.

# Chapter 5

At Cam's softly spoken words, Haley's rag fell to the floor. Dismay came first, then embarrassment, as she stooped down, but Cam gently took her wrist and pulled her up.

With a small smile that didn't quite mask the sorrow in his eyes, he touched the frame. Running a finger over the dusty edge, he remained silent.

Haley watched as with exaggerated care, he returned the picture to the mantel.

"This was taken a little over five years ago," he finally said. "We met in high school—"

"Don't," Haley said quickly, lifting a hand to stop him. "You don't have to."

"I know. I want to." He stared at the photo. "I've not spoken about it except to my family in all this time...." His gaze met hers then. "But I want you to know."

She knew what he was doing. He was going to open up, share himself, in the hope she'd do the same. But she'd done nothing to deserve him or his friendship—nothing but lie. She couldn't possibly feel worse. "Cam."

Taking the rag from her hands, he ran it over the glass in the frame. "Lorraine was gorgeous, smart. Funny. Everything I could have asked for, except one thing." His eyes pierced hers. "She couldn't be honest to save her life."

Haley's mouth opened. Then closed.

"She lied indiscriminately, about anything. Everything. Where she'd been, what she'd done. Strangely enough, not about other men, but about everything else... I know now she couldn't help it. She was sick. But it drove me crazy." He stared at the picture. "By the time I finished college, we'd been on and off so many times I'd lost count, but I wanted her. No matter how many times she hurt me, I wanted her." He sighed, then slipped his hands into his pockets, and she knew his hands were fisted. "She kept lying, and I kept wanting. We had no business getting married, but I... Well, I was stubborn."

He let out a little laugh. "The way I went through women during our off times before our wedding drove Lorraine mad. She came after me one night, I think to skin my hide, but we ended up taking it out in passion instead."

God, she didn't want to hear this, but she couldn't tear herself away. And the pain and regret on Cam's face squeezed her heart.

"She got pregnant." His melancholy smile disappeared and Haley's stomach tightened.

"I worked as a stockbroker then—fourteen, maybe fifteen hours a day." He broke off at her look of surprise and nodded grimly. "Yeah, believe it or not."

Something ached inside Haley at the look of pure torture on his face. She dreaded whatever was coming next. "Cam—"

"I worked hard and long," he said harshly, ignoring her. "No matter what, regardless of what Lorraine wanted. I don't know why, really. I hated the work, but I was driven. And I hated the lies. Always, more lies. But I wanted that baby." He shook his head. "I was working the night she went into labor, and because she'd been paging me nightly for no particular reason except she was lonely, I didn't call back right away. Didn't want to stop working."

He closed his eyes and Haley reached for him, unable to stop herself from offering comfort she knew wouldn't help. She touched his shoulder and he opened his eyes to look at her, his deep, dark brown eyes shiny and full with emotion.

"She died ten minutes after my son did. I wasn't there."

"Oh, Cam," she said softly, "I'm so sorry." The words were hopelessly inadequate. Awkwardly, because she had never become accustomed to giving any part of herself, she stepped closer. He might resent her sympathy, or reject any offer of comfort, but she found she had to try because watching him suffer hurt. So, for the first time in her life, she reached out to another human being by choice and gave what she had.

He went unhesitatingly into her arms, making her understand how actions could soothe more than words. *This was what life was really about,* she thought, awed. The intermingling of lives, love...death. Her own life had been so sorely lacking in these experiences, so sheltered, she could only hold him, and hope it was enough.

Silently they stood there, locked together, grieving; him for what had been; her, for what *never* had been.

Max came upon them that way, and his joy at finding two of the people he cared most about in the entire world proved too much. Yipping and jumping at their feet, he peed everywhere.

Haley leaped back, hopelessly flustered and a little embarrassed. The puppy just sat in the puddle, wagging his tail and panting happily.

Cam gave a hoarse little laugh as he studied the wet dog, who didn't look in the least bit humiliated by his faux pas. "The least you could do is *pretend* to be humbled." And when, amazingly, the puppy did, bowing his little head, Cam bent to rub his neck, murmuring sympathetically, "I've told you, buddy, you can't show your eagerness so quickly. Make them come to you." Cam obligingly hunkered down when Max rolled over to offer his belly for scratching. Then Cam rose, shaking his head at the puddle. "All right, Max. We've put this off long enough because I understood how you felt about such things, but we can't delay this another minute. *Bath time.*"

Max stood, too, looking unusually alert and wary.

"I'll clean this up," Haley said quickly, needing to escape the unfamiliar closeness. She moved to get a mop.

"Don't, I'll get it." Cam lifted his head from the dog long enough to give her a smile, though sadness lingered in his eyes. His voice sounded husky, intimate. "I don't expect you to clean up this kind of stuff."

At a loss for words, Haley picked up the forgotten rag, then stuffed it awkwardly into her bucket of supplies. Cam was still looking at her in a way that made thinking difficult. She moved toward the door, then stopped. He'd given her something new. *Closeness.* She felt she had to give something back. "Cam?"

"Yes?" Their eyes met, clung.

She felt something pass between them, some sort of silent awareness. "I'm...in trouble." She braced for the barrage of questions she knew was coming.

But he said nothing; just waited, his expression so open and unexpectedly patient, her eyes suddenly stung. "I am—was— in charge of a team of geologists. And I'm on the run."

"From the co-worker you told me about?"

"Yes."

"Are you safe here?"

"Yes."

"Are you sure?"

Now her vision wavered behind her unshed tears. She'd lied to him, hurt him, and what he cared about most was her safety. Well, she cared about his, too. "I'm sure."

He didn't move, as if he knew she was on the very edge and would fall apart if he so much as took a step toward her. "How come you're telling me now?"

"You— You're not like anyone I've ever met."

His gaze heated and her body reacted similarly.

"Why, Haley, I do believe that was a compliment."

"It was."

"Thanks for listening to me before," he said softly. "I didn't realize how much I needed to talk."

"I'm glad I was here." But she winced at the breathy sound of her voice. She gripped the doorjamb, feeling as though his gaze pinned her to the spot.

"Maybe I could return the favor," he suggested. "You could tell me more. About you."

"Cam—"

He just shook his head at the warning in her voice. "I'm not trying to push, Haley." Grimacing, he shoved a hand through his hair in an unusual show of frustration and said, "Okay, maybe I am. I want to know more."

And after what she'd just found out about him, she could understand why. She certainly understood his edginess at how she refused to be honest. It hurt him, and made her feel ashamed.

"It's the first time in a long time for me," he said. "I want to know everything."

What was he saying? That despite it all, he was still attracted to her? It was hard to believe that he felt anything more than a passing fancy. Or perhaps she didn't *want* to believe, because the thought was more than a little terrifying.

"Do you understand?" he asked, gingerly holding the wet, squirming puppy. "I want to know more about you. You're a *geologist,* for God's sake. Tell me more."

"Why?"

"Because I care about you."

Oh, Lord. Her stomach went all fluttery. Had anyone ever said that to her before? "It's only been a couple of days."

"My caring is not a death sentence," Cam said, a little smile playing about his lips. Only his eyes showed the lingering hurt from what he'd told her about his wife. Or had *she* caused that?

"Letting me get to know you won't hurt all that much."

She laughed nervously. "Don't be too sure."

*She'd called her old apartment.* The knowledge caused a smile. After searching for her for days—*days*—waiting for her to make a move, she had.

Now there was proof that Dr. Haley Whitfield was indeed alive.

That little fact would have to be remedied. Soon.

As soon as her location was pinpointed.

Sleep was impossible. Haley gave it up at dawn. She showered, dressed and opened her front door to admire the gorgeous fall morning. Dark still prevailed, but to the east she could see the sharp outline of the mountains as the sky above them lightened perceptibly. The trees rustled noisily in the early wind. Somewhere a rooster crowed. Another minute passed. The sky turned purple, then red, then a glorious yellow as the sun appeared over the tops of the peaks.

Taking a deep breath of the crisp, clear air, Haley found herself smiling at the glory of it. How often in her life had she taken time for sunrises? Never.

Wrapping Cam's denim jacket more tightly around her, she started walking toward the big house. The air seemed to vibrate with the sounds of birds and insects, and since the path was heavily lined with fallen leaves, the ground crunched pleasantly beneath her feet. Her breath crystallized in front of her. Soon it would get even colder and snow would come.

*Would she still be here?* Silly to hope so, but she did. And hard to believe she felt so content with this life after the one she'd left—or was it?

It wasn't until she was nearly to the ranch house that she realized she hadn't once used her ulcer medicine. Yes, she still suffered from insomnia, but the headaches that had plagued her for years had gone, too.

Amazing what a week keeping house in the country will do for stress, she thought wryly. Now, if she could just stop thinking entirely, she'd probably be able to sleep more.

But she'd never been able to turn her brain off. She thought of the journal she'd stayed up all night writing in. A waste of time, she knew, but she'd actually enjoyed the emotional outlet so much, she couldn't bring herself to stop. She'd described Cam's kisses as if she were a love-struck teen.

She felt like one. Haley-the-Virgin had gotten serious weak knees over the cowboy's kisses. Had he been able to tell how inexperienced she was? Oh, well...she hadn't known how to cook, either, and she'd done okay.

A distant drone cut through the quiet morning air. The birds went silent, and so did everything. Haley froze as a plane came into view, making a slow, lazy circle overhead.

*They'd found her.*

This time, it was real. She'd been found. Knowing what they were capable of, and knowing everyone she cared about lay sleeping in the big house, she took off running.

By the time she'd gotten to the side door, the plane had made another slow sweep of the area and was coming around once again. Chest heaving, Haley threw herself at the back door, yanking it open with fingers that didn't want to work.

She sprinted through the empty kitchen and into the long hallway, giving a passing thought to using the telephone to call for help, but she had to warn everyone first, before it was too late. Cursing the sheer size of the house, she ran through the living room, pausing at the foot of the stairs to drag a breath into her screaming lungs.

Head down, she lunged up the stairs, taking them two at a time. She opened her mouth to shout a warning, but as she lifted her head, the only thing that came out was a squeak.

At the top of the stairs, wearing nothing but white boxer briefs that hugged his muscular flanks, stood Cameron.

"Haley?" He ran a hand over his face, looking rumpled and groggy with the sleep from which she'd obviously woken him. "What's going on?"

She'd skidded to a halt at the sight of him, but the sound of the plane brought her back to reality quickly enough. "The plane," she huffed. "It's coming."

Giving her a strange look, he meandered—so slowly she

nearly screamed—over to the floor-to-ceiling window at the end of the upstairs hallway. Tipping his head back, he studied the plane for a long moment, then turned and gave her another strange look. "That's Tex. Our neighbor. He's checking his herd. Does it once a week or so."

*Not again.*

She hadn't really made a fool of herself again, had she? As the now familiar heat flooded her face, she turned away from his curious gaze, but he merely came forward, took her hand and wordlessly started walking down the hall.

Her resistance was met with more stalwart silence. When she dug in her heels, he merely tugged harder, and when she opened her mouth to protest, he spared her a glance over his shoulder. "Shush, darlin', or you'll wake the house up."

The thought of them all witnessing this spectacle was enough to keep her quiet as he pulled her into his bedroom and shut the door.

Leaning back against it, he studied her. She did the same to him, then wished she hadn't. He stood there, completely unconcerned with the fact that what precious little he wore hid absolutely nothing, only enhanced. And man, oh, man, did it enhance. The man stood there, practically, deliciously, nearly naked. Haley's mouth went dry and she tried to drag her gaze away, but she couldn't.

There was no way she could have known what a magnificent body he had, until now. Tall, lean and incredibly sculpted, he had muscles and contours in all the right places and then some. And this wasn't a gym-made body, either. Nope, she thought dizzily. This body was born of pure physical labor.

*Who would have thought?*

"You figured you'd been found, didn't you?" Cam crossed his arms over that wonderful, bare chest and lifted a brow.

She chewed her lip, forcing herself to look somewhere, *anywhere,* else. "Maybe," she mumbled.

When he remained silent and still, she risked a glance at him. And found him looking at her, his eyes swimming with the knowledge that he'd thoroughly flustered her with his near nudity. The man, damn his gorgeous hide, appeared to be enjoying every minute of it.

"Okay, Haley, let's review. First you're a housekeeper without a job. Then you're a housekeeper on the run. *Then* you're a *geologist,* still on the run, but from a co-worker who can't find you. What was the latest? Oh, yes. You're in charge of a *team* of geologists. Now..." He paused and smiled politely, coldly. "*Now* what's the story?" He dropped his arms and strolled toward her. "Keep in mind, here, I probably won't believe you."

He spoke lightly, but she could see the tension in every line of his body. And after what she'd learned about his dead wife, could she blame him? Guilt swamped her. "I didn't lie yesterday."

"No?" He stroked a finger down her cheek and looked at her with a mixture of angry frustration and reluctant affection that made her swallow hard.

He didn't deserve this. "I *am* a geologist. And I'm on the run because..."

"Because...?"

"Just because."

Regret filled his gaze. Regret and defeat. "You know what I discovered yesterday? That I'm ready to try again. I wanted to try again with *you.*" He shook his head slowly and dropped his hand to his side. "But I can't do it. I can't survive another relationship based on mistrust and lies, no matter how much I want you."

"I'll..." She swallowed hard. "I'll go pack."

"No." He caught her shoulders. "No. I don't want that. You seem to be safe here. I just wanted you to know how I feel. I wanted you to know how hard it is to walk away from you, but I have to. God, Haley, I *have* to."

The emotion in his husky voice made her throat clog. "I barely know you," she whispered. "I don't trust easily."

"You know me well enough. What you see is what you get."

Well, what she saw had her knees going weak at the moment. "I need to think. I can't do that around you."

His gaze swept over her body. "That makes two of us."

Her mouth worked, but nothing came out. He was *that* attracted to her? She wanted to sit down and laugh, but she was afraid it would sound hysterical. She was the nerd, the butt of all the rocket-scientist jokes. And this man had no idea, no idea at all.

He pulled her closer. Though her mind demanded a protest, she flowed smoothly toward him, colliding gently with his warm, hard—and very nearly nude—body. "I...I thought you were going to walk away from me."

"I am. In a minute. I need to kiss you first," he told her huskily. "Because I can't seem to get that last kiss of ours out of my head."

His lips lowered to hers, and she had one final coherent thought as her arms rose up over those wide, sinewy shoulders and around his neck.

The cowboy felt damn good.

As his mouth moved purposefully over hers, igniting an incredible heat, his hands slid up so that his thumbs rested just beneath her breasts. The blood rushed from her head as her body arched against his, hungry for more.

Cam ended the kiss and lifted his face, staring into her eyes. "Now that just gets better and better, if you ask me. Shame to walk away, isn't it?"

Hugging her tightly, he raked his teeth alongside her neck, evoking a set of delicious shudders that his clever hands then soothed away. Mindless, she clung to him, her thoughts drifting from one new sensation to the next.

"Haley?"

His tongue played with her ear, teasing, arousing. She forced her mind to work enough to answer. "Hmm?"

"Tell me who you really are," he whispered, his mouth hot against her skin. "Tell me the truth."

It took a good second for her thoughts to return, but once

they settled, she shoved back and stared at him. "That was low."

"What?"

Those guileless, sexy eyes didn't fool her. The mind that lurked behind them was as sharp as hers. "You thought you could seduce me into telling you..."

"Into telling me what?" His intense gaze contrasted with his easy, relaxed manner.

*People were dead because of her,* she reminded herself. *Dead.* Someone had used her discovery to make a catastrophic earthquake in South America, *just as a test.* An entire village had been wiped from the planet. Forever gone—because of her.

Cam might hate what she'd done, but she could tell him. And in doing so, she would risk his life. And Zach's, Nellie's and Jason's, too. Could she do that, just to unburden her mind? "I did tell you the truth. You just didn't believe me."

"*Make* me believe you." Frustration wasn't even close to what Cam felt. He wanted to shake her, wanted to demand answers, wanted to know what really haunted her, day and night. But most of all, he wanted her warm and pliant in his arms again. And the knowledge he couldn't force her to do any of those things hit hard. He had to do as he'd said. Walk away.

Struggling for calm, he said, "Apparently I've made the right decision."

She took a deep breath, obviously torn. And damn her, but he wanted to know why. "I'm sorry," she said, turning away. "I'll go—"

"No," he said quickly, his heart twisting at the thought. Reaching for her hips, he turned her to face him. "If you left now, Nellie would never forgive me. I meant what I said, Haley. Stay. You're safe here."

She leaned back to look at him, bracing her hands against his chest. He wanted to think it was because she just had to touch him, but knew by her expression that she did it to force his distance.

"I just meant," she said, looking uncertain, "that I should

go get breakfast started." She hesitated. "I wasn't lying when I said I was on the run, Cam. I appreciate the place to stay."

Worry had a taste, he discovered. Bitter. She wasn't lying about the terror; no one could be so convincing. "Why won't you let me help?"

"You can't."

"It's dangerous," he stated flatly. Questions raced through his head, and so did that insidious gut-wrenching fear that he was being a fool—again. But he understood pressuring her would do no good. And he wasn't about to start sounding like a nagging husband. No way. Not again. "It's seeing you so stressed that gets to me. It's not right."

"I'm used to stress," she said carefully, removing herself from his arms to cross hers over her chest. "It's this *other* I'm not so used to."

"'Other'?"

Looking uncomfortable, she pulled back. "This... You know."

He couldn't help it, he laughed. It relieved him to know she was as hopelessly attracted as he was. "No, I don't know. Tell me."

"I'm not used to *you,* all right?" She glared at him when he tucked a strand of her hair behind her ear. "You touch me a lot, you know that?"

He touched her some more. "Yeah. I noticed you usually touch me back."

The sound that escaped her was more like a growl than a sigh. Her hands fisted. "You think I don't know that?" Looking confused, she shook her head. "This is all very new for me, Cameron. And I have to be honest, I don't think I like it. Not one little bit."

So they were back to full names. "You know what I think, Haley? I think you like it plenty. It just makes you nervous. Well, that's fine, really it is. I told you we can't do this without honesty, and I meant it. If you want to meander through this thing until you trust me, that suits me just fine. Take your time, darlin', that's just my speed, anyway." He met her disturbed gaze and found himself lost in those heavenly blue eyes. "To be honest, I'm not sure I can walk away."

"Cam—"

"But I have to try. I'm not going to lie to you and say this thing between us isn't pleasant. It is. It's the most pleasant thing that's happened to me in a long time. But I can't do it your way."

"If...if I wanted to do this your way," she said haltingly, her voice so low he had to bend close, "all I'd have to do is tell you about me?"

"Yes."

She looked doubtful. "You mean *I'm* in charge?"

His smile was more grim than amused. "When it comes to the affairs of the heart, you women rule the world. The power is all yours. Us men just get to sit back and beg for favors."

Her mouth hung open a little in surprise, as if that thought had never occurred to her, and in another time and place he might have laughed.

She clasped her hands tightly together and ducked her head. "I've always considered myself a loner," she said quietly, touchingly shy. "And I can tell you, *no one* ever begged me for favors."

"No?"

"No."

Her unexpected admission banished some of his frustration. "I would have."

She ignored that. "I don't seem to work too well with others."

"You've worked fine here."

"I mean with *others*...as in a male-female type of relationship."

"I see," he said slowly, though in truth he didn't. "But there's no one here but us, and we do okay."

"That's because you don't really know me. Believe me, if

you did, you wouldn't want to..." She trailed off, obviously embarrassed.

"I wouldn't want to what?" He moved toward her again, reaching for her. "I wouldn't want to be with you? Haley, darlin', I don't mean to doubt your intelligence, here, but that's the stupidest thing I've ever heard you say."

She laughed, surprising him. So he squeezed her waist gently, until she looked at him. "All you have to do is tell me. Tell me everything."

"I...need to think."

"Okay."

"And I want to work here for a while longer," she said quietly. "It's probably unfair to all of you, but that's what I want to do."

"That's what I want you to do, too."

"You don't hate me?"

Was she serious? "No, Haley, I don't hate you."

"I want to be friends."

"Friends with Nellie, you mean."

"Yes. And Zach and Jason."

"Oh."

"And you," she said.

His eyes narrowed as he realized where this was going. "Friends. You want to be friends with me. Just like with Zach and Jason."

She nodded emphatically. "I don't know how long I'll be here and it'd be nice if we all got along—"

*"Friends,"* he repeated, interrupting her without a qualm. "And you don't know how long you'll be here." He nodded as if he understood perfectly, while his thoughts whirled with confusion. Had he been the only one to be completely bowled over by that last kiss? No, he remembered, she'd been just as affected. To prove it, he still had the fingernail indentations on his arms where she'd gripped on to him for dear life.

"So, one of these days," he said conversationally, "you'll

just wake up and decide—it's time to move on. And you'll go. Just like that.''

Her eyes locked on his, she nodded. "Just like that.''

He stared at her. God, she had his stomach in knots like it hadn't been since... He straightened. He didn't need this. He'd already told her he was walking away. He just needed to do it. Forcing calm, he took a deep breath. "That's fine,'' he said smoothly, maybe a little stiffly. Purposefully, he moved his hands from her hips to his.

He'd play it her way, for now.

Then her gaze lowered over him and color rose in her cheeks. He looked down, too, and realized he hadn't pulled on any clothes when he'd heard her barreling up the steps earlier.

If she didn't stop staring at his body like that, she was going to get a quick, *very hard,* surprise. Confident enough not to cringe, and male enough to take pride in her obvious approval, he shrugged and sighed, weathering the moment. "Sorry." He moved toward the adjoining bathroom door.

She made a soft sound, one that, unless he was mistaken, was of muffled yearning. He became instantly aroused. Because she'd annoyed the hell out of him, and because he was suddenly feeling mischievous and a little defiant, he casually turned back toward her, watching her eyes follow the line of his body, down his chest—and stop.

She gasped, and he hid his satisfied smile as he shut the bathroom door in her face.

"Friends—like hell,'' he told his reflection in the mirror as he flipped on the shower and dropped his shorts. *She wanted him.* He grinned and soaped up.

Haley waited until she heard the water come on before she sank down on the foot of his bed.

If there was a sexier man alive, she couldn't imagine who.

That night Haley wrote in her journal, putting down the words on a legal pad for lack of anything else. To ease her mind from the South American nightmare, she described how she felt, knowing that Cam had meant what he said—they couldn't have anything together until she was prepared to offer him the truth and make him believe it. Well, that truth could kill him. She'd made the right decision.

She should go. Maybe even back to South America and face the music. No. She'd felt like a robot for too many years to count. The horrible pressure had been killing her slowly. She knew that she'd never forget that jolt of realization when she'd learned what had been done with her discovery. The deep, overwhelming horror of it. She didn't want to ever feel that way again. Being here helped. Being trusted helped.

She concentrated on channeling her fear into righteous anger. And she did what she always did with anger—she worked through it. She wrote, and dreamed, wishing she really did belong in Colorado, on a ranch, with the sexiest man she'd ever met.

It wasn't until sometime near dawn that she got up and read the newspaper she'd brought in from the big house. In the world-events section she got a shock. A huge store of uranium had allegedly been discovered in South America, by none other than Earthquake/Volcano Studies. It was now missing. Stunned, Haley read on. The report claimed that EVS had found this incredible lode during routine digging for a new computerized undersea system, then shortly after this incredible find, EVS's office had been destroyed in a suspicious explosion.

*Her* system.

Good Lord. No wonder her boss had wanted to keep her system a secret a while longer. Not only could her system be used to predict—and potentially to cause—earthquakes, it could uncover pockets of valuable ore. Haley shuddered as she began to realize the implications. No wonder someone was willing to kill for the system. It would be worth untold millions. And she was the only one who could make it work.

She had turned her pager back on immediately after reading the newspaper report, so Haley wasn't surprised when it went off the next morning. It was from her flat in South America, presumably from Alda.

"Wherever you are, you must get back here. Things have changed. Come to the park where we used to lunch. Noon, one week. Be there, Haley. It's life or death."

# Chapter 6

That night, Haley stood in the center of the kitchen, despairing of ever managing to pull together something edible. Then her white knight entered in the form of Nellie, toting a large, foil-lined bag that smelled heavenly.

"It's fried chicken," she said, smiling apologetically. "I hope you didn't already start something, because I couldn't resist."

"Are you kidding? I could kiss you," Haley told her, meaning every word. "I had no idea what I was going to make."

"You would have come up with something," Nellie said confidently. "That lasagna last night was terrific."

Even Haley had to agree, it had been pretty terrific. And surprisingly easy. Noodles, cheese, sauce. Noodles, cheese, sauce. Formulas again. Good thing she was so good at that. She reached for the bag of chicken. "Your neighbor called. He said it's beef time again. He wanted your order."

"Great. I'll call him later. Anything special you want me to buy?"

"Wait a minute." Haley stopped in the act of opening the

foil. "You run a ranch with cows on it—and you *buy* your beef?"

"That's right." Nellie grabbed a wing and sniffed appreciatively, sighing a little. She bit into the chicken without getting a plate, moaning with obvious pleasure, and then quickly took another bite. "We buy our pork and chicken, too." She picked up a drumstick with her other hand and laughed. "See?"

"But you have both right here on the ranch," Haley said, watching Nellie stuff her face indelicately. "I've seen them."

Nellie finished off the wing and laughed again, holding her belly with one hand, the drumstick with the other. "You're catching on to the Reeves way."

"I don't get it."

"The ranch makes money only on the horses. Cam's rule."

Strangely touched, Haley sat down and looked at Nellie. "Let me get this straight. You have all these animals, but you don't use them for meat?"

"Cam won't let us kill anything. We bought the pigs and chickens…oh, at least two years ago now, and he named every one of them. Jason told him that was his first mistake, but Cam held firm."

Haley didn't want to think about why that brought a smile to her face and made her feel…mushy.

"The piglets we get each year think Cam's their daddy. Before we sell them, they follow him around the pen faithfully. You should see it."

Haley tried to picture that; the big, tall, rangy Cam, leading the baby pigs around like a mama duck. Sadness speared her when she realized she'd probably never see that. She'd be gone in a few days. She had to make a move, had to face this thing. She'd go first to the USGS, then to South America, hopefully with an escort, and hopefully as a witness, not as a suspect. But it had to be done.

Alda had to be stopped.

Nellie stuffed her mouth again. "The foals eat right from his hand." She grabbed a biscuit, split it open and slathered butter all over it.

"Would you sit?" Haley demanded, with a small laugh, forcing the ache away. "And use a plate—you're making crumbs everywhere."

Nellie did, then smiled apologetically. "I'm starved."

"What's new?" Haley smiled, too. What they said about expectant mothers seemed to be true; Nellie positively glowed. "You're feeling as good as you look?"

"Yep." She proudly patted the baby. "Doctor says everyone's doing great. Even poor Jas, who turns green whenever the doctor discusses childbirth." She took a sip from her water and gave a huge sigh, absently rubbing her tummy in a gesture Haley thought sweetly maternal. She wondered if all pregnant women did that—held their babies before they were even born. She tried to picture her own mother pregnant, caressing Haley in her swollen stomach, and couldn't.

"Have you seen the guys?" Nellie asked. "Let's call them in before I eat all the food by myself."

"Zach's studying. Jason's chopping wood and—"

"Oh, God— *Chopping wood?*" Nellie groaned, then stood awkwardly. "We've got to stop him. He'll cut something off, for sure."

"He'll...*what?*"

Nellie's smile was fond and full of such love that Haley felt an unexpected pang of envy. "He's a wonderful man. They all are. Beautiful inside and out. But my Jas, he's not too careful. He tends to break things. Like his own bones."

"Oh, no." Haley stood. She remembered that first night when Cam and Nellie had told her about Jason falling off the roof, how she hadn't wanted to believe it could be true.

"What did you say Cam's doing?" Nellie asked. "Maybe I can get him to take over and save us all a trip to the hospital."

"Oh, he's working *real* hard," Haley said, tongue firmly in cheek. "You should see him." She tossed her head toward the window where Cam could be seen in the yard, lying still in a hammock that swung gently between two large pines. Beneath the hat that covered his face, his sun-streaked hair lifted in the breeze. His hands lay lightly clasped, low on his belly. Even now, Haley could remember exactly how flat that beautiful stomach was beneath his shirt, how strong and long his legs were, and it had her jerking away from the window.

"Poor baby," Nellie said, looking at Cam. "He's exhausted. Must have worked all night. But mm-hmm, he does look fine, doesn't he?"

She'd choke before admitting it. "I don't know what you mean," Haley said primly, fussing with the chicken.

Which only made Nellie grin. "Sure you do, honey. You're a woman, aren't you?" Her smile faded some as Haley sniffed indifferently. "You don't like him much, do you?"

Haley shrugged. How, oh how, had she gotten herself into this conversation? She felt like she was in high school, only she'd never been in a regular school, with regular friends who would have teased her about the male species. She was in foreign territory without a map and she felt at a total loss.

Nellie was still looking at her, worried. "Has he...done something to offend you?"

"No, nothing like that," Haley said quickly. She looked at Cam again, sleeping so peacefully in the sun, like he didn't have a care in the world. Something inside her ached. "He wouldn't."

Nellie's gaze followed Haley's. "No, you're right, he wouldn't. At least, not on purpose. Cam's the nicest, most gentle, caring man I know," she said faithfully. "And the most easygoing, laid-back—" She broke off at the look on Haley's face. "That's it, isn't it? He's out there sleeping the day away and it bothers you."

She hated to admit it was true. "It just seems so...leisurely," Haley finished lamely. "I'm sorry. I have no right to say something like that." She sank back into a chair. "Can we just forget it? And go rescue Jason, maybe?"

Nellie looked at her, her disappointment obvious. "Yes, of

course." She started to move away, then hesitated. "You know, Haley, I've seen you work. I know how seriously you take things, how hard you try, and how much effort you put into each thing you do. You're a planner, I'd guess." She smiled. "It's wonderful, really. Those are traits I wish I had more of, believe me. But those are also some pretty tough standards to judge others by."

"I'm not—"

"Aren't you?" Nellie sat and took her hand. "Please, please, don't take this wrong, Haley. It's easy to underestimate that clever mind of Cam's. I know. I did it, too, at first. It's so easy to be dazzled by the looks, the voice, the overall outer package. But you'll just have to trust me on this—it'd be a shame if you made that same mistake. You really can't judge a book by its cover."

"I know that. But Cam's not exactly a book."

"No, he's not," Nellie said quietly. "But if you're thinking he's slow and lazy, you couldn't be further from the truth."

"I wasn't thinking slow," Haley told her, remembering exactly how quick he could be. "Lazy? Maybe." She thought of the lemonade he'd called out to her for, an hour ago, when he'd seen her through the window. He'd given her that indolent smile of his and looked at her with eyes that would have melted the Arctic. The crazy thing was, she'd actually done his bidding and brought him the drink. "And definitely spoiled," she added.

At Nellie's stricken look, Haley relented. "I'm kidding, Nellie."

"He's not spoiled."

"I know. I know he's had it rough. He told me about his wife."

"He— He told you?" Nellie sputtered. "He *never* talks about Lorraine. Certainly you can't believe he's lazy now—not if you know how hard he worked."

Haley didn't know what she believed, except that maybe it was better not to have loved at all than to have loved and been destroyed, like he had. "I guess I don't understand how he can be happy here, doing so little, after the busy life-style he had."

But couldn't she? Wasn't that exactly what she was doing?

Nellie looked sad, but for whom, Haley couldn't tell.

"Things aren't always as they appear, Haley. And I'm not minding my own business very well," she said. "Jas would tell me to shut my trap." She took a big bite from a chicken leg.

Jason appeared in the doorway, shirtless, damp with sweat from chopping wood, and looking every bit as good as a cover model showing off his stuff. He waved his slingless arm, looking proud of himself.

"Check it out, baby," he told Nellie, flexing his muscles. "Everything works just fine. Healed and ready to go." He gave her the once-over with his eyes and both women laughed.

"It's only a matter of time, cowboy," Nellie told him. "You'll trip over your feet, break something and be out of commission again." She ran her gaze up and down his body from beneath coyly lowered lashes. "Speaking of that...maybe we ought to make the most of the time we've got."

Jason grinned broadly and wrapped his long arms around her, steering her toward the door. "I do like the way you think, Nel. I like the way you think very much."

"Oh, man," Zach complained as he passed them and came into the kitchen. "They're at it again."

Haley laughed. "Yes, they are." She'd gotten past the embarrassment days ago, and now knew that what Nellie and Jason shared was very special and unbelievably good.

And honest.

She'd never had anything like that. Her gaze fell to the window again, and to Cam, still asleep. A yearning, surprisingly strong, swept through her.

"Look at that," Zach said, shaking his head in disgust as he caught sight of his brother. "Sleeping the day away again."

"He worked all night," Haley said quickly, coming to Cam's defense without thinking. "He's exhausted."

Zach flashed her that Reeves grin, mixed with startled wonder. "I know that, Haley."

"You— Oh." Embarrassed and flustered by Zach's curious gaze, she looked away. "I just thought... Actually, I don't know what I thought."

"You were defending him to me." Zach laughed. "Oh, man. You've got it bad. Don't worry. I'm told we're pretty irresistible, but it'll pass soon enough."

Haley managed to roll her eyes and laugh it off, but his comment stuck long after he'd filled a plate and left. Did she have it bad? She sure didn't want to. She thought of little else as she prepared a plateful of chicken and struck out for the yard, some half-baked idea in her head that she could take out these feelings on the person who'd caused them—Cameron Reeves.

Dusk settled quickly in the mountains. Locked into that short, glorious period between day and night, long shadows fell over the grass as she walked. She wouldn't mind the dark, which would hit at any moment. She'd discovered she liked the nights here, once she'd gotten past the fear of what she couldn't see. Colorado nights were like none other on earth. The smooth black sky flowed with stars so bright and clear they looked like scattered diamonds on black velvet.

But she wasn't outside now to enjoy the sights.

Miffed at herself, and thoroughly prepared to share it, she stopped before the hammock and cleared her throat. Cam didn't budge. None too gently, she set the plate on his stomach, watching with amusement as he started, then lifted the hat from his far-too-alert eyes.

"You weren't sleeping," she accused.

"Nope. Just thinking." He picked up the plate and smiled as he carefully sat up. "Thanks. I'm starving."

"Really," she said dryly. When wasn't he? The man ate constantly, as did his brothers. She could only imagine their food bill.

"You served me." He grinned. "I think you're falling for me."

"Don't bet on it." She watched his teeth sink into the chicken, trying to remember when she last ate. His cheek muscles bunched as he chewed, and he sighed in pleasure, going for more. Her mouth watered hungrily and she suddenly wished she'd brought two plates.

He must have read her mind, because he scooted over. "Come on, share mine."

She eyed the narrow hammock. "I couldn't."

"Sure, you can. You just open your mouth and chew."

"No," she said, rolling her eyes. "I mean, I *couldn't*. I couldn't possibly fit in there with you."

Almost before she'd finished the sentence, he'd lifted the plate in one hand and scooped his other around her waist, heaving her up and in with him. For one horrifying second, the cotton hammock shifted wildly from side to side and Haley thought they were going down. She screeched and clutched at Cam, who just laughed.

"Have more faith, darlin'. I'm a hungry man. Do you think I'd dump my plate?" He lifted a piece of wonderful-smelling chicken to her mouth. "Eat," he commanded.

She shook her head, and she was so close to him that even that small movement had her hair flying in his face. They were touching everywhere; shoulder to shoulder, hip to hip, thigh to thigh. It seemed incredibly intimate—certainly more than she'd bargained for when she'd brought him the plate of food.

And since when, she thought helplessly, had she been so constantly aware of another body like she was his? She saw everything: the way his shirtsleeves had been rolled back, revealing strong, tanned forearms, how his soft, faded jeans molded his long legs.

"Eat," he repeated, gently touching the chicken to her lips.

How could she when she could hardly breathe? But somehow, she managed to take a bite. He watched her mouth intently as she chewed and when she swallowed, his lips curved. "You're a sight, Haley Williams."

She felt a pang as she heard the false name on his lips. Another lie for the man who hated them. But it had to be that way. "I'm sure I am. I'm wearing clothes that don't fit me, my hair smells like the lemon I accidentally squirted all over myself while making iced tea, and I've got circles under my eyes." She gave him a look daring him to defy her description.

"You're beautiful."

Her heart somersaulted crazily. "I wasn't fishing for compliments."

"And compassionate. You have a sense of humor, too, though it's got a wicked streak—"

"No. Don't." She struggled to get out.

Without warning, and very quickly for a man who claimed he liked to move slowly, he cupped her head, pulled her toward him and nibbled at her lips. "Mmm, you're wearing that lip gloss. Tastes like strawberries."

She pushed back, bracing against his chest, and tried not to spill the plate. "Don't do that. You said you were walking away from me, remember?"

"Yes, but *you* came to *me*. I can't resist that, I'm afraid."

Good Lord, he was something, all rugged man and sweet smile. "You'll make me forget I'm mad at you."

"That was the idea...but okay," he said agreeably, settling back. "Then just eat."

"You keep pushing me to eat. You sound like a mom." But she took the bite he'd put to her mouth.

"*A* mom? Not *your* Mom?"

She stilled, the chicken a solid, unswallowable lump in her throat. His gaze searched her features and something he must have read there made him take pity.

"Take my mom, for instance," he said easily into the awkward silence. "She didn't have to nag us boys to eat. We ate her out of house and home."

"Mine didn't have that problem," Haley said carefully, pushing away the next bite. She'd lost her appetite. "And you're changing the subject. We were discussing my being mad at you."

He crunched into the corn on the cob, licked the butter off his wet lips and smiled innocently. "What does your mother think of your eating habits now?"

Her mother could care less, but because that hurt to admit, she forced a smile. "Wouldn't you rather know why I'm mad at you?"

"Oh, I already know that. I'd rather know why you won't talk about yourself."

"You're impossible." She sat up, determined to wriggle her way out of the hammock, but once again, she'd underestimated him. With one fluid move, he'd gotten rid of the plate and had her stretched out, flat beneath him. They rocked gently from the movement, every inch of her body touching every inch of his. There was something incredibly erotic about the motion.

"So you don't want to talk about yourself." He played with her hair and smiled into her stormy, furious eyes. "We can do something else. Anything. You pick, darlin'."

"I don't think so. You're crowding me, Cameron."

"Ah, we're back to formalities." He cupped her face, wishing those eyes didn't hold so many secrets, wishing she didn't resist him so. He didn't like how pale she seemed, how fragile she felt under him. Or how weary she looked. "Is your stomach better?"

"There's nothing wrong with my stomach."

Every muscle tightened. "I thought you said you weren't a liar."

She pushed at him, stiff with anger, embarrassment, and who knew what else. "Move. Just *move*."

Frustration purled from deep within, and for once, he couldn't find his patience, his gentleness, his innate kindness. "Damn it, Haley. How can you let yourself go like this?" He gripped her shoulders tightly. "You shudder in fear when you think no one is watching and you jump if someone so much as walks up behind you. I *know* you're frightened and you won't let me help. Now, I've agreed not to push, even though you admit you're on the run, but you've been clutching at your stomach like you're going to die. I can't just stand by while you're in pain. Don't ask me to.''

Since he still lay over her, he was well aware of the fact that she'd gone rigid with tension. Her eyes closed, and she inhaled deeply. He felt her slowly relax, then her eyes opened on his. "I'm sorry. I've not been very fair, have I?"

He shook his head, waiting. The day had fully disappeared into night, but he had no trouble reading the misgivings in her expression. "Do you need a doctor for the ulcer?"

"No, it's better." Her smile seemed bright—too bright, as if, once again, she associated her pain with weakness. "Much better."

He just looked at her.

"It *is*," she insisted. "I haven't had any trouble in days. You set your food down. I thought you were hungry."

"Now who's changing the subject?" He kissed her once because he couldn't help himself, then because she seemed so uncomfortable with him plastered to her, he sat and pulled her up next to him. Immediately he felt the loss of her soft, warm body. "Now tell me why you're mad at me."

She crossed her arms and gave him that sassy look he was so fond of. "I thought you said you already knew."

"I do. I just want to hear you admit it." Idly, he pushed his foot to the ground and set them into a gentle rocking motion. He tugged her hair. "I want to hear you admit you're mad because you can't stop thinking about me."

She sputtered with that, then finally tipped her head back and laughed. "You're something."

"I thought I was impossible."

"That, too." She tilted her head and studied him. "I've never known anyone like you, Cameron Reeves."

"I'm not sure that's a compliment."

Her smile had a touch of wistfulness in it. "It's not. Your ego's big enough without my help."

"A little confidence never hurt anyone."

She shook her head. "You've got more than a *little* confidence. All of you Reeveses do."

"And that's a bad thing?"

She looked at him and inhaled deeply. "No, actually. I find yours unsettlingly comforting sometimes."

He gave her a quick squeeze, touched. But she stiffened on him.

"I've got to go."

With his arm around her, the beautiful night making soft sounds all around them, and swinging in his favorite hammock, Cam was hard-pressed to think of anything more important to do. "Do you now? How come?"

"I've got—"

"Work," he finished for her, at the same time she said the word. "You *always* have work. Haven't you learned yet?" He was absolutely earnest about this, desperate for her to understand. "Work will wait. Life won't."

Before his eyes, her face changed. Her sorrow became a weight even he could feel burdened under.

"You're right," she said softly. "Life *is* precious. It won't wait and it should never be taken for granted." She rose. "Excuse me," she whispered. And then, without another word, she ran off.

He watched her go, wondering, worrying, at the glint of tears he'd seen.

He didn't wonder long. Early the next morning, rising before everyone else, Cam picked up the morning paper, needing a distraction from the woman he couldn't stop thinking about. He'd promised himself he'd stay clear of her, he'd get over whatever strange, unaccountable sense of lust he felt.

It hadn't happened. Even his suspicion of all her lies and secrets had dissipated in the face of her fear. He'd convinced himself—nearly—that Haley was fiercely protecting someone by keeping her troubles to herself, and he had the uneasy feeling that someone was *him*.

It got to him, as little else could have. He felt something for her, something deep and abiding, and he had come to the realization it wasn't going to go away. Hell, if he was going to be honest, he had to admit he'd *never* felt like this before.

Mentally skipping away from that thought, he skimmed his eyes over the paper. His heart stopped when he saw the headline. Fear and fury raced with equal strength through his veins but he forced himself to read the report, even though every word was like a knife to his chest.

When he was done, he folded the newspaper.

Haley *had* told him the truth. She was a geologist, and undoubtedly on the run. But she had left out several critical little facts. Like her real last name. And the fact that the South American authorities wanted her for questioning in association with several bombings, the missing uranium and several murders.

She was a criminal.

God, she *wasn't* like Lorraine; she was far worse.

Cooking breakfast, Haley couldn't get the night before out of her head. The way Cam had looked at her with warmth, affection and hunger; the way his body had felt strong and hard over hers in the hammock. She crashed a pot down on the stove, taking pleasure in the loud, satisfying noise.

He had no right to remind her how wonderful life should be. How precious. She *knew* that. Just as she knew that she'd always feel partially to blame for the uncountable number of deaths her undersea system had caused.

But, dammit, it had been someone else who had killed and destroyed—*not* her. Someone had used her, and with the discovery of uranium, that person was going to be very wealthy.

She knew Cam's computer had on-line capabilities, but she didn't want to risk being caught or traced. She wondered about the library in town. Would it be updated regularly with newspapers? Trade magazines? Certainly, there would have been a story about Bob. Maybe it would have more info. She had to do something, take some action.

She yawned. It had been a long night. Even writing in her journal hadn't given her the release it had before. Now her words sounded pathetic and full of self-pity. She'd written about how she wanted to ease the strange, unbearable ache Cam caused, how she'd seduce him if necessary. But when she'd reread what she'd written, she'd had to burst out laughing. She couldn't do it. She'd thrown the tablet across the room into the trash, vowing to give up writing if she couldn't come up with something better than fantasizing about her boss.

Nellie popped her head into the kitchen, a big, warm smile on her face. "Hey, Haley. I dreamed about pancakes. Big, thick, mouthwatering, delicious pancakes. Do you think you could... Oh, never mind." She cut herself off, obviously glimpsing Haley's horrified expression. "It's too much trouble, I'm sure."

She looked so hungry, Haley thought, with rising compassion for anyone who had to waddle rather than walk. She managed a smile. "You want pancakes, you got pancakes. Just give me a few minutes, all right?"

*"Really?"*

"Really," Haley promised, wondering what in the hell pancakes were made of. "They're easy to make."

The second Nellie had disappeared, Haley whipped out the thick cookbook, opened it to the pancake page and started memorizing. Formulas, she reminded herself. It was all formulas.

"Whatcha doing?"

Haley jumped, then turned around and forced a smile for Zach. "Just looking something up."

"Nellie said something about pancakes." He looked around hopefully.

"They're not ready yet," she said between clenched teeth forced into a smile. "But I'll let you know as soon as they are."

"Well, since I'm here, I'll help." He looked over his shoulder to make sure they were alone. "Don't tell anyone, but I cook *great* pancakes."

"Why wouldn't you want anyone to know?" she asked desperately, with a last, longing look at her cookbook.

He grinned that bone-melting, Reeves smile. "Because then I'd *have* to make them. Nellie would hound me day and night."

"Oh," she said, torn between wanting his help and wanting him to leave so he wouldn't guess how helpless she was. "Don't you have work to do? The horses—"

"Can wait a few minutes. It's early yet."

Great, she thought, beginning to panic. He took out a bowl, went to the cupboard and pulled out a container.

"What's that?"

He looked at her strangely. "The pancake mix." Then, because she didn't move or make any effort to stop him, he measured some out. "Am I stepping on your toes?"

She knew he was asking if she wanted him to leave. But if he could really come up with pancakes, she sure as hell didn't. "No. With bacon or sausage?"

Flashing that killer smile, he licked his lips. "Both."

Relieved, she left the pancakes to him and started the meat. She had it sizzling in the skillet when she realized Zach was staring at her.

"What?" she asked, self-conscious. She looked around. "Why are you staring at me?"

"It's nothing." He turned back to the pancakes, flipping them high into the air and catching them in the pan with an ease that surprised her.

"Okay." But before she'd turned back to her pan, he was looking at her again. She set down her fork and put her hands on her hips. "Zach. *What?*"

"You don't know how to cook, do you?"

Oh, God. What had she done to give herself away? "What— What do you mean?"

"Haley," he said in a gentle voice that made her want to cry. "You have to separate the bacon before you put it in the pan."

She glanced at the pan, then back at Zach. "Oh."

He raised his eyebrows, obviously expecting a better answer.

She sighed and busied herself separating the bacon. "So I don't know how to cook bacon. Maybe I don't like it."

"Maybe," he conceded. "But I think there's probably another reason."

What would she do if they demanded the truth? These people she'd grown to care about in such a short time would never stay idle if they knew the truth. They could never understand the danger—Zach and Cam would butt in and get hurt. Or killed.

"What other reason would there be?" she asked in a tone of defiance she didn't feel.

Zach's eyes were calm and quiet, as was his voice. There wasn't any accusation when he said, "Such as maybe you're not really a housekeeper."

"I thought you weren't a cop anymore. You sure sound like one."

"Do I?" he asked in that same mild voice. "Hmm. It's just natural to me, I guess. So...are you a housekeeper?"

She laughed weakly and rubbed her temples. "Did I mention your one-track mind?"

A corner of his mouth turned up. He deftly flipped the next batch of pancakes with a skill she could never have faked. "That goes along with the lawyer thing. It's a requirement. Are you, Haley? A housekeeper?"

"You doubt it. Have I done a poor job, then?"

"Of course not." With a small sound of dismay, he turned back to his pancakes and lifted an edge of one. Sighing with obvious relief that he hadn't burned them, he scooped them out and poured more batter. "But that's not the point."

She hated liars and she'd become one. The thought of what that would do to Cam killed her. "What *is* your point?"

"I think something's wrong."

"You've been talking to Cameron," she stated flatly. She should have guessed; they were family, after all.

"No," Zach said. "I haven't been talking to Cam about you." He searched through the cabinets, slamming things around until he found the syrup, which he plopped down on the table. "Listen, Haley, I care about him and his feelings. I also care about yours. All I'm trying to say is that if there's trouble, or you need something, maybe I can help.''

The meat sizzled in the pans. So did her pride. "Maybe I don't need help."

Cam came in at that moment, and found them that way. His brother and the woman he couldn't decide whether to strangle or kiss, facing off with cooking utensils in their hands as though preparing to do battle. "Problem?"

"No," Haley said quickly.

"Yes," Zach said at the same time. Zach and Haley exchanged a stubborn look until Zach added, "I burned the pancakes."

Cam didn't know what the hell to think, but Zach shot him a glance that said, *Don't ask*, before saying carefully, "Haley told me I would. But that's what I get for showing off."

Haley's look of muted surprise had Cam wondering, but he was so churned up with emotion from the newspaper report, he couldn't think about it. "Zach thinks he's a man of all trades," he told her. "Truth is, we only keep him around because no one else will have him." Zach growled and Cam went on. "Now, Thea, that pretty librarian in town, she just doesn't know better. I'd go down there and tell her myself, but for some reason she doesn't have eyes for anyone but Zach, here."

"Oh, shut up." Zach scraped the pan clean and poured more batter into it.

Nellie and Jason came in, wrapped in each other's arms. "Oh, great, it's you two," Zach said. "I thought Cam told you to have that damn bed of yours moved away from the wall. You kept me up, *again*. Don't you people ever sleep?"

Cam watched Haley bite back a smile. God, he hurt. *Don't believe it,* a little part of his brain commanded. *The report was wrong somehow. She's not a criminal. Be patient and she'll tell you the truth.*

"I *did* move the bed," Jason claimed, after muffling Nellie's giggle against his chest. "I guess I didn't move it far enough."

"Build that couple a guesthouse," Zach said, with heartfelt disgust to the room in general. *"Please."*

Cam watched his family coax smiles and even a laugh out of Haley while they ate. As usual, she didn't prepare a plate for herself, so for some reason he couldn't have explained to save his life, he did it for her, even managing to cajole her into actually having a few bites.

He had no idea why he cared. "I know this isn't the junk food you seem to prefer," he told her as they cleared the dishes a little while later, after everyone else had left. "But you've got to eat more." *Please, tell me,* he nearly demanded. *Tell me everything.*

She stopped at the sink and looked at him, her hands on her hips. There was a hint of amusement in her eyes when she asked, "Why? So I could look more like Nellie?"

He managed a laugh and came close to where she'd turned to start washing dishes. Moving up behind her, he grabbed her hips, then slid his hand over her flat stomach. He closed his eyes, every inch of him yearning, aching. "There's only one way you're going to look like Nellie, darlin'," he said with a lightness he didn't feel. "In fact, I have some interesting ideas on that."

She rolled her eyes. "You need help, Cam. Serious help."

He hugged her from behind, closing his eyes at the way her body fit to his. "Just an offer." His voice sounded husky, even to his own ears. God, he was pathetic. "I'd certainly be willing to oblige you in any way I can."

"Now why doesn't that surprise me?" She shouldered him away, then sent him a saucy look over her shoulder, soapsuds flying.

He'd never thought the mundane chore of dishwashing as particularly sexy before. But there was something about the way her hips wiggled slightly, the quick, precise movements of her arms.... It became incredibly seductive. She reached for more dishes, stretching, and he lost track of what she said next.

"Well?" she asked, giving him another one of her smart-ass looks she had no idea made his blood hum.

"I'm sorry. I didn't hear you." He encircled her hips with his hands again, letting out his breath in one loud whoosh as she planted her elbow firmly in his stomach.

"I warned you not to crowd me."

He backed up, alert, hopeful. "Did you have something else in mind?" Would she tell him now?

"Actually, yes." She reached and flipped off the water before turning to look at him. "You have a library in town. How current is it?"

Her earnest expression wiped away his joke about Thea-the-Librarian. That busy mind of hers was whirling. "Hard to answer a question when you only asked half of it," he said carefully.

"Can't you just answer the part I asked?"

He reached for a large green apple from the fruit basket on the counter, biting into it to play for time. "It's current," he said finally. "What're you looking for?"

"Nothing important." She reached for a towel to dry her hands, but he put his apple down and captured her hands in his. Eyes narrowed, he studied her, ignoring her struggle to pull back from him.

"It's important enough," he guessed. And he wasn't going to miss it. "I'll drive you."

"You don't have to—"

"Yes, I do. Especially if it has anything to do with what's keeping you up at night." Short of coming right out with the newspaper he'd read, he couldn't have given her a better opening.

"I'm sleeping fine."

He touched the faint, purple shadow beneath one eye. "Another lie."

With a disparaging sound, she looked away, biting her lip. "Fine," she ground out. "I'm having a little trouble sleeping. Okay?"

"Not okay." Before she could evade him, he took her shoulders. "My guess is that you know damn well you're lying. You even know what it's doing to me. And you hate it. You also don't want me to know that, so you'll tell the truth wherever you can to ease your conscience."

"I'm not—"

"It only gets worse, Haley, I promise. You'll drown beneath the weight of them one of these days. Believe me, I know."

"I can't do this. I can't keep reminding you of Lorraine, having you wonder what kind of jerk I am that I can't tell you the truth." She sighed. "I want to look something up. Something in the newspaper."

"Something to do with what you're running from?"

"Yes," she whispered, resting fisted hands against his chest and bowing her head. "Yes."

"You'll let me in this time," he insisted, gently running his hands down her arms, massaging gently.

"No. *No.*"

He studied her quietly, then murmured, "Let me put this another way." Tightening his hands on her, he pulled her closer. His mouth found hers.

Heaven. Hot, wet, deep heaven.

More shaken than he cared to admit, he slid his hands up to cup her face, pouring his fear for her, all his longing, into that kiss; and when she trembled and pushed closer to hold him tight, it only aroused him all the more. Her flavor, her scent, the feel of her beneath his fingertips—it wasn't enough. He wanted more, needed more.

"Haley," he whispered, sliding his lips over the soft firmness of her neck to nuzzle at her throat, licking the frantic beat he found there. "God. You're driving me crazy."

"I'm not ready for this. Not yet." But she still held him to her, tightly.

He rubbed his forehead against hers and took a deep breath. He said the words his heart already knew, for she was in serious trouble and he instinctively knew she wasn't a criminal. "You're not like Lorraine. I'm sorry I said you were."

Taking a steadying breath, she backed up, into the sink. "I told you as much as I could."

"But—"

"What I'm dealing with is dangerous, Cam. People have... died." Her voice broke. "I'm afraid for you."

Moving forward, he bracketed her hips with his hands against the tile. "I'm not going to walk away from this. Don't ask me to. Do you understand what I'm saying? I'm telling you that I'm here for you, no matter what it is."

"I don't need a hero."

"Good," he said with a little laugh. "Because I'm not hero material. But I'm your friend, and much more, if you'd only say the word. I'm not going to let anything happen to you."

Her eyes seemed huge and luminous in the morning light. And full of shadowed, hopeful surprise. That she didn't expect anyone to back her had an unexpected tenderness and that strange possessiveness once again flowing through him.

"What if I'm used to handling my own problems?" she asked tentatively.

"Independence is nice. But a little help never hurt."

"This will require more than a *little* help, Cam."

"You've got whatever it takes, darlin'. That's a promise."

No one had ever offered Haley so much, so simply. And genuinely. She didn't fool herself. She could read the steely determination in his gaze and knew he'd decided he was in. He'd never give up. If she didn't come clean, he'd go find out the truth on his own now. But she wanted him in. Wanted to share. The need to cling to him hit her hard. Useless to struggle against it, she decided. It seemed coy to pretend he didn't affect her when he did so very much. She reached for him, wrapping her arms tightly around his neck, and for the first time, *she* kissed *him*.

Hunger and passion, hope and promise—they were all there for the taking. She would have pulled away, stunned by the depth of her feelings, but Cam deepened the kiss. Even as she struggled to hold something back, she became aware that she wouldn't be able to do that for long. Had she ever been needed like this? Wanted like this? Her heart filled, and she just barely managed to rein it in, unbearably close to giving him everything.

"Too fast," she whispered, pulling back. The blood swam in her head. "Way too fast."

"No," he denied, but he stepped away, too, obviously as shaken as she was. "But taking you in my kitchen with my nosy family around isn't my usual style." He cupped her cheek with warm fingers and sent that sweet, irresistible smile her way. "Ready for a ride to the library?"

She smiled a little shakily.

"Good." He squeezed her to his side briefly. "Afterward, when you've gotten what you need, we talk, if I have to tie you down."

She owed him. "Yes," she whispered. "We'll talk."

The city library was not only a beautiful brick building, but held a surprisingly large selection and a wonderful, efficient staff.

Haley couldn't contain her small, knowing smile when Cam introduced her to Thea.

"Is she the one?" she whispered, when the pretty brunette had walked away to answer a question from another patron.

"Yeah." Cam grinned. "But I was teasing Zach before. *He's* the one that has a crush on *her*. She doesn't know he exists."

"Oh, how sad."

Cam laughed. "Don't feel sorry for my big brother, Haley. Women flock to him."

"That's what Nellie said about you."

"Did she, now?" He sent her a look with those sexy, dark eyes. "So how come *you* don't?"

Thankfully, she was spared having to answer by Thea's return. The librarian gave them an apologetic look. "Sorry, we're busy today. How can I help you?"

"Do you have the Los Angeles *Times?*" Haley asked.

"Of course. How far back do you need?"

"The past three weeks."

"Well, you're in luck. We just got our computer system up and running again. You can have any date you want. First room down the hall to the left."

Cam followed her, but at the door, Haley stopped and gave him a firm look. "Go find a book to look at," she suggested.

He grinned. "Shh, darlin', we're in a library."

Oh, he was in fine form today. "How about a magazine?"

"They don't carry the kind I like to read."

No matter that she'd promised to tell all, she simply wasn't prepared. "I'm sure there're picture books to entertain you. Try the children's section."

He let out a soft laugh that made her heart flip-flop. She glared at him, but at the look in his melting brown eyes, couldn't maintain it. He hadn't left her, despite the fact that she'd done nothing to earn his trust. He deserved much, much more from her.

She was going to give it. "Cam." She licked her suddenly dry lips. "I discovered something. Something that had much more power than I could ever have dreamed." She spoke the words in a soft rush before she lost her nerve. "Only someone evil got a hold of it and now I'm the only one left alive to tell."

He stared at her for a fraction of time, then moved so fast she could only let out a startled squeak as he hauled her close in a hug that spoke volumes. "God, Haley." He buried his face in her hair, ignoring the soft buzz of the busy library around them. "I thought you'd never tell me."

"You— You knew?"

"Some of it. You were in the paper, darlin'. I've been dividing my time between wanting to shake you silly and kiss you senseless."

"It's...a long story."

"But you'll tell me now. All of it. The entire truth."

"Yes." Having his warm, strong arms banding around her broke all resistance and for a moment, she squeezed tightly, never wanting to let go. "Stay," she whispered. "I want you to. I don't know why I keep pushing you away—"

"Shh." He kissed her once—a soft, tender kiss full of promise. "We've got work to do."

The computer was no problem. She'd mastered them long ago. And on her last job, she'd used one every day. With Cam silent and supportive, sitting next to her, Haley started reading files. She figured the story of Bob, who was well-known in their industry, would be first-section news, maybe second-page. What she didn't figure on was today's paper, and a full-blown picture of Alda on the front page, with a long article beneath the shocking headline.

### Prominent Geologist, Alda Jones, Found Dead of Overdose

It got worse, far worse. The next article was on Haley herself. It seemed she was missing. And wanted—for murder.

# Chapter 7

Shock and grief hit Haley as she sat there in the silent library, reading the article about her colleague's death. According to the report, Alda had been missing since the mysterious death of Dr. Bob Herntz. Both deaths were being investigated because of their strange and curious nature. Herntz had died in a car fire, but the autopsy had determined that a blow to the head had come first.

The facts sank in. Alda was well-known for her antidrug position, and yet she'd died of an overdose of a wild assortment of street drugs. The USGS had gone on record to say that although Bob and Alda hadn't worked for them in years, they deeply regretted the loss of two of their most intelligent and well-liked geologists. The police were currently looking for a Dr. Haley Whitfield, the only known connection left to the bombings, the murders, *and* the missing uranium.

They meant *suspect,* of course. They thought she had murdered, for her own gain. It filled her with a sense of panic so great, she couldn't breathe. If Alda *had* been involved, she had paid the ultimate price.

And so would Haley—if she left Colorado. So would Cam and his family, if she came out of hiding and revealed herself. She simply couldn't breathe.

"Haley?"

She brought her hands up to her neck, as if that could make her lungs work. Nope, she thought vaguely, not working. She was going to suffocate and die. As her vision grayed, she pictured the headline.

### Prominent Geologist, Haley Whitfield, Dies of Self-Suffocation

"Haley?" She felt her chair swivel and then Cam knelt before her, his hands on her arms, his concerned face inches in front of hers. "Christ, Haley. Breathe. You're turning blue. Come on, darlin', breathe." He gave her a light shake, then slipped his hands around her face. "A deep breath, Haley. Come on, give me another one. That's it. Again."

She did, her eyes locked on his as if he were her lifeline. Her hands gripped his on her face as she struggled. Then the strangest thing happened. Once she started breathing, she began to hyperventilate.

Her panic tripled now, every breath coming quicker and quicker, harsher and harsher. Frederick. Danyella. Lloyd. Bob. Alda. All of them, gone. She couldn't control herself, it consumed her—the deep, gasping breaths. And no matter what she did, she couldn't stop. Not even when she hiccuped painfully with each intake. Not even when the tears streamed down her face. She just couldn't stop.

"Haley, Haley." Cam held her face firmly and his eyes never left hers, as he forced her to concentrate. "You're okay," he said in a soothing voice. "Just slow it down. Come on, slow.... Good." He wiped her tears away with the pads of his thumbs. "You're okay," he said again and again, and when finally she felt in control, she sagged against him, exhausted.

He lifted her and took the now empty chair she'd vacated,

holding her close to him on his lap. He scooped the hair off her wet face and managed to come up with a napkin for her to blow her nose. She waited, painfully aware of what a fool she'd just made of herself, yet he remained silent.

The funny thing was—here in the circle of his solid, sure arms, she'd never felt safer. "I'm fine," she said eventually.

"Don't."

Cam hugged her tight and she felt his muscles tremble. "Watching you have that panic attack took ten years off my life." He drew a ragged breath. "I thought I could be patient for the rest. I can't. You've got to tell me what the hell's going on."

"I didn't commit murder."

"You may be able to lie smoothly enough to give me the chills," Cam said roughly, still rocking her. "But I never thought you could kill."

*She'd* caused those stress lines in his face, the tightness of his jaw. His gaze seemed weighted with worry, concern, and even fear. She squeezed her eyes tightly shut and held on to him. "I need out of here."

Cam didn't push Haley for answers on the long drive back. He parked his truck in front of the ranch house, then turned in the seat to look at her.

"Ever been on a horse?"

That was just about the last possible thing she expected him to say. "A horse?" She cleared her rough throat. "A couple of times. At school once. I knew someone who took me riding. I'm not very good."

He nodded, got out of the truck and came around for her, holding out a hand. "You know, Haley, that's the most you've ever volunteered about yourself." For once, his deep eyes revealed nothing. "Let's go for a ride."

"A ride," she repeatedly stupidly, coming to a stand before him. The day was cool, the sunny sky streaked with light clouds. But her chill came from deep within. Did he really believe she was involved? And if he did, could she blame him? She hadn't exactly been forthcoming with information. "I don't think so."

"Why not?"

She let out a little laugh, then rubbed her temples. Had he forgotten? "I'm tired, Cameron."

"You look it."

The words were brutal, in complete contrast to the absolute kindness of his voice. She snapped her head up to look at him and saw the burning questions and, yes, the basic affection and warmth she'd come to count on. She also saw his frustration. His pain and confusion over the lies. No, he hadn't forgotten.

"I just thought you could use a diversion."

There were a thousand reasons not to. "I'll slow you down."

"I'm not in the mood to race."

"I have—"

"Work?" he interrupted, with a small shake of his head. "Heaven forbid you forget that for even a few minutes." He gave her a ghost of a smile. "You can give up that pretense for now, don't you think?"

The sad thing was, she didn't want to. What she wanted most was to dive into the kitchen and work. "I don't want to."

He just looked at her.

"I *want* to work." She could panic over this, she realized. What if he wanted her to go, when what she wanted most in the world was to stay?

"We need to talk, Haley."

She studied her shoes. She smelled the aspens. She listened to the grass grow.

"Hel-l-o-o-o."

"I know. It's just that I was kinda hoping to…"

"Put it off?" He shook his head. "You're going to make me mad, Haley."

She rubbed her aching temples.

"Come on. Just a ride. Just you and me and the mountains."

He had her wait while he saddled up the horses. The ranch house sat at the base of a series of rolling hills that in spots still held their lush summer green even though winter was nearly upon them. But most of the tall grass had turned to a dull canvas brown. Soon, snow would fall, but for now, the last of the warm autumn days held. Beyond those hills were the high ridges of the Rockies, pasted against a mottled gray sky.

A perfect day for a ride.

When he led out the horses, Cam saw that Haley still sat on a large rock by the barn, just where he'd left her. The haunted look hadn't faded from her face.

"Just us," he said easily to her, forcing a calm he didn't feel. If *he* wasn't calm, there was no way he could get *her* that way. And that was exactly how he wanted her—relaxed and compliant. She wouldn't talk otherwise.

She stood and ran her hands down the thighs of her jeans. Her eyes had gone wide at seeing the horses. "They're...big."

"Yeah," he said, laughing a little. "Which is why they carry us, not the other way around." He reached for one of her busy, nervous hands. "This big guy here, he's mine. His name is Sal. The lady is Mrs. Twisted. She's Nellie's, which explains the name." He placed her hand on the horse's neck, holding it when she would have flinched away. "She's the sweetest, tamest horse we have, unless Jason's around."

"She doesn't like him?"

He could tell she didn't want to get on any horse, much less a temperamental one. "She's just jealous. You've seen Jason and Nellie."

"Yeah."

He wondered at the flash of emotion he saw. If he didn't know better, he would have sworn it was envy. Did she, like him, both admire and wish for what Nellie and Jason had?

"So I just hop on?" she asked.

"Need a hand?" He imagined touching her, helping her up. His hands would brush over her hips, her thighs....

"I can do it," she said quickly, moving past him.

He watched as she pulled herself up with an ease that spoke

more of her physical strength than experience. He'd noticed that for a tiny thing, she was tough as nails. And had a tight little body to go with that toughness—one that happened to drive him crazy every time he looked at it.

He got on Sal and they started for the hills. Haley sat naturally in the saddle, which didn't surprise him. She wouldn't like to be less than good at anything. She didn't smile, or even look at him, but then, he hadn't expected her to. Nervousness vibrated from her, and he knew she was thoroughly braced for his barrage of questions.

She'd have to wait.

He had no intention of grilling her. That would get him nowhere with the stubborn woman riding next to him. No, it would take much more finesse to get what he wanted. Though, in truth, he wasn't sure *what* he wanted from her. The rest of the facts, certainly.

But even that didn't matter so much as banishing the fear from her eyes. The woman was a bundle of contradictions. Seemingly aloof, but really just shy. Her domestic "front" was merely a facade for a slick professionalism and a need to succeed at everything she tried. Bravado covered up her almost-desperate need for approval and affection.

Haley pulled Mrs. Twisted to a halt and lifted a shoulder. They'd come to the top of the first hill. "Which way?"

Her dark hair blew against her pale, serious face. He wanted to see her laugh with abandonment, talk with ease. "You pick."

Without another word, she chose the path that would take them past the rolling hills and into the wooded area at the base of the craggy, jutting mountains. The only sound came from their horses' hooves pounding the dirt.

"It's beautiful here," Haley said, speaking for the first time in long minutes. She ducked beneath the low branch of an aspen. "I hear water running."

"There's a creek. There're also some cliffs a mile or so ahead. Jas, Zach and I camped there overnight once."

"You must have played here a lot as a boy."

He brought Sal alongside Mrs. Twisted. "No. I grew up in Denver. I only bought the Circle C several years ago."

"Oh. I thought— Never mind."

She'd turned away, embarrassed, and shifted in her saddle. "You'd thought what?" he pressed. "It's okay to ask me, Haley. Contrary to *some* people I know, my life's an open book."

She flashed him that haughty, annoyed look, but said nothing, not even when he lifted his brow and silently dared her.

They came out of the woods into a clearing. The creek ran noisily through, rushing past rocks and boulders. "This is my favorite spot. I came here a lot when I first bought the house." He glanced at her. "I bought it after Lorraine died. I wanted to change my life-style. Completely. I dumped the suits, quit the job." He looked around at the beautiful woods he considered his. "I had no intention of really running the ranch, I just wanted to...disappear, I guess."

He saw a flash of surprise light her face. "I can understand that," she said softly.

"I thought maybe you would."

She dismounted and so did he. The horses turned to the spots of green at their hooves, looking for something to graze on.

Cam walked to the water's edge. "Jason came with me. He'd had some trouble with college, then on a job. He was as desperately unhappy as I was. But within a week of being here, that changed. He's got a knack for working the place. It's really amazing. And then he met Nellie. Things have been good for him."

She came up beside him, the wind teasing color into her pale cheeks. "And Zach?"

"Zach came later. He'd been working as a cop. Saw a lot of junk, and it burned him out. Then he went to work on another ranch, so it was only natural he'd come here. He and Jason make this place work, not me."

"But you love it, too."

He watched a squirrel dash across a branch, chattering busily. "I do." He looked at her and decided to take the plunge. "You want to start at the beginning, or at what happened in the library?''

Turning her face away, she sank to the ground as if her legs wouldn't support her. Her nervous fingers played in the dirt. She was silent for so long he didn't think she'd answer, but she surprised him. ''I used to work with her. The geologist who died.''

''Did you steal the uranium?''

Abruptly, she stood and stalked toward the horses.

Catching up with her, he whirled her around, spurred by that temper he so rarely felt, and by his fear that Haley could still prove to be no different from Lorraine. A horrifying thought, since he figured he was already halfway in love with her. ''Answer me.''

''I didn't steal anything! And if you think I could, then I was wrong about you.'' She shook herself free. ''I'm not going to tell you anything. I don't have to.''

Like a knife in his heart, he thought. And when the hell had he forgotten his promise to walk away? ''No,'' he agreed, dropping his hands from her. ''You're right. You certainly don't have to. I guess I'd just hoped you'd *want* to. Forget it. You know what? This was dumb. Let's go back.''

He expected her to stomp off, or to at least stare at him in stoic silence as usual. The last thing he expected was for her to touch his arm and meet his angry gaze steadily.

''No, wait. I'm sorry, Cam. I'm so on edge.'' She closed her eyes for a moment, and when she opened them, they were damp. ''There were five of us in South America. We were a team, working specifically on earth movement. Our office was blown up, one week after we made a particularly critical discovery. The reports are saying that the discovery was uranium, but I never heard anything about that when I was there. If they found it, they kept it a secret. But we did discover something else that day, something just as unbelievable.''

''Okay.'' He crossed his arms and stared at her, hardening his heart to the appeal in her blue eyes. ''More.''

"Alda was the last to die. Every one of them is now dead except me." She drew a ragged breath. "I'm next."

She was next. God. He couldn't begin to imagine what it would feel like to lose her. Yet she looked like she expected him to push her away. "I'm sorry."

*She was sorry.* He yanked her close, closing his eyes when he felt her nuzzle her face into his neck. He wrapped her in his arms and wondered how he could feel so much. "Haley—"

"Please. Just this. I'm about to explode from the tension."

He could feel it in her trembling form. "Okay, darlin', okay."

She clutched him. "I don't want to fight. Not with you."

He wrapped his arms tightly around her, feeling the vise that had gripped his chest loosen slightly. "We're not fighting, it's all right."

She snuggled against him for a bit. "It's a good thing, Cam," she said with ironic wit, "that you walked away from me."

He let out a little laugh. "Yeah. I sure showed you, didn't I?"

She was quiet for another moment. "I'm too screwed up for anything more than this. You know that."

"No."

"Friends, Cam. That's all this is." She sounded panicked. "You promised."

God, had he really ever agreed to anything so asinine?

"Hold me," she whispered, her eyes closed, her arms around his neck.

He did, even knowing his heart was in big trouble.


Cam found Zach in the study. He slapped the article he'd had faxed down on his brother's desk. "Got it."

Zach pushed aside the large lawbook he'd been studying. "And?"

"The uranium was indeed stolen. No suspects other than Haley."

"And we're so absolutely certain it isn't her."

"Absolutely," Cam said in a steady voice, ready to do battle.

"And her boss?"

"Lloyd Branson. Reported dead in the bombing, but according to the USGS, with which I just got off the phone, there's no body."

Zach frowned and picked up the faxed sheets. "They didn't just tell you that."

Cam grinned devilishly and affected a British accent. "Of course not. As Lloyd's youngest nephew, I deserved to know. I have memorial arrangements to make, you know."

Zach shook his head in amazement. "Does Haley know?"

"That I called? No." Cam sat on the edge of the large oak desk he'd made last year. "She's terrified. For us. It's what has kept her silent. She'd flip if she knew we'd started investigating on our own."

"If Haley is found here, they'll extradite her to South America and try her for murder."

"That's why she won't be found," Cam said with finality. He tapped the papers and tried to ignore the ball of tension growing inside him. "Haley says the entire team is dead—except her."

"You really think she's safe here?"

"Yes." He had to believe it. The brothers looked at each other, mirror images of strain and concern on their faces.

"What about Nellie?" Zach murmured. "If danger comes looking for Haley..."

"We'll protect what's ours. Are you going to fight me on this?"

"Could I?"

Tense, they stared at each other. "No," Cam admitted.

Zach stood, laid a hand on his brother's shoulder. "We'll help her. But if she's innocent—"

"She is."

"Then maybe we should call the police, let them prove it. It might be the best way to keep her safe." He lifted a hand when Cam's expression darkened. "Think about it."

He was so close to gaining her full trust, so damned close.

"They'll take her, you know they will. And what if they *can't* prove her innocence? Or they have to send her back to South America?"

"You can't make her accept your help," Zach said quietly. "Or you."

Welled-up fear for Haley had him shrugging off his brother's hand and stalking to the window. The day had faded, leaving nothing but a black sky. It matched the terror in his heart. "Do you think I don't know that?" The decision was painful, but he saw no choice. "Her safety comes first. When we can no longer provide that for her, we call the police."

"How long?"

"A couple of days. Just give me a couple of days. If we haven't come any closer to flushing out the danger..." God. "We'll call and let the authorities help her." Just the thought chilled his blood. "I can't let anything happen to her, Zach."

"You can't control this." Zach paused. "Just like before, with Lorraine. What happened to her and the baby...you couldn't have stopped it. It wasn't your fault."

"You're wrong." Cam paced the room, unbearably restless, frustratingly helpless. "I *could* have called Lorraine sooner that night. If I had, I could have gotten to the hospital faster. I might have seen my son alive."

"But he still would have died." Zach watched him pace, his expression holding a deep sorrow Cam wasn't sure he could bear. "It's the truth, Cam. You couldn't have stopped what happened."

"I can this time. I can protect her." Or he'd die trying.

Haley sat on the split-rail fence, next to where Nellie leaned on it, and bit back her laughter. Hard to believe she could feel like laughing, but that was exactly what she wanted to do.

Nellie, unable to hold anything back, held her stomach and roared.

In the pen, the three Reeves brothers—rough-and-tough cowboys—struggled to corral the largest pig for his shots. The pig wanted nothing to do with it.

The guys, covered in mud and dirt, took a break and huddled, discussing strategy. The pig stood his ground, staring at them defiantly. The brothers straightened, looked at each other, then nodded in unison. Zach went left, Jason veered right, and Cam handled the center as they stalked the pig.

"Does it always take the three of them?" Haley asked, giggling helplessly as both Zach and Jason dived for the pig, and missed. They collided in the mud. Cam still stood, shaking his head in obvious disgust.

Nellie swiped at the tears of mirth that rolled down her face. "Oh, this is good. Better than 'Oprah.'" She sniffed and sighed. "Usually Jason handles the animals' inoculations. But this pig— Cam calls him King—is pretty stubborn."

King continued to reign. Cam approached slowly. "Now, King, buddy…this isn't going to hurt but just a bit." He smiled the charming smile that never failed to turn Haley's heart on end.

King wasn't moved in the least.

"Come on, King," he cajoled. "You've got to have some gratitude, here. You could be bacon."

Nellie howled with laughter, clutching her stomach. "Empty threats, Cam, and he knows it!" she called.

Jason picked himself out of the mud and spared a frown for his wife, even as concentration banded his face. "Nel, honey, you keep laughing like that and you'll drop that baby right there in the dirt. Go inside."

"You just catch that pig, cowboy. I'll worry about this baby. Besides," she yelled, a mischievous smile on her face, "watching you is so much fun!"

Zach muttered something obscene under his breath as he brushed himself off and turned toward the pig again. Slowly, carefully, he made his approach. "*Now,* Cam."

Cam dived for the pig, landing directly on top of him. With

King thrashing beneath him, he pushed down in the dirt and lifted his head. "For God's sake, Jas, hurry up, would ya?"

As both Jason and Zach hurried to help, King squirmed and squealed, splattering each of them with mud. When they finally managed to stick the pig with the needle, Nellie cheered.

"My heroes!" She laughed. "My dirty, stinky heroes."

All three brothers scowled at her. Despite the weak sun and cool air, Jason whipped off his shirt. Unsnapping his jeans as he went, he walked toward the house. Zach followed suit. Cam pushed up from the mud, dirt and sweat streaked over him. He spared a halfhearted disgusted look for the women who'd been no help at all, who were in fact still laughing hysterically, and turned away. With his back to them, he, too, pulled off his filthy shirt and started after his brothers.

"Goodness," Nellie whispered beneath her breath, her eyes riveted to the men walking away from them. Muscles rippled and glistened in the sun. Three sets of wide shoulders tapered to lean waists that disappeared into jeans. "That's certainly a sight."

Haley, whose mouth had gone dry, had to agree.

And that was the image she kept with her for the rest of the day and long into the night.

When she lay in bed, writing in her journal, she remembered Cam telling her he *wasn't* hero material. Well, as she saw it, he'd been wrong, for he was indeed the stuff heroes were made of.

## *Chapter 8*

Haley attacked her chores with a vengeance that did nothing to ease her tension or her troubles. Dusting, mopping, vacuuming—all of it failed to soothe her the way it had for the past couple of weeks.

Both Cam and Zach had tried to get her to stop working so hard, but it was all she had. She stood in the downstairs hallway, wrapping the cord to the vacuum when she heard a scuffle. Her head whipped up.

It was Nellie.

"You startled me," Haley said with a nervous smile. "You're amazingly quiet for such a pregnant thing."

Nellie didn't smile back. Her eyes, full of worry, tipped Haley off, and a dread spread through her. "What is it? You in pain? Having a contraction? You've got to sit more, dammit."

"I'm fine, Haley."

Regardless, she took Nellie's arm, fretting over the unusual paleness of her face. "Come on, let's go to the kitchen. I'll get you something to drink. You can keep me company while I put the breakfast dishes away."

Nellie went with her, and sat at the table. "I just came from the barn. The guys are out there." She put her feet up on another chair with a sigh. "They didn't see me, of course, or I never would have heard them talking about you."

Haley's hands fumbled on the pitcher of tea, nearly dropping it. *They were talking about her.*

With her back to Nellie, Haley stared out the window over the sink. The day, as per Colorado usual, was glorious. Long silver clouds streaked across the brilliant blue sky. Rain clouds, she could almost hear Cam tell her. A nostalgic pain hit her with the force of a gloved fist.

She was a wanted woman, hunted by the law.

Would Cam ever again want to dance with her in the middle of a thunderstorm, with only the rain and lightning for their music? Would he ever again kiss her with the aching tenderness he had in his truck? Or with the barely restrained furious passion he had the morning she'd burst into his house after hearing the plane?

She doubted it. Just as she doubted Nellie could possibly understand the predicament she now found herself in.

"I thought we were friends, Haley."

*Friends,* she thought, wincing at the hurt tone of Nellie's voice. Oh, how she'd wanted that. More than anything, she'd wanted that. She forced herself to turn and face Nellie. "We are."

"You're in trouble. A friend would have come to another friend for help."

"You already helped me. Gave me a job. A home."

"You know what I mean," Nellie said in the harshest voice Haley had ever heard from her. "Dammit, you *know* what I mean."

Haley found that by concentrating on carrying the tray to the table, she could almost steady her hands. Almost believe things were normal. "I couldn't involve you. I don't want to see you hurt."

Nellie took her hand and pulled Haley into the chair next to her. "Do you really think Jason, Zach or Cam is going to let me get hurt? It's *you* I'm worried about. I heard them say what serious trouble you're in. They're trying to figure out a way to help you. Cam was talking about going to South America."

"He's been doing his homework," Haley said grimly. She jumped up, unable to contain herself. Dammit, dammit. The welling panic shook her. How could she stop him?

Nellie watched Haley pace. "Don't be mad at me for listening."

Haley halted abruptly, letting her shoulders droop. "I'm not mad. How could I be?" She felt Nellie come up beside her. "You're the first friend I've ever had, Nellie. Did you know that?"

"You're a geologist. You must know lots of people."

Haley sighed heavily. "No. Not really."

Nellie touched her shoulder, her eyes bright with emotion. "You never talk about yourself. I know— I mean, I could tell you're not used to people. Not really."

"I'm not used to people like you. Nice, loving, caring people. I didn't grow up like this." Haley turned away from the compassion, the understanding, feeling as if she could simply shatter from the pressure. "I tried to explain that to Cam, but he didn't want to understand."

"It's not easy for him. You must know that. He feels he has to protect you."

"But that's ridiculous. I don't want him to protect me."

Nellie's face softened. "After what happened to Lorraine, can you blame him for his desperation to keep you safe?"

Haley moved away, went back to the sink, leaning against it because suddenly her feet wouldn't support her. "I'm not his wife."

"He has feelings for you."

"He told you that?"

Nellie laughed. "Of course not. He has pride. Too much of it. But then again, all the Reeves men do. No, he didn't say a word. But I can see it in his face when he watches you. Oh, yes," she said at Haley's glance of surprise. "He watches you. Just as you watch him when you think no one's looking."

"Oh, great. I must be a great source of entertainment for all of you."

"No. We think what's happening between the two of you is the greatest thing to happen to Cam in a long time. We care about you, Haley. Maybe if you and Cam—you know—got together, you'd stay."

A nice dream, Haley thought, closing her eyes. "This is very difficult for me, Nellie."

"Are you saying you don't have feelings for him?" Nellie crossed her arms and gave her a knowing look. "Go ahead, Haley. Try to tell me. But I'm warning you, you're not a very good liar. I'm on to you."

"Isn't there something—*anything*—else we can talk about?"

"Absolutely." Nellie's eyes were serious, probing. "Let's talk about us helping you."

"No." If she did, they'd die. "I won't risk getting you hurt."

Nellie looked like she might protest, but didn't. She came close and gave Haley a quick, fierce, very protective hug. "Then promise you'll stay here."

"I can't."

"Honey, for me. Promise."

"Nellie," Cam said mildly. He was leaning against the doorjamb. "Leave it alone. You can't force her."

Haley's heart all but stopped at the sight of him. He moved into the kitchen, his long, lean limbs working with their usual grace and fluidity. They hadn't had much time alone in the past few days. Now she knew why. He'd been busy butting into her life. His face was void of expression, but he couldn't mask those eyes. Filled with unleashed heat, they landed directly on her with the impact of an explosion. The physical pain of it made her look away.

"But, Cam," Nellie protested. "If she leaves, she could get hurt."

"You heard us, then," he said flatly. "Jason will be upset, Nel. He won't want you worrying about this."

"Yeah, well, he should have told me himself." Nellie put a hand on her hip and gave him a long look. "And for the record, *I* don't need your protection, *she* does! Do something, Cam, to make her believe that. Do it right now before she gets hurt."

Without waiting for him to make a move, Nellie turned to Haley. "Please, Haley. Listen to me. Zach used to be a cop. He's got lots of connections. He can help."

Sure. He could help extradite her. Then she'd go to trial for crimes the South American authorities were already certain she'd committed. She'd be executed before the next sunrise.

"Nellie, could you give Haley and me a minute?" Cam sent Nellie a special sister-to-brother look, communicating without a word.

Nellie locked Haley in a quick bear hug. She repeated the motion with Cam, whispering something in his ear that had him nodding his head solemnly.

"Thanks, honey," he said to her, leading her to the kitchen door with an arm around her waist. "Now go rest. And stop worrying about this or Jas will have my hide."

He waited until they were alone before turning back to Haley. His gaze pinned her to the spot. "Nellie was drilling you."

"Kindly, but yes." Haley had never felt so...sick. She'd destroyed any chance she would have had with the most wonderful man on earth. "I know you're upset with me."

"Do you?"

"Yes. And I completely understand. I can leave, but I'd like to wait until—"

He let out a disbelieving laugh. "You understand nothing, Haley. Absolutely *nothing,* if you can calmly discuss my wanting you to leave."

"You...don't want me to go?"

A muscle worked in his cheek and into his eyes came the warm light she'd wanted so badly to see. "God, no." He came toward her, but stopped short of touching her.

"What *do* you want?"

He let out a low laugh. "A lot of things. To know you, for one."

"You know me."

He just looked at her, then opened the leather jacket he wore. From the inside pocket he took out two things she recognized immediately. He held up the tiny notebook and the pocket phone book she always kept in her purse.

"I found these under my desk. I'm guessing they came from your purse. The funny thing is," he said in a deceptively calm voice, "I consider myself a smart man. Not terribly motivated, I admit, but that's another story." He flipped through her notebook. "These notes might have been written in Greek for all I understand. Lots of geology talk. Magnitudes, intensity, seismic waves, that sort of thing. I'm guessing they have something to do with South America."

"Yes," she said harshly. "Thanks to those notes, people's lives have been destroyed. Thanks to me, there's been earthquakes, a bomb set off, and uranium found, then lost because of greed." She gulped hard. "Thanks to what's in those notes, my life has been turned upside down and I'm a wanted woman, on the run from God-knows-whom *and* the law."

Cam tilted his head and studied her thoughtfully. "Feel better?"

She did. Letting it all out felt a whole lot better, but hell if she'd admit it when she was so keyed up, that if he so much as touched her, she'd explode. "That's my phone book, too," she snapped. "Hope you enjoyed your little sneak peek into my life, Cameron." She reached for it, a little surprised when he gave it right over.

"I didn't enjoy anything," he said quietly, his voice gentle and incredibly apologetic. "I just was hoping you'd tell me why you don't have any non-geology numbers listed in there except for an Isabella Whitfield in Manhattan. Is she a relative?"

"She's my mother, though I have no idea if that's the current address for her. We...sort of lost touch." Another lie. Not told to avoid danger this time, but for self-preservation. How could she admit her mother didn't want anything to do with the nerd kid she'd never understood? "There's no one else in there because, as I told you, I don't have anyone else."

"You have me," he said, startling her by taking her shoulders. His eyes held so much, her own grew wet. "You keep forgetting that."

"No, I don't forget. I just..." Just what? What would keep him safe? "I just don't want you."

"Really?" He pulled her to him, his eyes dark and intent. She braced herself, but his kiss was tenderly devastating, and she had no defenses against it. She moaned and held him close, trying to memorize each and every sensation, to keep it all in her heart forever.

Cam pulled his head back a fraction. "Don't want me, huh?"

She was wrapped around him like cellophane on candy. She flushed.

"It's all coming back to haunt you, isn't it?" he asked roughly, giving her a little shake. "Lies have a nasty habit of doing that, you know. I warned you." He inhaled deeply as if it hurt to breathe. "I told you, I can't do this anymore, and I meant it." He sank his fingers into her hair, forcing her to look into his terribly hurt eyes. "But you can't stop, can you? You can't stop lying. Not even to yourself."

Anger surged, hurt seeped deep. She pushed him away. "Dammit, I'm not Lorraine! I'm not lying to you about getting my nails done, or spending too much money on clothes! This is life and death and...*God.* I don't want to witness yours." She shoved at him again, the tears she didn't want to acknowledge threatening to spill. "You have a terrible habit of crowding me, Cameron. I keep telling you that." She whirled from him, then leaned over the table on stiff arms.

He came up behind her—she could feel him, though he didn't make a sound. She closed her eyes against the deep, yearning ache he invariably caused.

"I'm not going to die." His voice, by her ear, was gravelly

with emotion. "And neither are you. I won't let it happen. But, Haley, you've got to trust me—at least with how you feel for me. You're killing me, here."

She felt wretchedly ashamed now. In his voice was something she'd always wanted, something she could have, if she would only reach for it. But she couldn't. He couldn't know what it did to her heart, to be offered something she'd wanted her entire life—trust—and then to have to turn it away. "I'm going to leave, Cam."

He dropped her notebook on the table in front of her. It clamored noisily in the silent kitchen. "I wish you could believe in me. I want that more than you could know. But even more than that, I want your safety. I don't want anything to happen to you, Haley. You want me to stop crowding you. Fine. I will. But don't leave."

She felt his fingers brush over the back of her neck in a soft, loving caress. She held herself rigid, knowing if he so much as touched her again, she'd give in and fly into his arms.

"Don't go," he whispered. Without another word, he left the kitchen.

She waited until the door shut before sinking into the nearest chair, dropping her head into her arms. The tears she'd been holding back fell freely, but it didn't matter.

Nothing mattered.

She'd done this to herself. She'd fallen in love with a man she could never have. Her sobs echoed around her, like her dashed dreams, crushed hopes and broken heart.

Much later, Haley thought to check the pager, which had been ominously silent.

Nothing. She shouldn't have been so surprised, but she was.

The service had been disconnected. There would be no more messages.

She was completely alone.

Cam pushed the papers littering his desk away and shoved ten fingers into his hair. Haley was going to leave, if he didn't stop her. He'd call the police and turn her in before he let that happen. But what would that do to her—that final betrayal?

Without stopping to think about the wisdom of it, he pulled out her mother's phone number and dialed it.

An English guy answered. He turned out to be the butler, giving Cam the third degree. By the time Mrs. Whitfield came on the line, Cam had started to regret the call.

"Mrs. Whitfield," he said in his most charming Southern voice. "I'm a friend of your daughter's and—"

"Haley?"

Well, who the hell did she think? "Yes, Haley. I know you haven't seen her lately, but she could really use your support right now—"

The woman laughed, long and coldly. "I paid for her education, which was more than most would have done. I'll not give her another penny."

"But—"

"Tell her to capitalize on her brains. For whatever they're worth."

Something deep inside Cam chilled when he pictured Haley as a little girl, with this icy woman for a mother. No wonder she felt she could rely on no one but herself.

"I'm sorry," Mrs. Whitfield said. "I have another call."

She wasn't sorry at all, except for the fifteen seconds she'd wasted. But he had to try one last time. "Your daughter is in trouble. Aren't you in the least bit concerned? Or even curious?"

"Frankly, no," she replied. "I've tried to make my mark in that woman's life, tried to show her what was important, but she never listened. Haley has made a lifelong habit of living her life as she saw fit. She'll continue to do so, with or without me."

Unbelievable, Cam thought, his hand shaking as he hung up the phone. Absolutely unbelievable. Her mother didn't care. How different from his own mother, who before she'd died of cancer five years ago, had butted into all her sons' lives night and day, all out of love.

So much about Haley made more sense now. The way she hesitated to lean on anyone, her stubborn insistence on doing everything for herself, her incredibly low self-esteem. His hand slammed down on his desk as anger vibrated through him.

All he wanted was to show her how life could be, show her patience, kindness...love. And all she wanted to do was fight those very things as hard as she could. Understanding her motivation didn't help.

He hoped to God she managed to stay out of his way until he could rein in his feelings for her. If not, he'd kiss her again, or humiliate himself and beg her to feel a fraction of what he felt for her. He'd chase her away, and send her into the unknown danger she feared so.

A small noise had him looking up. The subject of his thoughts stood in his doorway, watching him with wary, vulnerable eyes. Damn it, she looked beautiful. And he wasn't close to being prepared to face her. Not yet.

"I'm busy," he said evenly, tapping his pencil against a file.

"I'm...sorry. I just wanted to talk to you."

He tossed his pencil aside before raising his reluctant gaze to hers. She wasn't going to make this easy for him, but he'd face it. If only to keep her here. "I thought you were all talked out."

"I thought so, too." She moved into the room, bringing the light, sweet scent that was so uniquely her. She'd changed into a pretty floral dress that he remembered as Nellie's, but he'd never remembered it being so...alluring. It swept to her ankles, its fitted bodice emphasizing her thinness. She'd lost weight, he realized with a pang of alarm. It wouldn't be good for her health. If only... Well, there were a thousand if-onlys.

"It's going to rain," she said inanely, her voice that throaty whisper that always brought visions of hot, lusty sex to mind.

Which added frustration to his growing bad temper. "Yes. And as I doubt you've come to ask me to dance in it, you might as well spill it." He would absolutely *not* plead with her to give him what he wanted. Her twiddling fingers spoke of her own nervousness, but he couldn't cater to her feelings now. He had his own to protect.

She sank into the chair in front of his desk. "I came to ask you to not be mad at me."

The fight drained out of him in one sweep at the urgent, almost-desperate need on her face.

How was he supposed to remain distant when all he wanted to do was wrap himself around her, comfort and protect her? As he rose and went closer, the signs were there for him to see and agonize over. She'd been crying, and as she lifted drenched eyes to his, he could see the tension, the pain blazing in them.

He squatted before her, tried to take her hands in his, but she gripped his desk so tightly, he couldn't pry them off without hurting her. "Haley," he murmured, guilt racking him. *Selfish,* he berated himself. *He'd been so selfish, thinking only of himself.* "Come on, darlin'," he urged, stroking her hands until she loosened her grip. He turned her toward him, bringing her hands up to his lips. "I'm not mad at you."

Her eyes closed, her voice filled with exhaustion. "Oh, please. Not you, too, Cam. Don't *you* start twisting the truth."

"All right." He couldn't contain his reluctant smile at her self-demoralizing tone. "I *was* mad. I was also acting selfishly. Come on." He stood, still holding her hands. "I'll walk you back to your house. You should sleep. It'll probably help the headache."

"How did you know?"

"I know you better than you think. Or at least, better than you want to admit." He tugged her gently to her feet, giving in to the impulse to pull her close.

He slid his hands up, cupped her jaw and brought his face closer to hers. God, he could drown in those eyes. "Haley, I know I agreed to walk away, to be just friends." His fingers sank into her lovely, silky hair. "But I don't want to anymore."

"Cam—"

He didn't want to hear it so he covered her mouth with his.

Under his fingers, her muscles went lax, even as her pulse raced. *Slow and soft,* he reminded himself, though his body urged him to hurry and possess. The change in her—the gradual, hesitant response—was so irresistibly sweet, he pulled back just to look at her.

Tears streamed down her face. Making a sound of dismay, he ran a finger over her wet cheek.

"I can't do this, Cam." She backed up, shaking her head, touching her fingers to the lips he'd just kissed. "I can't. I won't hurt you." And she turned, stumbling toward his door.

"Wait."

She didn't, and as she yanked the door open, he tripped over the chair she'd pushed in his way. "Dammit, wait." Shoving the chair aside, he moved, only to stop short again in the middle of the room when she paused to look at him. One more step on his part and he knew she'd bolt. He lifted his hands in a silent plea, hoping he'd say the right thing. "I believe in you."

She gripped the door. "I'm not a good bet."

"Why? Because your mother says so? She's a joke, Haley. Don't let her influence your life."

"My mother?" She gaped in disbelief. "You— You *talked* to her?"

He nodded reluctantly, and her eyes widened. He said quickly, "I called her, thinking she could help you—"

"You *what?* How could you? Never mind, don't answer that." She stiffened. "Just do me one favor—*stay the hell out of my life!*"

He stiffened, too. "As long as you stay here."

"Are you going to hold me prisoner, Cameron?" she asked softly.

"If that's what it takes to keep you safe, you bet," he replied grimly.

Without another word, she left the office.

# Chapter 9

Cam watched Haley go. *He'd have to follow her,* he thought wearily. If only to make sure she didn't try to leave the ranch, which he simply couldn't allow. He hadn't realized how late it had gotten. The house, as he moved through it, seemed dark and empty. The silence assured him that both his brothers and Nellie slept. But just in case, he didn't flip on any lights. He didn't feel like answering questions from a well-meaning but pesky sister-in-law.

Which was exactly why he tripped over a soft, warm bundle in the kitchen and fell flat on his face. Before he could let out a curse, Max was yipping loudly and licking his face all over.

"Shh!" Grappling in the dark with the wriggling mass of excited puppy, Cam couldn't get a good grip. "Come on, boy, calm down." He couldn't even get up with the excited dog jumping all over him. "Max, if you don't put a cork in it, I swear I'll wrap that tongue around your scrawny little neck."

Undaunted by a threat spoken in the kind voice he'd grown to love, Max jumped on Cam's chest and continued to both bark and lick whatever skin he could reach—which was plenty.

Finally, drenched in puppy slobber, Cam managed to grab hold of the puppy and sit up. "It's all right now, boy," he whispered, feeling Max quiver. "I probably scared you as much as you startled me." He stroked the dog, thankful when the high-pitched barking stopped. "Did I hurt you when I stepped on you?"

He got another kiss for his question and found himself able to laugh despite the ache in his chest. "Up for a walk?" That proved to be a silly question, and one that started the dog hopelessly wriggling with happiness. "Okay, two rules. One, no more barking. Two, no peeing on me. Got it?" Even in the dark, he had no trouble detecting Max's eagerness. "Let's go find Haley."

At the name, Max perked up even more, if that was possible. The night was cold, dark and bleak. It matched Cam's spirits. Max didn't notice. He ran from tree to tree, leaving his mark, making happy little sounds in his throat that almost had Cam wishing for the carefree, easy life of a dog.

Haley's cottage looked deserted, but he knocked, convinced she'd gone straight to bed. Not surprised when she didn't respond, he knocked again. "Come on, Haley," he called out. "I just want to make sure you're all right. Open up."

After two more minutes, he decided the hell with being polite. "Haley?" Max pushed ahead of him, whining softly. "It's just me."

No sound, no light. Moving quickly now, goaded by fear, Cam stepped from the main room into the small hallway. The bedroom door was closed, but that, too, opened with just a push. She'd left the shutters wide-open so what little light the stars provided spilled into the room.

At first he thought she was in bed, but as he sat on the edge and flipped on the lamp, he realized his mistake quickly enough. It seemed the housekeeper didn't bother with making her own bed. The empty pile of blankets and tangled sheets only looked like a body.

Haley hadn't come back.

"Damn." He looked at Max, who had his nose deep in the trash by his feet. A bright yellow legal pad in it caught his attention.

It looked like a ledger, and it was filled with writing he now knew to be Haley's. He picked it up and brought it closer to the lamp. Haley's journal.

His first reaction was to put it down. He could still remember the diary he'd started in the back of his math notebook. He'd been thirteen and in lust with Sally Michaels. Jason had found the notes, copied them, and sold them to his classmates for a dime each. It had taken all eighth grade to get over that humiliation. And on top of it all, Sally had dumped him.

No, he couldn't read the journal. But still, he hesitated, holding it, staring at the writing. Here at last was a chance to maybe find out the truth about the woman he wanted in his life. The pad was flipped open to a page with writing halfway down. He stared at it, warring with himself and his scruples.

Then his name stuck out from the writing.

*She'd written about him.* Max looked at him, tilting his head, obviously wondering what the big deal was. It was a weak excuse, but simple curiosity won, and Cam scanned the page.

It was the last thing he expected of her—a personal diary. The most recent entry was dated days ago, a day he remembered all too well. Their trip to the library. The day he'd held her in his arms as she'd cried in grief and fear. He read her words.

I can't stop myself from thinking about Cam, can't seem to stop myself from dreaming about what it would be like to make love with him.

Cam's mouth fell open. Utterly incapable of stopping now, he read on.

Since I can't imagine he'd really want to be with me, I guess I'd have to seduce him. Ha! As if I'd even know how. I'd probably start with candles.

Cam groaned out loud.

In my fantasy, I'd have the sort of body that would make a grown man beg, so that when I took off my clothes, the gentle light would flicker over my body. I'd be so beautiful, he wouldn't be able to turn away. We'd step into a hot, deep tub and he'd lose himself in me. I wish—

The writing stopped abruptly. Dazed, Cam lifted his head and stared at her rumpled bed. *She wanted him.* She'd fantasized about him. He could almost see the candlelight flickering over her body, see her dripping wet from the tub, feel himself sinking into her.... God. If he'd ever been more turned-on, he couldn't remember.

Then he looked up and went still. Haley stood in the doorway. Her dark hair framed her lovely face, the flowered dress she still wore dipped enticingly low in front. He could imagine lifting her up, carrying her into the bathroom and fulfilling her fantasy. That her bathroom had a shower, not a tub, and that there wasn't a candle in the place wouldn't have stopped him.

But her expression did.

"What are you doing here?" she asked, her voice low and controlled. Only the way she gripped her hands told him she was upset.

"I...ah..." He'd lost track of that when all the blood had drained from his head, rushing to his lap.

Her eyes narrowed on what he held, then widened as she took it all in; him sitting on her bed, holding the journal she'd written. "That's mine."

"I'm sorry." He stood just as she grabbed the pad of paper from his hands. "I—"

"Oh, my God," she whispered, staring down at the opened pad. Her face reddened, but still she met his gaze evenly. "You read this."

He nodded, watching as she closed her eyes in misery and mortification. "No," he said, reaching for her. "Don't do that. I'm sorry I invaded your privacy, but—"

She jerked back, covering her cheeks with her hands. "You're *sorry?*" She choked out a laugh. "You read my most private thoughts, thoughts I can never get back, and you're sorry?"

Turning from him, she plopped down on the edge of the bed, then dropped her head into her hands. "Go away," she said quite clearly. "Just go away."

He sank to his knees before her and gently pried her hands from her still-red face. "I'm very sorry if I embarrassed and hurt you. That's the last thing I wanted to do."

"You should have thought of that first. Before you read my things."

He felt like the lowest form of life. "I know."

"You keep butting into my life," she said in amazement. "I don't know why, but you do. I don't like it." She shook her head. "And to think I'd gone looking for you, wanting..."

He leaped on that—*anything* to change the subject. "Wanting what?"

"Never mind now." She lifted that stubborn chin. "You ask impossible questions, dig where you shouldn't be digging, and now this!"

"If I'm pushing where I said I wouldn't, then I'm sorry for that, too. But I'm worried sick about you. You're holding your head like it hurts so much it's going to fall off. You've given yourself ulcers. You need sleeping pills. And you've lost weight." He surged to his feet. "Yeah, I'm going to push now. I told you I wouldn't, but I can't hold back the concern, and dammit, I won't be sorry for that."

She'd gone completely still. "I can't believe how much you care."

At the moment, he couldn't, either.

"I'd come looking for you to tell you I...didn't mean it before. I don't want you to stay out of my life. I trust you, Cam.

And I've never said that before, to anyone." She bit her lip at his stunned silence. "I just wanted you to know."

He gave her a little smile. "It means more than you could know to hear you say that." He just barely resisted the urge to add, *finally*. But he couldn't think beyond the journal. "Haley, about what you wrote..."

She made a little sound of protest and closed her eyes. "Don't remind me."

Again, he hunkered down before her. "It was thrilling to know you felt that way. That I wasn't the only one."

"You told me you wouldn't do this thing between us. That you couldn't."

"You know why I said that," he said gently.

"It wasn't meant for you to see." Haley tipped her head back and stared at the ceiling. This was, without a doubt, *the* most embarrassing thing that had ever happened to her.

He squeezed her hands, ran his thumbs over her knuckles. His gaze heated, holding hers. "When I read your words, something happened to me. Then I saw you standing there watching me and I could have devoured you alive. God, Haley, I've been dying to know what it would be like to be with you since that night we danced in the rain. You felt so good, wrapped around me—"

"Stop it," she said quickly, his words making her heart tattoo against her chest. She dropped her spinning head to their joined hands. "This is very embarrassing, you have to know that."

"Because you're as attracted to me as I am to you?" He loosened their hands to frame her face, lifting it. "That's one of those silly-girl things, isn't it? Wanting to keep it a secret?"

"Stop it," she said miserably, rolling her eyes when he smiled. "This isn't funny."

"No," he agreed. "But then, neither is the fact that I want you more than I've wanted anyone since Lorraine died. I didn't think I *could* want again, but I do. And I'm glad, so glad. You've opened me up, brought me back to the living. I want so much, Haley. And I want it with you."

What exactly did that wonderful man see in her? And could she see enough in herself to even give it a chance? "You've read my innermost thoughts. I'm not sure how to deal with that."

He rose and sat next to her, his weight dipping the bed down a little. His hands rested on either side of her hips. "It was wrong for me to read what you'd written and I apologize for that. But when you ran off, I got worried."

"So you just came on in? Didn't it occur to you I wanted to be alone?"

"I was *worried*," he repeated. "When I flipped on the light, I saw the yellow paper in the trash. My name just sort of stuck out at me. I shouldn't have, but I read it. I know it makes you uncomfortable and I understand that you're a woman who doesn't easily share herself. What I don't understand is why."

Now she had to look away. This was uncharted territory for her. Just as everything else with this man had been. "I've told you, I'm sort of a loner. I always have been. I like it that way."

"I don't believe that."

"It's true." She gave a little laugh that even to her own ears sounded high and nervous. Just sitting close to him did that to her, but now she had the added disadvantage of Cam knowing exactly how badly she'd wanted him. "I don't get along well with others," she said uneasily. "Just ask any of the teachers I've had over the years."

"Maybe no one gave you a chance."

That was just close enough to the truth to have her taking a deep breath.

"I hate to see you hurting so." He touched her, his fingers brushing over her forehead. "And I hate to think I had a hand in causing that headache."

She took a deep breath and spoke the honest truth. "It's gone." Facing him on her bed, where she'd lain dreaming about him so often, seemed a bit unreal. She caught sight of her journal lying on the floor near where Max was sprawled out, asleep.

"No," he murmured, touching her face until she turned it back to him. "Don't relive it. You'll make me feel bad again."

She lifted an eyebrow, but caught his smile. "You don't strike me as a man who would brood for long."

"Only when it comes to you."

With a sudden restless movement, she stood, brushed past his tough, rangy body and went toward the window. The rain had come; she could hear it hitting the earth, smell it in the air. "I meant what I said before. I trust you. I trust you with the real me. But you don't really know that woman."

"I'd like to."

She could see him in the reflection of the window, still sitting on her bed, watching her.

She took a deep breath and a big mental step when she moved back to him and took his hand. "I'm not a regular type of person, Cam. I'm...different. I don't even know who my father is. All my mother would say was that he was unsuitable."

"That doesn't matter to me."

"When I was two, I recited the past presidents of the United States, their political parties and the dates they served office."

"Impressive," he said dryly, trying to picture the uncaring woman he'd talked to tonight on the phone caring for a vulnerable, brilliant two-year-old Haley.

"Not to my mother. She told me how unladylike too much knowledge was, and demanded I forget what I'd learned."

"When you were *two?*" When she nodded, he said softly, "Oh, Haley. Darlin', I'm sorry."

"By the age of five I had read every book in the house and had mastered Spanish from an English-Spanish dictionary I found at the library in school."

Pride for her shot through him. "A child prodigy. I'd think your mother would have been proud."

"No," Haley said wistfully. "I was an odd little thing. Often sick, always weak. I never wanted to play with other kids. I read every spare second of the day and that embarrassed her, too. A

Whitfield lady was to make her place in society, not lose herself from reality."

She looked around at the small, comfy room, with the soft light from the lamp, the beautiful homemade quilt. Homey. So different from the rooms she'd had over the years. She could so easily get used to this life here, but she was afraid it wasn't meant to be.

"What did she do with you?" Cam wanted to know.

She hated his pity, but was determined now. She wanted him to understand. Everything. "At first, she'd send me to my room to keep me out of sight." Where she'd hidden away, reading for hours. "But eventually she shipped me off to boarding school."

"When you were five?" He looked horrified.

"At least the teachers recognized immediately I wasn't like the other kids, so I was sent to a special school with other supposedly 'gifted' children. But what they really were was a sad little group that no one understood, or wanted to understand. All they wanted was to find out what we could be taught, how much we could learn."

Cam made a sound of regret and sympathy, one that, instead of making her cringe, somehow made her feel better. "I hated it."

"Pretty different from my childhood," he said lightly. "My parents tried not to expect too much from us. Of course, they had three wild, out-of-control boys. They were just thankful we didn't destroy the house on a daily basis."

She smiled a little, and found it felt good. "My mother didn't have that worry. I'm an only child. She enjoyed the freedom of having me away at school. She could continue her social obligations untethered. So I stayed in boarding schools and the path was set."

"Were you unhappy that whole time?"

No one had ever thought about her happiness. No one except Cam. "At first. I got sick a lot. Stomachaches, headaches, that sort of thing. Stress, they determined. So they lightened my load.

But school was all that mattered to me at that time, so I got worse.''

"Did you go home?"

"No."

He'd gone still, except for his eyes, which searched hers. "I have to tell you, Haley. I don't think I like your mother very much."

She laughed a little. "You know what? I don't like her, either."

"What happened when you got out of school?"

"I finished high school when I was ten. I got my first college degree at twelve. My second at fourteen. By the time I was sixteen, I had my doctorate."

He stared at her, obviously stunned. "At sixteen?"

"Yeah." She smiled, pleased by how much better talking had made her feel. Then, because he looked so cute flustered, and because she felt so light, she giggled. "I have a quick learning curve. School was all I knew, Cam. So I just kept going. And going and going..."

Cam gave her a little smile, but his eyes were filled with anger and compassion, and she found that felt good, too. "Even the Energizer bunny gets a new battery occasionally."

Some of her humor faded. This was the tough part. She'd told no one. "By the time I was twenty, I suffered from insomnia, chronic stomach trouble, exhaustion and was so near a mental breakdown, I could have reached out and touched it."

His mouth tightened, his expression turned grim. "Couldn't anyone see what this was costing you?"

"There was no one *to* see."

"*No one* close to you?"

"No."

"No friends?"

"Just acquaintances."

His disbelief was plain. "You're gorgeous, Haley. You must have been fighting the guys off at every turn."

That made her laugh again. "Hardly." She wrapped her arms

around herself, dropped her gaze. "For some reason, you look at me with rose-colored glasses. The truth is, I never had to fight off a single man. I think I turned them off because of..."

"Your brain?" He grinned, then sobered. "I can't believe that no one ever saw you for what you are."

"What? A nerd?"

"An intelligent, strong-willed woman—as lovely on the inside as out."

"Thank you," she whispered.

"What happened between you and your mother after you grew up?"

"Not much. I did try, but I knew what a disappointment I was to her, which didn't help my self-esteem." To her horror, she could feel the tears build. "Inside, I was so desperate. Even after all those years, I found myself still wanting her love, her attention. But she just couldn't give it."

"No wonder you were a loner. You'd been brought up that way from the start."

"Maybe. It definitely made it difficult for me to get along with others. Especially men. I— I never— Well." She smiled nervously. "Let's just say men were, and still are, a complete mystery."

He sighed and pulled her close. "Your mother is an idiot, Haley. And so are all the men that passed you over—" He stopped. *"A complete mystery,"* he repeated slowly, looking shell-shocked. "You mean you've never—"

"No," she said shakily, pulling away. She needed distance for this—lots of it. "I've never been with a man before. Pretty pathetic, huh?"

Those amazing dark eyes caressed her. "No. It will mean all the more for you this way. And me."

"You don't understand," she said, flustered by the way he was looking at her. "I think I'm what they call...'repressed.' You know, 'frigid.'"

A laugh escaped him, but it died quickly enough when she didn't crack a smile. Cupping her shoulders, he turned her toward him. "The woman who can kiss me senseless—the same woman who wrote about wanting to seduce me so that I couldn't even remember where I was...*that's* the woman you think is repressed? Frigid?" He started to smile again, then read the truth that must have been in her eyes, and straightened. "My God, you're serious. Haley, darlin', you're one of the most sensual women I've ever met. I mean it," he insisted when she scoffed. "I watch you cleaning the house in Nellie's clothes, wearing that clingy thing under your pale blouse. Drives me crazy."

"The camisole?" she asked in surprise. It was plain white and very comfortable. It was also all she had. *But just when had he been trying to see beneath her clothes?*

"Yeah." His voice was soft and unbearably husky. "The camisole. When you stand in the living room dusting, the sun shines in from the picture window and the blouse turns sheer. It's heaven."

Her lips curved, even as embarrassment dictated some sort of indignation should be shown. "Ever thought about looking away?"

"No." He grinned and flicked a finger lightly over her heated cheeks. "Then I see you hugging my jacket close against you and I imagine it's *me* keeping you warm instead. I have to admit, I've never been envious of an item of clothing before."

She just stared at him. "You're making this up."

His hand ran down her side, squeezed her waist. His hungry gaze followed the movement. "You may try to hide it, but you have a hot little body I can't seem to get out of my head."

Thinking was difficult whenever he looked at her like that, with passion and promise, but she had to try to get back on track. "My life has been tied up in my studies. I've never taken the time for anything else."

"Because it was easier not to."

"Maybe." She shrugged, and his other hand shifted to her waist, as well. "Things changed when I went to work."

"Changed how?"

She took a deep breath. "Well, work was good. Great, actually. Fulfilling and all that. But the pressure was rugged, the work very intense and the schedule always grueling. My health…suffered. I—''

''Wait.'' He frowned. ''What do you mean, 'suffered'?''

It still hurt, still embarrassed her, to admit this last weakness. ''We were under a lot of pressure, there were so many secrets, which are just starting to make sense, but then all I knew was that I had to work. Insanely, around the clock. I lost a little weight, was feeling tired all the time.'' She shrugged again and backed from his touch. ''Then we made that discovery, one that would have revolutionized the way we handle earthquakes.'' Unable to sit, she bounced up and paced the room while he watched with serious eyes. She stopped before the small dresser with the round mirror above it. Her face, wan and wretched, stared back at her. Visions of the lives her undersea system had destroyed wavered in front of her. Her fault? *No*. She knew that now, accepted it. But it had been her creation that had started it. ''People died, Cam. I blamed myself for those deaths.''

''No. Darlin'—''

''Wait. Let me finish, or I'll never be able to get it out. In South America, after I found out, everything suddenly felt like such an effort.''

Tension filled the air, thickened it.

''What do you mean, Haley, by everything?'' His voice seemed muted, strangled.

''You know, life in general.'' She shrugged, pretending a lightness she didn't feel. ''It was too difficult, it seemed, to go on. I didn't want to.'' She looked at her hands and whispered, ''On the plane here, I thought about dying. How easy it would be. How maybe I deserved it.''

He lurched to his feet, pale and stricken. ''Haley.''

She smiled a little, but still couldn't meet his eyes. ''I got over it, Cam. I came here. And within a day, things had changed. I *wanted* to live. Quite desperately.'' Now she did turn to face him, and found him standing right before her, looking ready to do battle. *For her*, she realized with a sweet pang.

"You did that for me," she said softly, touching his face. "You and the others."

"Well, thank God for that." He hugged her fiercely. Then he cupped her face, his eyes searching and intense. "Promise me you got over those other feelings—the ones that made you feel you couldn't go on."

"I promise."

Relief came into his expression. But the worry remained. "Haley, I'm not used to keeping my feelings inside, like you. I just can't do it. You're going to have to hear them."

She tried to duck her head, not wanting to see his pity and disgust, but he made her look at him. Surprisingly she saw neither; just compassion, understanding, and far more emotion than she was equipped to handle.

"I hate what you went through," he said gently. "I know there's a lot you've left out, but you'll tell me the rest."

"Yes."

"I hate thinking about you sick, afraid, alone. Feeling worthless." His eyes turned grim. "Wanting to end it all." He kissed her very tenderly. "I'm just so thankful that you made it here. I can't regret that."

He had a way of putting things, she thought, as she felt herself being enclosed in his warm, reassuring embrace. "I'm not sick now," she said, a little amazed by it. She hugged him close, buried her face in the crook of his neck, where he smelled so good. "It's funny, but since I've been here, my stomach has gotten better and I hardly ever get a headache."

"Good. We'll get through this," he said with quiet strength.

How she wanted to believe that. She closed her eyes, listening to the rain pummel at the earth outside.

"Together," he whispered. "We'll do it together. And then, we'll go from there."

*Together.* The word implied so much. She dug her fingers into his waist, knowing she must look half-wild as she lifted her head. "I've been so afraid for you and the others."

He let out a wordless sound of amazement, of remorse, and pulled her closer. "Darlin', I can protect myself and the others."

"I...care about you."

His eyes went opaque. "Say that again."

"Cam." She let out a little laugh. "You know I do."

"You don't know how it makes me feel to hear it. Say it again," he demanded.

Still uncomfortable with the words, she rolled her eyes and said obediently, "I care for you more than I've ever cared for anyone, but—"

"No," he said gently. "No buts." He kissed her, pouring everything he felt into that one sweet connection. "No more secrets," he declared when the breathless kiss had ended.

"No more," she repeated softly. Then she stole his heart when she pulled his head back to hers.


From half a world away, the shadowy figure finally got another lead.

It had been badly needed, since the last one had petered out when the call from Haley had been untraceable.

But now there had been several phone calls to the USGS—anonymous, of course. Someone was trying to get information on EVS—specifically on the deaths from the bombing—and that someone was just outside Colorado Springs, Colorado.

Dr. Haley Whitfield? There was no one else left.

Triumph surged. It was just a matter of time now.

# Chapter 10

The next morning, Haley took one last swipe over the kitchen floor with her sponge. The tile gleamed from one corner to another, giving her a surge of satisfaction.

When the phone rang, she let out a frustrated sigh. "Of course," she muttered. She stood in the far corner, the length of the huge kitchen away from the telephone.

*Ring...ring...ring.*

Eyeing the beautifully clean, *wet* floor, she debated. Let it ring, or make tracks on her perfect tile? She made a face and hopped across the wet floor, leaving the dreaded prints.

"Hello?" she said, breathless.

Silence.

"Hello!" she demanded, letting her irritation show.

"Do exactly as I say and I won't kill any of them."

Her heart stopped, the breath clogged in her throat. "What?" she whispered.

"You heard me."

"Lloyd?" Lloyd Branson, her boss. "But...you're dead."

The gruff voice laughed and the evil sound sent chills up Haley's spine. "Am I?"

Mindless, she sank to the wet, pine-smelling floor. Her jeans soaked up the water, but she didn't notice as she leaned back against the counter for support. "You're alive."

"Yes. And everyone else is dead."

How could this have happened? "Alda told me—"

"Exactly what I forced her to tell you. She served her usefulness. She's gone now."

Terror, mind-numbing terror. "You're insane." She sounded so calm, Haley thought. Until she realized. "You know where I am."

"Oh, yes." His voice hardened, sounding unlike the quietly determined, kind man she'd always known him to be. "Pay attention now, Ms. Whitfield. Your freedom's over. You work for me again."

"No." *Never.*

"Oh, yes. I want you to make a little trip."

"No."

"Back to South America. We have a project to finish, and I'm flying with you to make sure you don't get cold feet or do something stupid...like bring someone with you. You'll meet me at the gate at seven o'clock."

*Only hours from now.* "No," she whispered.

"Don't forget your passport. I wouldn't want to have to fit you in my suitcase." He laughed softly and goose bumps rose over her skin.

Dear God, he was here. In Colorado. And he knew exactly where she was. "Don't come here," she said quickly. "Please. I'll come to you."

"See that you do."

"Please. Please, don't hurt anyone."

"Follow directions, Haley, and see that I don't have to."

Her stomach turned. She was cold, clammy, and very close to being sick. Her nightmare was coming true and all she could think was that she just might throw up on her newly cleaned floor.

"Dr. Whitfield, are we in agreement?"

"Yes," she whispered, starting to shake. She gripped the phone until her hand went numb. She couldn't see the pretty kitchen, could only see Zach, giving her that sweet, shy smile. Nellie and Jason—and oh, God, their unborn baby. And Cam. She loved him, oh, how she loved him. And now, if she wasn't careful, she'd destroy him.

"Don't hurt them. If you do—"

"No bargains. Now listen up. Once we're back in South America, you'll re-create that undersea system for me. The earth-movement detector. I want another one."

"I can't."

"You can," he insisted roughly. "If you don't, everyone around you will be very, very sorry. I want you to show me how to use the system by myself. I also want your notes. I want your observations. I know you took them with you when you left here."

She hadn't. The small notebook in her purse held only a tiny fraction of her work. Her other notes had all been destroyed in the office bombing. "Okay," she said, afraid to make him angry, just wanting him as far from Colorado as possible.

"When we're done, you will turn yourself in. You'll tell them you stole the uranium and sold it, and that you bombed EVS."

And because everyone thought him dead, he'd be free. With the uranium—which she had no doubt he'd sell to the highest bidder—he'd be wealthy beyond imagination. He'd never be found.

He'd get off, free and clear. And he'd be able to use her system as he pleased. She wouldn't let this happen, she vowed. She'd stop him somehow, and she'd gladly die to do it. "Why are you doing this?"

"Greed," he said simply. "Pure greed. You were the head of my team. The smartest and the best. Certainly the only one capable of creating a system to predict earthquakes and volcanoes that any first-class government would pay an arm and a leg for. I'd much rather use you than kill you, Haley, but I'll do what I have to.''

She could hear the hissing of his breath over the wire, could see again in her mind the dead bodies of Frederick and Danyella as they lay covered in blood. Could imagine Bob's and Alda's death. He'd do the same to everyone here without a qualm.

''Haley?'' It was Zach now, standing in the kitchen, looking down at her strangely. ''You okay?''

She stared up at him from the floor, the receiver still against her ear. She could see his lips moving, but couldn't make out the words over the roaring in her head.

*''Don't screw this up, Haley. You'll be very sorry if you do,''* Branson said in her ear. ''The airport. Seven o'clock.'' He hung up.

Haley lowered her gaze from Zach to stare dully at the receiver in her hand. What the hell was she going to do? Then she dropped the phone as though it could burn her hand.

Zach bent and took her hands in his. ''Haley? Look at me.'' When she did, he frowned. ''Are you sick?''

*Branson would kill them,* she thought, fear skittering up her spine. If she didn't do exactly as he said, he'd kill them all. She blinked away the haze of panic and straightened, then forced herself to smile at Zach. ''I'm fine. Just got dizzy for a minute there, that's all.''

''The cleaner's pretty strong stuff. You shouldn't use so much of it.'' He reached for her, helped her to her feet, his gaze never leaving her face. ''You don't look good. Let me help you into the living room.''

She was too weak to protest.

''Wait here,'' he said, when she'd slumped into a chair. ''I'm going to get you some water.''

When he left, she dropped her face into her hands.

She'd have to go back. *Back to hell.* How would she survive it? Would she even be allowed to?

"Here." Zach was back, pressing a glass of water into her hands. He sat on the coffee table before her. "Are you sure—"

"I'm fine now." Sheer strength of will had her lying more fluently than she'd ever done before. Smiling and even laughing a little, she stood. "But you're right about the fumes. I think I'll go lie down for a little while." She had to lock her knees together to keep them from giving out.

Zach nodded slowly, carefully examining her face. "That sounds like a good idea." He patted her hand. "Don't worry about lunch or dinner, okay? We'll be fine."

She smiled again and just managed to walk from the room without falling into a heaping, sobbing mess.

She couldn't call the police; they'd take her away, leaving the Reeveses vulnerable and unprotected for when Branson came for his revenge.

She would have to leave the world she'd come to love beyond her wildest dreams. She *had* to. Then she could call the police, if she got the chance before Branson killed her.

But first, she had to make her fantasy come true. She deserved that much, at least. She had to get Cam to make love with her. She couldn't face her death without that.

Cam sanded the oak rocking chair with loving hands that soothed and coaxed the best from the wood. He'd never made a rocker before, but he'd wanted to give Nellie and Jason's unborn baby a special gift.

And someday, he wanted his own baby to be rocked in this chair.

That thought startled him enough to straighten and stare into space with a dreamy expression on his face.

A baby. *His baby.*

He'd thought he'd never want another, not after having lost his son before he'd even gotten to hold him. But oh, he did, and he wanted one with Haley.

*Haley.*

He'd stayed up until dawn trying to figure out what to do.

There was simply no way to keep her safe and hidden for the rest of her life. It wasn't right. She had to turn herself in and fight. He'd be at her side, of course. His entire family would. But coming to that decision and convincing Haley of it were two different things. She had to go willingly, for he simply couldn't handle the thought of calling the authorities behind her back. He had to make her see reason, and he had to do it today, before it was too late.

He looked up as the barn doors opened, letting in the sunlight and the scent of late autumn. Wind and leaves twirled through the opening as Haley stepped inside.

A greeting died on his tongue at the look of immeasurable sorrow on her face. But the moment she saw him, her expression was transformed. The promise of passion took his breath. He dropped the sandpaper and went to her, reaching for her hands.

"Haley?"

She managed a smile, but it seemed too bright, and Cam felt the first inkling of dread. "It's freezing outside and you're not wearing a coat."

She gave a little laugh, completely without mirth.

He tightened his grip on her fingers. "What's wrong?"

"Nothing," she said quickly—too quickly, which did nothing to relieve the pit in his stomach. "I just...have something I want to do."

She reached up on tiptoe to set her lips on his. He jolted in surprise, and would have pulled back, but she threw her arms around his neck to hold him still and teased the corner of his mouth with a flirty pass of her tongue. Instantly, his heart drummed hard and fast against hers as she pressed her body to his. *Wait*, he tried to say. He wanted to look at her, assure himself she was okay. He could feel her tremble, could feel how cold and clammy she was, and he couldn't shake the sense that something was terribly, horribly wrong. He thought he could taste her desperation and fear, her needs and doubts....

"You're thinking too much," she said.

And then he couldn't think at all because she'd slipped her hands up beneath his T-shirt to streak over his bare, heated skin.

"I want you," she whispered huskily.

His hands, which he'd lifted to her waist, froze. "You— *Now?*"

She let out a sound that might have been a laugh. She tipped her head back, and he could see the shadow of fear in her eyes, though she kept her gaze steady and level on his. "Yes, now."

"Are you sure?"

Her lips curved. "Are you going to turn me down, Cam?"

It was easy to ignore the soft sarcasm when he still couldn't get past the feeling that something wasn't right. "You've waited a long time for this, Haley. I just don't want you to regret it. I don't think I could stand it if you did."

"You *are* going to turn me down." With a sound of impatience, she moved away from him. "I'm really not very good at this, I knew that." She let out a little laugh. "I actually thought... Oh, never mind." Stumbling, she went for the door.

His heart broke at the rejection he'd seen flash on her face. "Wait." He reached for her and gently turned her back to look at him. "You thought what?"

Face reddening, she leaned her head back against the wall and closed her eyes. "I thought I could seduce you. Silly, huh?"

The yearning grew and spread until his body ached with it. How could she not know what she did to him? "No, it's not silly." He traced her jaw with his fingers. Her skin felt so silky, so soft. She wore the peek-a-boo blouse tucked into a long skirt that brushed against his thighs. He'd never seen anyone look so beautiful or desirable. "You've been seducing me for weeks with little to no effort from you at all."

She gripped the front of his shirt with tight fists. "Then make love with me. *Now.*"

Need and longing swirled inside him, so deep and so strong it was amazing to him that he could remain on his feet. The cold, crisp air blowing in the door did nothing to cool him down.

She wanted him, and yet...the absolute sense of urgency, the desperate look in her eyes told him that something *was* wrong.

Haley mistook his silence.

Squaring her shoulders, she gave him one of her regal looks. "Never mind," she said. "I can see the idea of making love with me just thrills the hell out of you." She spun away, but before he could so much as take a step toward her, she whirled back, fury emanating from her every pore.

"Wait a minute," she said unevenly, pushing her hair from her face. "All my life I've been doing this. Accepting casual criticism without a murmur. Taking rejection silently, painfully. I won't do it anymore, Cam. Not even for you." She jabbed his chest with her finger, her eyes misting, but her voice remained calm. "I thought you were different. These past few weeks have meant something to me."

"Haley—"

She evaded his touch. "No, don't. I'm sorry." She shrugged. "You know what? I've got to go."

When had the conversation taken this bad turn? Cam found his limbs and grabbed for Haley as she rushed out, but she fought him with a strength he hadn't guessed she had. Finally, unable to do anything else, he wrapped his arms around her from behind, restraining her.

"Dammit, Cam," she muttered, fighting wildly. "Let me go."

"You're wrong, Haley," he said gruffly into her ear. "Wrong, if you think I was playing with you, that I don't really want you." He turned her in his arms and shook her gently until she looked at him, her glorious blue eyes bright with humiliation. He couldn't stand it. "I wasn't rejecting you just now. My God, you think I could? You just startled me, that's all." He had to laugh at himself. "You came in here with the offer I've been waiting for and I lost all capability to think."

He realized that, given her limited experience, she might have no idea what he was talking about. "Do you understand what

I'm saying?'' he asked, because he still couldn't believe that a woman who looked and felt like she did was a virgin.

She shook her head, her eyes wide on his, and his blood surged.

''God, you're sweet,'' he said, giving her a quick, hard kiss. ''You make me ache for you, Haley, everywhere.'' With a slow, easy gesture, he grabbed her hips and rubbed them against his. He knew by her sharp intake of breath, she hadn't missed his very unmistakable desire. ''Yeah, *that's* what you do to me, darlin',' '' he whispered, then nearly died of pleasure when, with an instinctual movement, she slid herself over him again.

At the connection, her mouth fell open, her head dropped back. ''Oh!'' she whispered, obviously finding equal pleasure. Cam wanted to lose himself in her, but he had to make one thing clear. He gripped her waist in his hands to keep her still, waiting until her glazed eyes met his. ''Haley,'' he murmured. ''Listen to me. You'll never have to scramble for affection, or attention with me. *Never.*''

She blinked and braced herself by clutching his arms tightly. ''That sounds nice,'' she said, her voice whispery and breathless, making Cam hesitate one last time.

''What is it?'' he murmured. ''What else is it?''

But she only shook her head. ''Come with me,'' she said in that throaty, sexy voice that could drive a grown man wild. ''Please?'' Without waiting for an answer, she took his hand and led him outside, her skirt billowing in the gentle breeze. The storm from the day before had vanished, leaving everything sparkling and clean and gorgeous as only the day after a rain could be.

''I'll never forget this day,'' she vowed with a vehemence that surprised him. ''It's beautiful.''

''It is.'' Her hand felt small and fragile in his, and as she led him, he could only see the back of her petite frame. Her urgency, coming on the heels of her hesitation of weeks, seemed out of character. ''Haley?''

''Hurry, Cam.''

At the front door of the main house, she paused. "Nellie and Jason went to Colorado Springs to shop for the baby." She chewed her lower lip in a gesture he knew to be pure nerves. "Zach went to Tex's ranch to help out with something or other." She stepped inside and twiddled her hands together. "We're alone."

He reached for her. "Alone is good."

"I hope you don't mind, but I have something to show you upstairs."

He followed her, watching the swaying of her narrow hips as she climbed the stairs. There was only one thing now that could ruin this—the unexpected return of his family. "Ah, Haley?" He wasn't worried about himself; he could take the ribbing he knew would be meted out often, especially at the dinner table. But Haley... It would mortify her. "Maybe we should go to your place. Nel's been in a mood ever since the doctor told her she has three weeks left to carry that basketball. Jas won't be able to tolerate her for long."

She only gave him a quick, indecipherable glance and pulled him into his own bedroom. She stopped before his bathroom door, startling him with the mix of emotions he saw in her expression. Hunger and need combined with a strange aura of fear that confused him.

"Are you afraid of me?" he asked, concerned. "Of this?"

"No."

"Are you sure? Because—"

She laid her finger over his lips. "I'm not afraid of you, Cam. Or this. Well, maybe just a little nervous."

He touched her face and kissed her gently. "If it helps, I'm nervous, too." He smiled past the almost-unbearable ache in his heart caused by his feelings for her. "I've never been someone's first." She smiled, and her lips brushed over his fingertips, causing a surge of blood that pooled in his groin. "I don't want to hurt you, darlin'."

"You won't."

Her faith in him gave him strength, but it also fueled the

hunger, the need. "This is just the beginning between us," he promised, stroking her jaw. Beneath his fingers, she paled. "Haley?"

She only shook her head, then reached up and unbuttoned her blouse with trembling hands. "I have no standard formula for this." She pulled the silky material away from her shoulders, revealing the virgin-white teddy she wore beneath. No frills, no lace, just creamy silk and smooth, pale skin. His mouth went dry as one of the teddy's thin straps slipped off her shoulder.

"And no guidelines," she admitted. Her fingers started on the long row of buttons down her skirt. "So instincts and needs are going to have to be enough." She straightened as the skirt fell away from her hips, dropping to a puddle at her feet. "But, if it matters, I've never wanted anything so much in my life." She reached for the other strap of her camisole.

"It matters." If her motions had galvanized him, her words stirred him into action. But, God, that body. She was moving too fast, when he wanted to go slow and savor. He stopped her fumbling fingers by brushing them with his. "Let me." His rough palms slid over the silky camisole, feeling the softness of her skin beneath.

Fascinated, he let his hands roam over her as he dipped his head to seek her mouth. Her body seemed as taut as a wire and he tried to use his hands to reassure as well as seduce, attempting to convince himself that her unnatural stiffness was indeed just nerves. "Darlin'?" Even to his own ears, his voice sounded thick with arousal. "Tell me again that you're sure."

He could feel her force herself to relax. "I'm sure." Her voice was husky. Sexy. Unbearably arousing. "I have to have this, Cam. Have to have you." She yielded against him with a sigh that humbled him to his toes. He understood this was much more than passion on her part; she was giving him her full and unconditional trust.

Her fingers slid up under his T-shirt. As her gaze met his, she brushed them slowly over his chest, moving from side to side, exploring...and just that light touch drove him to a pitch of desire he hadn't known before. He kissed her—long, wet, deep—and she moaned low in her throat, letting her head fall back against the door as he devoured her jaw, her neck. Mindless now, beyond thought, he swept his hands down her sides, then slowly back up, his fingertips teasing the undersides of her breasts.

Her low moan turned into a baffled whimper.

*Innocent,* he reminded himself. *Innocent.* And he had her backed to the door, pressed between the hard, ungiving wood and his equally hard, ungiving body.

"Not here, not against the bathroom door," he managed to say, grabbing her restless hands in his. He tried to scoop her up, but she stepped back and opened the door, her eyes naked and vulnerable.

Cam spared her one last curious glance before looking into the bathroom. His breath stopped. Simply stopped.

Lit by the soft glow of scented candles, the bathroom glimmered with shadows. In the center of the room stood his bathtub, filled with steaming water and overflowing with bubbles.

She'd done this for him, recreated the fantasy that had so gripped him last night. His throat tightened.

"Haley." He turned to her, brushed his fingers over her cheek. "It's beautiful. You're beautiful." He could feel her heart pounding against his, could feel the intriguing contrast between the silk of her garment and the smoothness of her skin. "I want you so much." He let his lips wander to the warm, sweet curve of her shoulder. "I've been waiting for this since that first night I saw you."

She arched beneath his hands, making a soft noise of agreement, of surrender, that boiled his blood. Closing her eyes, she fisted her hands in his hair and dragged his mouth back to hers.

He responded to her desperate urgency by tugging down her other strap and feasting on the skin he exposed one inch at a time. She made another sound, almost a whimper, and arched against him again, and his body answered helplessly in kind.

God, he loved her. "Haley—"

As if she could read his mind, she kissed him fiercely, stifling his words. "Just this," she begged. "Just this."

Frustrated, he kissed her back, hard. He finally knew how much he loved her—and she only wanted the mindless kind of passion he himself had always sought.

Fine. He'd show her it didn't take words. He lifted her up against him, giving her deep, drugging kisses as he carried her into the bathroom. The candles shimmered and flickered, creating warmth and the sense of intimacy he'd craved to have with her. He'd take it slow, tormentingly slow, and make sure she felt each and every pinpoint of pleasure he could give her. Inhaling the sweet scent of her hair, her skin, he brought his mouth back to hers, teasing her tongue with his, thrilling to each little sound he coaxed from her.

When he finally drew back, she murmured in protest and reached for him. "I'm not going anywhere," he assured her, pulling his shirt over his head. She stared hungrily at his chest, making him let out a laughing moan. "Come here, darlin'." He ran his fingers lightly down her arms, giving her the shivers. She stared at him wild-eyed as he smiled. "You're so lovely." Slowly, so slowly, he drew the camisole the rest of the way down, watching her face. He could see her confusion, her desire—a heady combination that made it easy to linger and savor, to temper his own need.

When she lifted a hand to cover herself, he bent his head to kiss her fingers, then gently lifted them away. Holding her hands in his, he lowered first his gaze, then his mouth to a small, firm breast. *Sweet, unbearably sweet,* he thought with a groan. He peeled the rest of the silk away, lost in her taste, her texture. Above his head, Haley's breath caught, and she gripped his hair in painful fistfuls.

"Haley, honey, do you like this?" He dragged his tongue over her tightened nipple.

She shivered and tugged on his hair hard enough to bring tears to his eyes. "Yes. Yes!"

"Good. That's real good." He worked his mouth over her

again and then again. She pulled even harder on his abused hair. "Maybe you could loosen your grip a bit, darlin'. Just a bit."

"Oh!" Her fingers released his hair, then slid against his scalp, soothing the area. "Just don't stop," she cried.

He smiled against her breast. "Not a chance." He straightened to undo his jeans, because if he didn't, he was going to do himself serious damage. He watched her watch him, her mouth slightly open, her breath coming in shocked little gasps, and it was unspeakably erotic. Shoving the jeans down his hips, he kicked them aside. Then he lifted her, setting her gently into the steaming tub. Water sloshed over the edges as he sank in after her, smiling when she laughed. Bubbles floated around them, candlelight flickered romantically, and the woman in his arms arched against him as warm, soapy water surrounded their bodies.

Dry, she had been a vision in white. Wet, she was a seductress, demanding long, heated kisses. He gave them to her and more, streaking his mouth over her neck, her shoulders, across her rib cage, tasting the beads of water pearled on her hot skin. She moaned and spread her arms to grip the sides of the tub, the rosy tips of her breasts peeking above the bubbles. "Please," she gasped, then jolted when he once again closed his lips over what she offered up. He scraped lightly with his teeth, and water rained out of the tub as she lurched beneath him, nearly bucking him off.

This was just how he wanted her—mindless and pliant with pleasure. He wanted to send her high into a delirium to mask the pain he knew would come, but he sent them both into ecstasy. He rose to his knees between her legs, and another shower of water hit the floor. Candles hissed and flickered from the rising steam. He skimmed his fingers up her slick thighs and she writhed beneath him, her eyes tightly closed. He loved the small, helpless sounds she made deep in her throat, and wanting to hear more, he caressed and kissed his way down her torso. Though they'd barely just begun, she clawed at the water. "Cam," she whispered in a choked voice. "Cam—"

That sexy voice had desire pumping through him. "Soon, darlin'. Soon." Her skin was so hot and slick. Oh, how he wanted to sink right into her, but he forced himself back, continuing to tease. When he finally allowed his fingers to brush over her and find the core of her heat, she convulsed, then reared up as he lightly tormented that creamy center. Flinging her arms around his neck, her breath sobbing in his ears, she rode his hand, and when she stiffened against him, he swallowed her startled cries as she came. Her head fell back as she gasped for air, limp as a rag doll against his chest.

Shaken, he could barely draw his own breath. The candlelight shimmered over her dripping body. He nuzzled her neck, murmured softly to her as he ran his hands over her back, then took her mouth again. But he'd overestimated his own control. Watching her come undone in his arms had put him on the thin, narrow edge and he knew he couldn't hold back much longer. Haley lay before him in the water, stretched out, her eyes tightly closed, every muscle quivering. He'd never seen anything so incredibly perfect.

"There's more," she whispered. "I know there's more."

"Oh, yeah," he assured her. "There's more."

"Show it to me, Cam."

He reached for her, touching her again until she lifted her hips, crying out softly. He positioned himself, holding her up. "Haley." His voice sounded thick and rough, even to his own ears, but with his heart pumping and emotion pouring, he couldn't help it. "Look at me, Haley. Look at me."

Her eyes fluttered open, dazed and clouded with desire. He waited until they cleared and focused on him before he sank into her as far as he could. She gasped softly and opened her legs farther, making needy, husky little noises. "Cam… Please."

"I love you, Haley," he said hoarsely, withdrawing—only to sink into her again, deeper.

She stiffened and let out a strangled cry that tore at him. She tried to pull back, but he held firm, wishing he could absorb her pain. "Give it a minute, darlin', just hold on," he whispered, his own heart in his throat at the thought of it being him to hurt her. He kissed her mouth, her face, her breasts, until he felt her loosen the bruising grip she had on his arms.

She felt so hot, so tight and wet, it took everything he had to stay still. Murmuring softly to her, stroking her rigid body, he moved gently, slowly, wincing when she made a small sound. He went still, and her eyes flew open.

"More."

"But—"

"Cam!" Her hips rose to meet his. She touched him then, and met his steady gaze with such wonder and love in hers, he was lost, so completely lost. Setting the rhythm slow and deep, it was *Haley* who speeded him up by wrapping her legs and arms around him; *she* who demanded more, *she* who brought them to a sudden helpless urgency that he could hardly bear. He could hear the splashing of water, see her lovely wet body shimmering in the unsteady light, feel her clinging to him with a desperation that matched his.

She shuddered beneath him with the thrill of it, the pleasure. There was an unexpected poignancy in this—having her surrender so completely, watching her explode over and over. It had never been like this for him—*never*. His body thrust into her like iron into velvet, and as she called his name in a dreamy voice filled with dazzlement, he buried his face into her sweet, damp hair and let her shatter him.

Haley lay still, even though the water had long since gone tepid and most of the candles had burned down to little stubs. She didn't want to move, ever; she wanted to stay drenched in the scent of Cam's skin, feel his heart still thundering against hers.

But reality intruded, and with it came the threat of tears.

How many such moments would they have? She had to leave—and soon. Branson would hunt her down if she didn't show up. He was too organized, too methodical, to let her go. Thank God for this last memory of Cam, she'd treasure it always; but just the thought had an unexpected sob nearly choking her.

Cam lifted his head, made a soft sound of dismay. "I hurt you."

"No," she said quickly. "It's not you."

He stood, clearly unaware of what a picture he made—that tanned, nude body with water sluicing off it to the floor. Bending, he scooped her up against his chest and carried her, dripping wet, to his bed. Covering them with his quilt, he hugged her close and kissed her with a soft, aching tenderness that only brought more scalding tears.

Her wildest fantasy had come true, with greater reality than she had ever thought possible. It had been beyond her greatest dreams, made that way by his love for her—and her love for him.

How could she leave him now?

She would hurt him so badly. He pulled her closer and she could only close her eyes and cry, desperately afraid and so full of sorrow she didn't know how to handle it. But she was strong, and used to such pressure. She *would* leave, she *had* to. She couldn't risk the person she loved more than life itself.

"Haley, what is it?" He smoothed the hair back from her face. "Tell me."

His voice was full of pain because he thought he'd done something. One last lie, she promised herself. Just this one last lie to save him. "I always cry when I'm happy."

He tipped his head back to study her face. "Are you hurting?" He shifted as if to get up. "Wait, I'll get you a warm, wet cloth."

But she held him close, preventing his escape, feeling the need to cling. "I'm fine. Great, actually." That much was true. Her body had never felt so deliriously tingly and alive. She hadn't thought she could need so much, or that a man could give so much.

But this man could. Cam had given her that and more. *He loved her.*

He framed her face, his own solemn and serious. "You're really okay? Not in too much pain?"

She had to lighten the mood now, or she'd start crying again and never stop. So she smiled and forced a teasing tone. "Are you asking me to rate what just happened? Because if you are, as you very well know, I have nothing to compare it to."

"Try hard," he suggested, narrowing his eyes as he caught her teasing tone. He grabbed her waist and squeezed gently. "Try real hard."

"All right." It was an effort not to giggle at his fierce expression as they lay side by side. She, Dr. Haley Whitfield, lay in bed next to this gorgeous man. *Who loved her.* She gave in to the luxury and skimmed her hands over his beautiful chest. "Like I said," she said slowly, concentrating on the rippling strength of him. "I have nothing to compare it to— Ouch!" She giggled as he bit her ear. "Okay, okay. It definitely went right off the scale as far as these things go."

He flashed her a very satisfied-with-himself male grin. "Are you sure? Because if you can't really remember, we could, you know...try again." He cocked a brow. "Just to revive your memory, you understand."

She let her fingers dance over his still-damp spine, marveling at the muscles she felt there. The sight of his lean, hard body seriously hindered her ability to breathe. But the euphoria he'd created dimmed when she looked into his deep brown eyes. The moments she had left with him were numbered and she knew she'd never again feel the sweetness of a time like this.

She'd never again be told how much she was loved, needed, wanted. "You know, you may be on to something," she whispered, meeting his smoldering gaze. "I think you should. Revive my memory, that is."

"Yeah?" He skimmed his hand over the length of her, his eyes following the movement as if he couldn't get enough of her.

"It would be just the thing I need."

He rolled her onto her back, holding her down possessively

with his body, and closed his lips on hers. "Well, then," he murmured, sliding his hot, open mouth over her jaw, down her throat. "Let me oblige you, darlin'."

Amazingly, Cam slept. He dreamed the light, weightless dreams of a very contented man. But even before he came fully awake, before he reached for her, he knew.

Haley was gone.

# Chapter 11

Cam stood in the center of the guesthouse, frantic. Haley had cleared out, damn her, without a word. She'd taken nothing, not a stitch of Nellie's clothes that he could see, nor any of the things she'd bought in town that first week.

But she was undoubtedly gone.

Storming into her bedroom, he stared at the neatly made bed. Dread and welling fury mixed now. On the small chair, neatly folded, lay his denim jacket—the same jacket she'd worn since the beginning. He scooped it up and the scent that was so uniquely, gloriously her wafted up.

He shook his head, as angry at himself as with her. He'd known it, had prepared for it, but it still hurt more than he could possibly have thought.

She'd run.

Max rubbed against his legs, whining, worrying. Cam scooped up the puppy and got a sloppy kiss that failed to bring a smile to his face.

*Why, dammit?* Why now?

"Cam," Zach said from the doorway.

"Go away." Cam didn't turn to face him, wasn't ready to see the I-told-you-so his brother would never utter, but that would be there so plainly in his eyes. "Just go away."

"Can't do that, I'm sorry. Cam…"

His brother's voice came low, controlled…and very shaky. Nothing rattled Zach—*nothing*—and Cam whipped around to look at him. "What?" he asked, fear lacing his voice. God, what else? "Nellie?"

"No." Zach took a deep breath and looked at Cam with things in his eyes that hadn't been there since—*since Lorraine had died.* The horror, compassion and gut-wrenching loyalty had Cam bracing himself for the worst. "It's not Jas, either," Zach added quickly. "It's Haley. There's something on the answering machine you're going to want to hear right away."

The day was cold, nearly frigid, and all Cam could think as he walked to the big house was that Haley had left wearing only her light blouse and trousers.

They strode in grating silence inside, to where both Jason and Nellie stood by the answering machine, ominously quiet. Nellie had tears streaming down her face and Jason held her tight. Cam looked at them, swallowed hard and hit the message button.

He listened to a harried Haley picking up the line just as the machine clicked on, recording her every word. Listened to the dark, threatening voice demand that she do as she was told and no one would be killed. Listened as Haley realized she'd been betrayed by someone she'd trusted. Listened as Haley pleaded for their lives, willingly giving up her own. *For them.*

*For the love of them.*

Sickness rose in him, and a dark rage such as he'd never known.

When the raspy voice laughed at Haley's fears, it sent chills down Cam's spine, but the sheer terror in Haley's voice shook him to the core. She believed every word the man said. *Every word.*

And she'd gone to him, back to South America. Back to the

hell she'd run from in the first place. *To protect him and his family.* She'd gone, knowing she'd end up dead.

Damn her for not trusting him enough to help her.

The machine clicked off and everyone looked at Cam, but he could only stand still, replaying every last tortuous moment of the day; how she'd come into his barn with that wild look she'd immediately replaced with hunger and passion; then the magical time in his bathroom where they'd made love by candlelight.

He'd known something was wrong, hadn't he? He'd seen the nervousness and terror shimmering in her eyes and he'd let her seduce him regardless, telling himself it was just first-time jitters, because he'd wanted her so badly.

Now she'd gone back to that place that had taken everything away from her; her pride in her work, her self-confidence, her simple joy in living. She hadn't had much of that, and he'd wanted nothing more than to give her everything she'd missed out on. Warmth, affection, fun. Life.

"Oh, Cam," Nellie sobbed. "He'll kill her. She left because she was afraid for us, and he'll kill her anyway."

"No," he promised her grimly. "He won't." He hit star sixty-nine on the phone, which redialed the last number used. As he expected, a taxi service answered.

Haley had called a cab.

Tersely he asked for information on a recent pickup and was told their computer system was temporarily down. "Dammit!" He slammed down the phone and moved to the door.

"Cam," Zach said sharply.

He didn't want to stop, not until Haley was back in his arms. He yanked open the door. Zach was there in an instant, pulling him back. Cam whipped around him, ready to fight. *Needing* to fight.

"Wait." Zach held his arms down with a surprising strength. "Just stop a minute."

"I can't. Dammit, Zach, back off!" Couldn't they see? It could already be too late.

Jason moved up behind Zach, obviously willing to be backup if needed. "We have to have a plan here."

Cam stared at them, and at Nellie quietly crying by the phone. His brothers, though worried sick, were together going to force him to listen. He didn't have time for it. "I want you guys to get out of here until this is over. Take Nellie to town and stay there. Call the police. I'm going to the airport."

"Jason'll take Nellie," Zach said. "I'm coming with you."

"No." Cam stepped over the threshold, daring them to stop him. "Call into town. Do what you can to round up help before you follow. Call the airport and warn them. Call the FBI if you have to. You know everything I do about this."

Zach nodded. "We'll catch up with you, or meet you back with Haley."

Cam moved toward his truck. "Cam?" Nellie called out from the door. "Bring her home safe and sound."

"I plan to," he said grimly. "I plan to."

The taxi ride was blessedly long, and it was dark, quiet. Haley shut off her brain, afraid to think. Leaving as she'd come, she had only the clothes on her back and a few dollars in her purse.

She caught her reflection in the rearview mirror of the cab. Yes, she looked like the same woman who'd come to Colorado. The fear was still there, the wariness. But something had changed on the inside. She no longer lived for the sole purpose of work. She'd experienced love, which made the hopelessness of this situation all the more unbearable and terrifying.

This time, she'd die. And this time she cared, because she had so much to lose.

The taxi came into Colorado Springs and she knew she'd be at the airport in a matter of minutes, then with Branson in no time at all. Every passing second brought a new and overwhelming sense of nostalgia. She'd never again see the deep blue skies of Colorado, never again see the sharp mountain peaks and lush pine foothills she'd grown to love.

Her heart started pounding the minute the airport came into

view and by the time they'd turned into the loop of terminals, she was near a full-fledged panic.

She couldn't go through with it.

Images of Cam came to mind: the way he'd looked at her that first night at the airport, accepting her without question, how he'd made her laugh, live…love.

He was her life.

But Haley knew she had to go inside. Knew, too, she had to hurry. If she didn't and Branson got tired of waiting, who knew what he'd do.

She couldn't risk it.

"Are you getting out or what?" The cabdriver tipped back his hat and gave her an impatient look.

He couldn't have been more than twenty, she thought dully. So many years left. Again, that impossible lump stuck in her throat. She felt like screaming at him, *You're so young, so free. Go live!*

Instead she paid him, her nervous hands fumbling for change. He sped off without a backward glance, leaving her to her private hell.

With a deep breath and a growing sense of horror, Haley stepped up to the terminal, her insides quivering with fear and regret.

What if she was doing the wrong thing? What if Branson hurt her friends anyway? He *wouldn't*, she assured herself, staggering slightly. *He wouldn't.* But she couldn't stop thinking about it. Her stomach roiled painfully, reminding her she hadn't eaten. A sharp pain stabbed through her. Her ulcer, of course. It was back with a vengeance, and worse than ever.

Pushing past a large group of Japanese tourists, she blindly ran down the hallway and into the first women's rest room she found.

She threw up, then rocked back on her heels and stood shakily. Staring at herself in the mirror, she slowly shook her head. She couldn't give in to self-pity. Not yet. Not until she was absolutely positive Branson was on a plane headed far away from the people she loved. Then, and only then, would she find a way to contact the authorities, to lead them to Branson. It would mean her own capture, of course, but she would have to trust the system to prove her innocence. Nothing mattered—except getting Branson put away.

She rinsed her mouth and took a long drink of water from the sink. Then she took her ulcer medication. She'd have to accept the fact that without the happiness of freedom, without Cam, she'd need it.

Other people shuffled through the rest room, giving her no more than a cursory glance. Even in her haggard state, she didn't look out of the ordinary—just like one of a thousand weary travelers. Head held high, she started back toward where she'd come. She checked the huge monitor overhead to see which gate she needed, then started walking, her mind carefully blank.

She'd forgotten how noisy an airport could be. People walked, ran or carted to their destinations. Talking, screeching, crying...in several languages. The dull roar seemed to vibrate mockingly in her head.

Ahead, she faced three sets of glass doors that led to the next terminal. This was it. But just as she reached for one of the doors, a steel grip clamped down on her arm, spinning her around by force. As she turned against her will, she swung her purse up, high and hard.

And clobbered Cam in the face with it.

He let go of her to grab his nose and she gaped at him. "Cam!" He winced and she took a step backward, colliding with the glass door. Oh, God, Cam. *Here.*

He tweaked his nose. "You nailed me."

"What are you doing here?" she whispered, glancing wildly around. *Please, please,* she chanted to herself desperately. *Don't let Branson see him.*

"That was my question for you."

If Branson thought she'd brought him, if he saw them together... "Get out of here. *Now,*" she demanded, pushing at him. He didn't budge and she shoved him again.

He dropped his hands from his face and looked at her. Everything he felt for her, everything he was, swam in those dark, aching eyes; and her heart—the one she'd been trying to harden over the past several hours—slowly cracked open.

"You had no right to follow me. No right at all." Her voice wobbled.

"I thought we'd covered all this." He shook his head and reached for her. "Some genius you are."

She backed up a step, unable to believe that this nightmare of hers was about to come true before her very eyes. "Cam, you've got to go. Now."

"Can't do that." Though she tried to evade him, he took one of her hands in a grip that might as well have been steel handcuffs. "I'm sorry, Haley," he said flatly. "But we're going to play this my way for a few minutes." He turned and half dragged her back the way she'd come.

"Cam," she whispered furiously, beating him on the shoulder with her free hand. "Don't do this. Please, don't do this!"

Capturing her other hand, he continued walking, moving even faster. "You could have told me, damn you," he said in a voice just as quietly furious as hers. Several people glanced at him as he muscled their way through a horde of travelers, but Cam paid no attention. He shoved open the front doors of the terminal and yanked her out into the cold, dark evening.

She stared at the beautiful Colorado night sky she'd not thought to see again. She tried again to squirm free of the painful grip he had on her wrists, but his bruising hold merely tightened as he craned his neck to check for traffic. Calmly, ruthlessly, he pulled her across the street.

"Cam, wait. You have to wait."

He didn't even look at her. On the ground floor of the parking structure, he headed purposefully toward his truck. Fury rolled off him in waves.

"Cam, stop!"

"Nope," he said in a deceptively mild voice, still tugging her along. Easily, he held both her wrists in one hand while he fished for his keys.

"Cam!"

"Save it, Haley," he ordered. "Later."

She had to get him safely away, even if she had to use his feelings for her to do it. "You're hurting me," she said quietly, letting her voice crack.

He loosened his hold with a surprisingly obscene oath.

"It's a free world. I can leave if I want to."

"Haley, *I know.*"

"Look," she said desperately, glancing over her shoulder to see how far she'd have to run back to make it. Quite a distance, she thought frantically. And she still had to get Cam to leave. "Sometimes these things just don't work out and—"

"*Don't,* Haley."

"I'll explain better in a letter, I promise. Now you just go home and I'll—"

He swore again. Grabbing her shoulders, he gave her a shake. "I already know! And I'm getting you out of here. *Now.*"

"No!" she cried, trying to break free. "I can't. I—"

"You're leaving," he said harshly. "With *me.*"

He opened his door while keeping a firm arm around her waist.

"Why are you doing this?" she whispered.

"You already know why," he said, giving her a not-too-gentle shove toward the open door. "*I love you.*"

Damn him, she thought, tears threatening again. "I don't *want* to go with you," she said, not having to force the little sob in her voice. "I want you to leave me alone."

He didn't even blink. "Well, there's a surprise. A lie." He shook his head. "I'm trying not to lose my patience here, Haley, but you're really pushing it." Again, he pushed her, but she fought him.

"I mean it!" she cried, holding the door so he couldn't shove her in. "I won't go with you. I'll scream if you try to make me!"

He stared at her for a minute, then at the guard at the end of the parking aisle. They both knew what would happen if she made good on that threat.

Then, very deliberately, he hauled her up against him until their faces were only inches apart. For the first time, she realized exactly how furious he was. His eyes shot fire. His arms quaked. His heart pounded against hers. But his voice remained quiet and calm. "You're doing it again, Haley. Testing me. Now listen carefully.... *It's not working.*" He shook her. "Are you listening? *I love you.* I always will. I think you love me, too, but we'll get to that later, since much as I hate to admit it, now's one of those times we've got to hurry."

"Hurry?" She could have laughed. He had no idea the hurry she was in.

"Yeah, hurry. I think Zach's taken care of it, but I want to be sure." His hold gentled, his gaze did not. "I know why you're here and there's no way in hell I'm letting you go. He won't kill you. He won't kill me. And he sure as hell won't kill my family. Now get in the goddamn truck so I can get you away from here." No longer nice and patient, he pushed her down into the driver's seat.

He leaned in, his eyes so dark and dangerous she nearly didn't recognize him. "Scoot over, darlin', and don't even think about bolting. I'm really quite angry at you, and believe it or not, I'm fast when I'm mad."

"Cam—" She squeaked and moved over a split second before he sat down on her. Reaching across her, he checked the lock, locked his side and thrust the truck in gear. "Get your seat belt on," he commanded and fastened his.

He knew. *He really knew.* But how? Could he be bluffing?

She reached for her door handle, but he slammed on the brakes, skidding to a halt right there in the parking lot. "Don't even think about it." He tried to glare at her, but sighed instead and closed his eyes for a second.

When they flashed open, the fury had dissipated. "Haley, I can't let you go. I just can't. Don't ask me to."

"I can't stay," she whispered.

"You don't have a choice." And he sent the truck screeching out of the lot so fast, she was thrust against the back of the seat.

Cam's mouth was a tight, grim line as he maneuvered them through traffic and onto the highway. *He wasn't going to let her go back.* She shivered, icy to her bones. He tossed her the denim jacket lying on the seat, the same one she'd worn the entire time she'd been in Colorado. "Wear it, you're cold," he said gruffly. "And next time you run away, be sure to take the correct clothing—I hate worrying about you getting sick."

He was so quietly furious, so absolutely rational. She, on the other hand, was going insane. "Please, Cam. Stop the car."

"Why? So you can jump out?"

He snorted his opinion of that. "Do us both a favor, Haley, and be quiet a minute."

"Cam—"

"Are you going to tell me why you left me without a word? Are you going to tell me why you didn't respect me enough to even wake me? Or why you even agreed to make love with me in the first place? *Are you?*"

"I— Oh, Cam," she said wearily. "Why did you come for me?"

He glanced at her in surprise, then shook his head. "You've got a hell of a lot to learn about me, Haley, if you can ask that." He drew a deep breath. "I heard the call you took." He reached over to take her hand in his large warm one. He ran his thumb softly over the wrist he'd bruised, his gaze hard on the road. His jaw was granite. "It got recorded on the answering machine."

She stared at him, at the tense lines in his face. "He'll never let me stay. He'll hurt—"

"No," he said flatly, driving fast. "He won't. Jas took Nellie into town. Zach's taking care of things, I hope, but I still want to get you out of here. He can't hurt any of us, Haley. Whoever *he* is." He brought her wrist to his lips. "I'm sorry I hurt you. You scared me to death." He whipped his truck around a slower vehicle, keeping her hand to his mouth. "Now, I need a favor. It's a big one." His breath fanned the skin of her wrist, somehow warming the chill that had seeped through her bones. "Okay?"

She tried to take it all in—that he knew, that he'd rescued her, that the others were safe. "What?"

"I need you to trust me." His eyes met hers briefly over their joined hands. "Tell me you do, and mean it."

"How are you going to stop him—"

His eyes were glued to the road, his teeth locked together. *"Tell me, Haley."*

She thought of how this was supposed to be, how she'd left him safely asleep, thinking she'd never see him again. She had everything to lose, and most of it was looking right at her. His eyes searched hers as he slowed for traffic.

"I do," she whispered. "I trust you," she said softly, meaning it with all her heart.

Instantly, the tension left him. "We have a lot to discuss, you and I."

She looked away from him, out the window.

"There're going to be questions, Haley. Plenty of them, and not from me. I wish I could take you far away from all this, but I can't. Not yet."

"What do you mean?"

"The authorities—"

"You're...going to turn me in?" she asked in disbelief. *This* was how he was going to repay her trust?

"It's the only way. You're innocent. We'll prove it."

He believed in her. No one else would, she knew. "We're going back to the ranch?"

"Yes. We'll meet everyone there."

Everyone. The police. Extradition. Possible execution. Her stomach sank.

"Haley?" He touched her hair, her face. "Are you ready for this?"

"Yes." She had no choice.

* * *

A short time later, he pulled the truck into the driveway and she opened her mouth to cry, *No! Wait! First let me have just a minute to think!*

But Cam wasn't looking at her—only at his house, and he was frowning. He'd stopped the truck at the bottom of the drive instead of pulling all the way up, as usual.

"What—"

"Shh!" He lightly squeezed her thigh, staring intently ahead at the house. Something was wrong; very wrong, he thought. The house was dark. Okay, so maybe Jas had actually done what he'd said and gotten Nellie out. *He better had.* And Zach was probably still at the airport with the cops, trying to apprehend the owner of the slick, evil voice on the telephone. But Cam knew how well prepared Zach always was. Because of that, Cam had expected to have house protection, as well.

"I don't think we're going in." He reached to put the truck in reverse.

"Cam, I—"

"Luckily for you, it'll have to wait." He switched his gaze back to the road, then the rearview mirror, and gripped the wheel tightly. "Oh, hell."

Haley's head whipped up and she looked at him. Her eyes widened. *"He's here,"* she whispered. "Oh, God, he's here."

He felt her freeze up beside him. Slamming his truck into four-wheel drive, he gunned the accelerator and headed directly over the wild grass between the barns and the house.

Haley gaped at him, then twisted in her seat to look behind.

A set of headlights slowly followed them.

"Police?" she asked hopefully. After all, when it came right down to it, extradition was better than dead.

Cam shook his head, staring into the left-hand mirror, as dread welled up. "Not in a black BMW."

She gasped. "He saw you. Oh, no, he saw you! And now he knows I've told. He'll—"

A gunshot rang out into the still night and Haley slapped her hands over her mouth, stifling her scream, as Cam fought to keep control of the truck.

The next shot ricocheted off the side of the truck with a loud ping.

Cam hated guns with a vengeance, but wished with all his might he had one now. He veered around the toolshed, dust flying up in front of the headlights and forming a cloud around them. Haley screamed as a third shot hit the back of the truck.

"Get down!" he yelled, turning off the headlights, plunging them into pitch-darkness. Another shot echoed in the night. He swerved onto the narrow horse trail he'd taken Haley on the fateful day of the library incident.

"He's still following," she announced fearfully, craning her neck. "He can see us in his lights."

"Not for long." He hoped. "Stay down." She bumped her head on the ceiling when he hit a dip in the dirt path. "Dammit, down!" he shouted again as yet another shot rang out. When Haley just stared at him, her eyes glossy with shock, he swore and shoved her head down between her knees.

Again a shot splintered the night. It plowed through the window precisely where her head had been a second before, and Cam's heart nearly leaped from his chest. Glass shattered and rained over them as Haley slowly raised her head.

"You okay?" he demanded, scarcely breathing. Cold air whipped over them as she brushed glass off her. "Haley!" he shouted. "Answer me!"

She nodded, but he could hear her choppy, panicked breathing. He started to sweat as he stared at where the glass had broken over her. The next bullet whizzed harmlessly by.

"I can't believe it." She gripped the hand he held out. "He's armed and I'm with the only cowboy in the Wild West who doesn't carry a gun." She swore when she bumped her elbow on the door as he hit another dip in the trail. "Where are we going?"

Cam prayed he had this path memorized as he navigated in the dark. At least twenty-five yards behind them now, the headlights of the BMW bounced eerily as the car hit every rut. "As far away as we can get."

"Can you even see?" she called out over the roar of the engine as he gunned the truck forward.

He imagined she didn't really want an answer to that one since it was obvious—no one could see. Everything around them—the trees, the rocks, the mountain, everything—was a dark blur that whizzed by. He whipped his truck around a large bush and over a fallen tree stump. A minute later he risked a glance at Haley and saw how pale, how absolutely terror-filled she looked in the eerie glow of the BMW's headlights. The image of her in the clutches of the nameless evil behind them had Cam tensed and coiled for the fight of his life.

He forced himself to concentrate when he took the next turn too wide and nearly dumped them down a small ravine. By the time he'd shoved into reverse and gotten them straight, the BMW had closed some of the distance between them.

They came to the top of the first hill and Cam knew they couldn't go much farther in the truck. The tires slipped on the sharp, jagged rocks as the trail grew steeper and all the more difficult because he could hardly see a thing.

"There's no moon," Haley whispered as he slowed. "It seems so black, so...scary."

He wished to hell he had a third hand so he could wrap Haley close to him. He could hear the panic, feel the terror vibrating from her, and he'd never felt quite so helpless.

"He can't stay on this trail as long as we can," he assured her grimly as he steered sharply to the right to avoid a dark shape. It turned out to be a huge tree trunk that would have stopped them cold.

Another quick turn saved them from a nice gouging by a low, jutting branch. Now the BMW was nowhere to be seen. Cam knew that to the left rose a high, sheer rock face and to the right was a steep, unforgiving cliff that fell to the canyon floor below.

Horses would have no problem on this trail—in fact this was the exact trail he'd taken Haley on before—but his truck was a different story entirely. His tires protested against the rocks. His back right tire slipped off the edge on his next turn, and he knew it was time to call it quits. He went just a little farther, to where the terrain had evened somewhat and the rock to his left had leveled out to a small wooded area.

The headlights behind them had disappeared, but he knew their pursuer was still back there, waiting, biding his time. The cliffs Cam and his brothers had camped out in last summer weren't far now—just beyond the creek and through some dense brush and trees. He could get them there. They could hide in a cave where no one could find them until daybreak.

Stopping the truck abruptly, he yanked out his flashlight from the glove compartment. "Come on. Quick." He pulled Haley out the driver's side, and then because she looked so damn petrified, he gave her a quick, hard kiss and took her hand. "Hurry."

"Hurry?"

The pop of a gunshot above their heads had her complying as they ducked and sprinted into the woods.

# Chapter 12

Running wasn't easy in the dark, but having been shot at was great motivation. Within a few seconds, the woods had completely swallowed up Haley and Cam, surrounding them in an eerie, echoing darkness.

Though he couldn't hear signs they'd been followed, Cam forced them to keep moving, knowing they shouldn't stop.

Deeper and deeper they went, up the mountain. "Hurry." Mercilessly, he tugged the panting Haley over rocks and branches, through trees, farther into the black woods. "Come on."

When she fell suddenly, she nearly tore his arm out of its socket. He dropped to his knees, groping for her. "Haley?" he whispered, frantic.

"I'm okay."

She didn't sound it, but he knew it was too soon to slow down. The sudden rustling of bushes from where they'd just come reinforced that feeling. "Can you walk?"

She surged to her knees, bumping her head on his chin so

hard he saw stars. "Oh, Cam, I'm sorry!" She reached for him with chilled hands.

He took them in his, gritted his teeth against the pain in his chin and pulled her to her feet. "Farther."

She groaned but moved, and they continued on. The sounds of their ragged breathing seemed loud to Cam's ears, but he couldn't control it. He could hardly see in the moonless night but he could hear the running water of the creek. The tall trees blocked any light the stars would have afforded. Twice he stopped to listen, pulling Haley close while he concentrated. A haunting silence filled the air; the kind of unworldly quiet that precedes a storm—just what they didn't need.

But finally there was no sign that they were being followed. Still, they ran. Near the creek, they stopped for a third time. Haley bumped into him from behind, gasping for breath. Turning, he held her tightly, alarmed by how cold she was, how she shivered despite their exertion.

"I think we've lost him." She nodded and pulled closer, burrowing her face and icy nose into his neck.

And right there in the dark, in the most dangerous situation of his life, his heart swelled with such an overwhelming protectiveness, it took his breath away.

"He couldn't have followed us this far without a light, could he?" she asked.

"No." He hugged her close for a moment, then made them go a little farther to a small clearing that was lined with sharp, jutting rocks. "We can't go back," he said. "Not until the sun comes up. It isn't safe." He pointed to the rocky side of a ravine close to them. "See over there? Some of those rocks cover shallow caves. We'll rest there."

He helped Haley climb up the rocks—not an easy feat in the dark. Several times he caught her as she slipped, saving her from a nasty fall. Finally, at the top, they settled with their backs against the sheer granite, covered overhead by an outreach of stone. Darkness loomed around them, so complete that Cam couldn't ascertain exactly how big an area their small cave afforded them. But if they didn't light a fire and they kept their voices down, no one could see them, even if someone passed directly beneath them in the bush.

Pulling Haley into the crook of his arm, Cam stared at the opening of their cave, his heart still thundering from their escape. When he could breathe normally again, he gave Haley a slight squeeze. "You okay?"

He felt her nod against his shoulder and he wished it weren't so damn dark. "We're safe enough for now." She shivered and he ran his hand up and down her arm, pulling her closer.

"He'll find us in the morning."

"Haley—"

She jerked back from him. "You're still mad at me, I suppose. I'm sorry, Cam. I know I deserve this, but you don't."

"You don't deserve— Come back here." His stretching fingers couldn't find her. "Where are you, dammit?" He crawled forward, found her huddled against the back wall. On his knees before her, he cursed the dark that made it impossible to see her expression clearly. "What the hell did you mean you deserve this? No one deserves to be chased with a gun through the wilderness, hunted down like an animal."

"I brought this on you," she said softly. "When all I ever wanted was to protect you. And the others. Where're Nellie and Jason? And Zach, Cam. Where are they?"

"They're safe. We heard your phone conversation. Jason took Nellie into town. And Zach was supposed to get help and be at the airport—"

"To arrest me."

"To protect you."

"You were going to turn me in."

"I wanted you safe, dammit."

"It doesn't matter. I would have turned myself in long ago, if it was that simple. I'm afraid for you. I wanted to draw him away from Colorado." Her voice sounded bitter. "But now we won't know if Zach, Jason and Nellie are safe, really safe, until we get back there. God, if something happened to them, any of them, it'll be all my fault.''

"No." He believed, *had* to believe, that Zach had gotten out. "Zach will be all right. He knows how to take care of himself."

"You have every right to hate me."

He touched her, found her sitting cross-legged, her head in her hands. "Hate you?" He slid his fingers into her hair and held her face, trying to blink away the darkness, struggling to see more than just her outline. "For someone so smart, Haley, you can be incredibly slow-witted. I told you how I felt about you."

She shoved his hands away. "You can't still mean it."

Flowing adrenaline had his usually nonexistent temper kicking in. "Stop it." Again he reached for her, but she'd started to scramble away. "Come back here."

"Too bad we don't have the cell phone. You could call the cops on me from here." He lunged after her but she evaded him. "I should leave, Cam. Now. It would keep the others safe if I did."

"No." One last tug and her heel clipped him hard on the chin. "Dammit, Haley." She rose. He yanked, pulling her down to the hard, gritty floor, ignoring the fight she put up—until she managed to knee him.

He sucked in a sharp breath of air and lost his grip on her.

Haley surged up to her knees, preparing to worm away from him, but he let out a pained breath and flattened her down with his hands. By the time he flipped her onto her back, they were both panting and furious. The dark prevented him from seeing her face clearly, but he had no trouble tasting her frustration.

"Let me go," she choked out.

"You're not going anywhere without me tonight, Haley. Not until this thing is over." Crawling up the length of her, he held her prisoner, but she renewed the fight. A flailing hand hit his chin, the chin she'd already bruised. Swearing, he gathered her hands together, then yanked her wrists over her head, anchoring them there. She squirmed and struggled beneath him, to no avail.

"Hold still a minute, would you?" he panted, resting his forehead on the ground beside her. "Please, don't scream." Who would have thought such a tiny thing could fight so nasty?

"I'm not a complete idiot," she retorted, giving up bitterly.

Beneath him, her chest rose and fell harshly, her breathing uneven and raspy. Warmed from their wrestling, she no longer shivered. But now that she'd stopped fighting him, her body became soft and pliant under his, and he had to quell the urge to turn their position into something sexual.

He must not have been entirely successful.

"Dammit." Her hands flexed in his as their hips slid together. "Let me go."

He lifted his head, but could still see nothing of her expression. "Not until you stop this. I told you, I would have used the police's help, yes, I'd do anything—anything—to keep you safe."

*"Why?"*

He sighed. "Because I love you, Haley. Someday you're going to believe that."

She fell silent, though he could almost hear the wheels of her brain spinning. Finally she said, "It's just...new for me. All these feelings. I...I still have things to tell you."

"Well, at the moment," he said, irony heavy in his voice, "I have nothing but time to listen."

She made a noise that might have been a laugh. "The man chasing us is Lloyd Branson. My ex-boss. I thought he was dead, but he's not. He's the one killing my team."

"Why does he need you?"

She wiggled her wrists entrapped in his hands. "You're hurting me, Cameron."

He loosened his grip, but didn't let go, still afraid she'd take off to surrender herself to save him. Beneath him, he could feel her every line, her every torturous curve.

"Branson needs me to go back because he can't re-create the system, only I can. He doesn't know how. I've studied earth movement, both above and below sea level, for years now. He was just a businessman, though a damn shrewd one."

"What, exactly, was this system?"

"It predicts earth movements."

"Earthquakes?"

"And volcanic eruptions."

He let that soak in. A cold breeze brushed over his skin, but he barely felt it. "I thought your system *monitored* earth movement."

"I never said that."

She hadn't, he realized. He'd just assumed, because in his wildest dreams, he hadn't imagined this. "A system like that would save a lot of lives."

The sound that escaped her was more like a choked laugh than an agreement. He let go of her, then eased up to cup her face. Concentrating hard, he found that he could just barely make out the outline of her features. He didn't know if it was because he could actually see, or if he was just incredibly in tune with her, but her pain and suffering became his own. "What happened to you down there, Haley?"

"My dream came true."

But it was bitterness and defeat he heard, not joy. "The system worked? You can predict?"

His fingers holding her face became wet. *With her tears,* he realized with great dismay, and his stomach tightened.

"Could. Before it was destroyed in the bomb blast."

"Oh, darlin', I'm sorry." He pushed up on his arms and knelt over her, awed by what she had accomplished. "Branson got greedy."

"We weren't allowed to go public and make the announcement. I didn't understand then." She sat up and covered her face with her hands. "I can't believe I didn't see it. But we were so high on our discovery...."

"Didn't see what?" he asked gently, holding her shoulders. More wind blew in and this time, he felt it. The chill seeped deep. "Haley, what didn't you see?"

She drew a shaky breath. "He killed them, my whole team. Alda must have suffered so—the others certainly did. I'd gone home to warn them, but was too late." Her voice came muffled in the dark and he knew she'd covered her face again. "There was blood everywhere—smeared on the walls, coating the floors... I was so scared, Cam."

He let out a violent oath, rage boiling so quick and strong he shook with it. He held her close, despite her brief struggle to move away. "Haley, I'm so sorry." Now he understood the mindless terror in which he'd found her that first night.

"Finding uranium was coincidental, but it made it better for him. Now he has the money once he sells the stuff, to stay hidden forever. He can just wait me out."

"Why did he bomb EVS?"

"So there wouldn't be any evidence. He didn't know my notes were there, or that I wasn't in our substation on the water as he'd planned for me to be. He'd flown me there earlier—he's a pilot, you see. But I'd left by boat. He must have thought he'd make me work with him after he'd killed everyone that had knowledge of it. But I saw our apartment—" She took a deep breath. "I had nowhere to go. I panicked. I hardly remembering getting to the airport, but I got on an airplane, the first one I could, and it took me to L.A. But I knew he could trace me there because I'd used my own name and passport, so I hopped on again, and came to Colorado Springs."

*Thank God,* he thought, squeezing her closer.

"Nellie was so kind to me. Cam, if anything has happened to her—"

"Nothing did," he promised, praying with all his heart that he was right. "She's safe. So's Jason." He couldn't think about Zach or he'd lose it. He could only hope that his brother had gotten out of the house. "Haley, darlin'...Branson thinks you can reproduce the system?"

"Yes, it would take months, maybe more. My notes were all destroyed. The U.S. government would probably pay him for it, but he won't give them the chance. Not now that he's discovered that by finding the weakest points and placing a certain type and amount of explosive there, he can *create* earthquakes as well as predict them.''

Cam leaned closer, unable to believe what he'd just heard. *''What?''*

''He can *cause* earthquakes. He can, in fact, hold the entire world for ransom. Blackmail whole governments. Or if he chose, destroy as much or as little land as pleased him.''

He sat back, stunned. ''My God.''

''He had a grand time in South America creating that 7.0. So many died. An entire village was wiped from the face of this earth.'' She stood abruptly, facing away from him. ''I won't make that system again, Cam. I won't. He'll have to kill me. But I wanted to get him away from you and the others first.''

He rose to stand behind her. A woman like Haley wouldn't take the loss of *one* life lightly, much less the thousands she'd talked about. No wonder she'd been in such a state of mind, he thought, aching for her. No wonder she hadn't cared if she'd lived or died—Branson had taken everything from her.

Cam could kill him for that alone, and this time the violent thought didn't give him pause. ''I told you, I'm not going to die. And neither are you.''

She sighed. ''I nearly had a heart attack when I saw you at the airport,'' she whispered. ''I knew if he saw you, he'd—I thought I was going to have to watch you die right in front of me.''

He closed his eyes. She loved him, he thought, his heart going a little crazy with relief. *She did love him.* ''We're going to get out of this. Alive.''

She let out a little disbelieving laugh. ''The optimistic cowboy. We're barricaded in a dark cave in the freezing mountains of Colorado, being hunted down by a psycho, and you tell me we'll get out. Only you, Cam. Only you.''

''Actually, you're the genius, here. So technically, you should be able to come up with something better. But seeing as you're distressed and not quite yourself...I'll let you slide.''

"This isn't funny."

"If you give up on me now," he said lightly, "I'll have to get tough." He stepped closer and dropped the teasing. "At least we're together." He heard her breath catch. "I thought I'd die, Haley, when I realized you'd left me. Don't do that again."

She wrapped her arms around her middle, bending slightly at the waist. "You hurt," he said in an unintentionally accusing voice, grabbing her shoulders. "Your ulcer?"

"Yes," she whispered.

He could feel her trembling. "Do you have your medicine?"

"It's in my purse. In the truck."

He pushed her gently to the floor. "I'll be right back. Stay here."

He was totally unprepared for her reaction. "No!" she cried, grabbing his arms and yanking hard. He stumbled forward, landing on her. She held him with the tenacious hold of a pit bull. "You're *not* going back to the truck. He'll kill you. Do you hear me, Cameron Reeves? You're not going!"

He lay sprawled on top of her, probably hurting her as he pressed her into the hard ground. He tried to lift his weight off, but she only held him tighter.

"No!"

With a sound of frustration, he stopped fighting and lowered his forehead to hers. "You're in pain, Haley."

"I'm fine."

He propped himself up on his elbows, searching her face in the dark. "No more lies, Haley. *Ever*. You're too good at it— it scares me. Promise."

"Will you believe me?"

"Yes," he said without hesitation.

"Then I won't lie to you again."

"Thank you." He ran a hand down between them, and touched her stomach lightly. His own body tightened as he felt her soft, giving curves. "Does it still hurt?"

He could barely see her face. She'd closed her eyes. Her

breathing hitched, but he didn't know if it was her fear or his touch that had altered it. "Does it?" he asked again.

"Just a little. I'll be fine without the medicine. Don't go."

"I'm not going anywhere," he promised, moving so his face hovered over hers. "Look at me, Haley." When her eyes fluttered open, squinting to see him, he said, "I think you're the bravest, most incredible woman I've ever met."

Her eyes shone brilliantly in the dark with unshed tears, and she tried to turn away, but he trapped her head between his hands. "I mean it," he told her, stroking her jaw with the pads of his thumbs. "We're going to get out of here alive. And then..." He bent to softly kiss her stiff, cold lips. "There's only going to be us, Haley. No more Branson, no more terror. Just us."

"I can't believe you're here, with me." She hesitated, then ran her hands over his shoulders, her voice suddenly shy. "I'm so glad you are. Cam...kiss me again."

"Kiss *me*."

She did, deeply and sexily enough to have him letting out an involuntary moan. "Haley—" He stopped for another drugging kiss, then nuzzled her jaw, her throat. "Why did you make love to me before you left?"

She ran her cool hands down his arms. "It's...silly."

"Tell me."

"I've never experienced lust before, not really. Not until I came to Colorado and met three of the sexiest men on earth—"

"Three?" Not one, *three?*

"Mm-hmm."

He squeezed her, growling deep in his throat, and she laughed. "But only *you* did something to my insides, Cameron. I know it sounds ridiculous, but you look at me and my knees go weak. You touch me and I want more. I didn't recognize it at first, but then I knew. I had to be with you that way, even if only once. It was my greatest fantasy." She sobered and gripped his arms tightly. "I never thought I'd get to touch you again."

"Touch me now," he commanded softly. The memory of

her—wet, wild and wrapped around him, first in his tub, then his bed—had him fully aroused in the blink of an eye.

Her arms wound around his neck and she pressed her body upward, arching into him. Hungrily, he took her mouth again, thinking she felt so good, so right. The relief that they both were safe for now made him dizzy. So did her kisses, and the choppy little whimpers that came from deep in her throat. He slipped his jacket from her, helping her pull out her arms and spread it beneath them as he lavished hot, openmouthed kisses over her throat and shoulder, working his way down. Through the thin material of her blouse, he kissed her breast.

"Cam!" She sounded shocked, yet she pushed upward, thrusting herself into his mouth. "Here?"

In answer, he kissed a path to her other breast, gently nipping the hard tip with his teeth. The fabric between his mouth and her sweet skin became wet, sheer.

"Cam..." She clung to him. "We shouldn't."

He slid his arousal over the sweet hollow between her thighs.

"Okay. Here," she decided breathlessly. "Now."

Impatiently, he unbuttoned her, shoving silk aside. A lacy bra hid her from him until he tore that away, too, baring her to the night and his hungry gaze. Then she was inside his mouth, against his tongue, and he revisited heaven.

Moaning, squirming, she tugged him close as he sucked. He lifted his head, just to shift to her other breast, but she made a protesting sound and yanked him back by the hair. Grinning against her, he thought that at this rate, he might be a bald man by the time he hit thirty-five.

He could care less.

She made him ache, unbearably, and he pressed her against his hips to show her exactly how much. She sighed and angled upward, trying to get closer still.

"The bath and candles were for me," she whispered. "It's your turn to pick a fantasy."

"You're it."

She ran restless hands over him, pulling at his shirt. Surging above her, he stripped off the rest of her clothes, then his shirt, but she quickly yanked him back down, pressing her lips all over his face.

The icy wind vanished. So did the hard, ungiving ground and their fear. The horror. He wanted, needed, to plunge in and ride deep. "Are you sore, Haley?"

"No. Now, Cam." She tried to wrap her legs around him to bring him closer, but with a little laugh at the wildcat he'd created, he held her off for a moment. He rose up on his elbows to see her better, wanting to feast his eyes on the delectable sight she made, stretched out before him, but he could barely see. Still, his blood surged hot and thick, centering between his legs. This frenzied need for her went beyond lust, far beyond mere wanting. "You take my breath away."

She reached for the snap on his jeans, then hesitated, suddenly shy. His fingers closed over hers, guiding them back. "If you don't free me soon," he said a little desperately, "it'll be too late, darlin'."

She laughed breathlessly, then slowly worked the soft denim open. He nearly died of pleasure when she took him in her hands. With a hum of approval, she stroked him and he just about erupted in her hands like a novice.

"Oh!" she gasped, yanking her hands back when his hips jerked. "Did I hurt you?"

He could still laugh. "Not quite." Striving for some semblance of control, he bent to her mouth.

Her tongue touched his. Her perfect body pressed up against him, and he lost himself in the emotions she created, in how she made him feel. He kissed her for all he was worth, on the edge already, and from just touching her. As if wanting her as desperately as he was, his fingers slid down over her, sinking into the silken curls between her thighs. She let out a surprised, thrilled moan, and pushed against his fingers for more.

*So very wet.* The discovery made his head swim with desire. Exploring, he found the tiny nub that drove her and gently, so gently, squeezed. She shrieked, and the sound echoed in the cave. More than satisfied by her response, he covered her mouth with one hand, while the other feathered and teased mercilessly. Whimpering and panting, she thrust her hips against his fingers. When her muscles clenched, caught in the torturous slice of time before climax, he stopped. "Wait," he murmured, sliding down her body slowly. "Wait a sec."

She moaned, sounding dazed, bewildered. *Desperate.*

He pressed her legs wide-open with his palms, brushed a kiss against her inner thigh. Then the other.

She stiffened. "Cam," she whispered, sounding a little panicked. "Stop. I don't think—"

"Just for a minute, darlin'." He reached up, took her hand and set it over her own mouth. "Hush now, okay?" He nuzzled, kissed her center softly, then lightly grazed her with his tongue. He expected the brutal grip on his hair this time, and he licked at her as if she were his last supper.

His sweet, modest Haley shucked all inhibition and went crazy beneath him.

He lifted his head. "You still want me to stop?"

In answer, she yanked on his hair, pressing his mouth back to her.

He laughed softly and used his teeth until she was sobbing his name behind her hand, and her thighs were trembling violently around him. Still, he stroked and laved and suckled until she all but shattered beneath him and was left quivering, dazed and sated.

He rose above her, shaken and needy, stunned by what she did to him.

"I want you inside me," she said, her voice thick and emotional, and she reached to guide him to her.

"Oh, yes." He barely held on as he sank into her slowly, gradually, deeper and deeper, until he had nothing left to give. She arched her hips to meet him, reaching blindly up for him, and he responded, bending over her for a long scorching kiss. He started to move, his firm, fluid thrusts matching the greedy, eager motion of her hips.

Whispering her name hoarsely, he surrendered to the ecstasy only she could create. She held him as he hovered at the brink, struggling to hold back a little longer. But then she shuddered—close, so very close. He rode her off the edge of sanity as his release pounded through him, rocking his body, his world.

"Wow," Haley said shakily into the dark cave, some time later. "That gets better and better."

Pulling her close with the last of his energy, he nuzzled her hair. "Well, darlin', I have to agree there."

She held him tighter, as if she'd never let go.

"You're not going to pull my hair again, are you?" he joked, "because—"

"No," she whispered, kissing his jaw. "Oh, Cam. I'm so thankful to be with you. You saved my life tonight. I still get can't over that."

"Why not? I love you." Catching the telltale glint of tears in the dark, he tucked her against him, cradling her head in the crook of his arm. "I'm sorry. Pull my hair all you want. I won't complain."

She didn't laugh.

"Did I hurt you?" he asked her huskily. "Was I too rough?"

"No, God, no."

He tried to smile, there on the cold, hard floor of the cave, but it was difficult. "It could give a man a complex, Haley, if you cry every time he makes love to you."

"You *love* me," she said in a small, choked voice, curling into his arms. "I have a hard time dealing with that. Or the future at all, as a matter of fact."

"You'll have to get used to it. Do you love me, Haley?"

"I've never loved anyone before. I—" She lifted her hands from him in a helpless gesture. "I don't know."

"Sure, you do," he said mildly, though nerves raced through his body. "You just have to listen to your heart."

"I'm not ready," she whispered, and though he couldn't see

for sure, he imagined her blue eyes wide with panic. "I told you, I can't face the future right now."

Ironic, he thought. His love scared her more than a gunshot missing her head by a scant fraction of an inch. "I can deal with you not being ready," he said, though it terrified him that she never would be. "What I can't deal with is knowing you still plan to go to Branson at the first opportunity. It's not an option, Haley. You're *not* going, even if I have to squire you away somewhere and hold you against your will." Gently he disentangled himself, sitting up to right first her clothes, then his, but when a little sob escaped her, he pulled her back to him. "Ah, Haley...it's going to be all right."

She shook her head, her swing of hair sliding over his face. "How, Cam? He won't stop hunting for us. In the morning—"

"We'll get out." Freezing night air blew in over them and he put his jacket back on her. Wishing they were warm and safe in his bed, he cursed the fates that had them in this cold, dark cave. "He works alone?"

"Yes."

"And no one else has a system like this?"

"No," she said firmly.

"We'll find a way to stop him."

"But how?" Sagging against him, she rubbed her face against his shirt sleepily. "I don't even know if our government will believe me." She yawned. "I'll rot in jail."

"No, you won't."

"Maybe the USGS will help." Again, she yawned. "But this is a pretty crazy story, and they're years behind where EVS was. Even if they believe me, they might want me to re-create the system, as well."

"Just tell them you can't."

"They'll know better than that." Her words had turned fuzzy, slurred with exhaustion. He rocked her against him. Amazement filled him over what this woman had accomplished, what she was capable of. Squeezing her close, he allowed his hands to sweep down her narrow back, over those slim limbs that drew him so. "Haley," he whispered, streaking his hands beneath her blouse just to feel her warm skin. Her body pressed heavily against his. "Haley?"

She'd become a dead weight against him. Knowing she was near complete and utter exhaustion, he tried to shift her to a more comfortable position.

She stirred. "Cam?"

"Shh," he whispered. "Sleep now."

"Can't...sleep," she mumbled, turning in his arms. "He might find us."

"I'll watch," he promised, lying on his side by her, still touching her. "Shh, now. Just sleep, Haley. Just sleep."

"Never had anyone...love me before," she murmured. "Never thought I needed it." She was silent for a long time. He thought she'd fallen asleep, but still he touched her, watched her, loving the luxury of having this unlimited access to her.

"It feels good, Cam."

"This does?" He continued to sweep his fingers down her arm.

One corner of her mouth curved drowsily. "Mmm. That, too." Her eyes remained closed. "But I meant...it feels good to have you love me.... Why does it feel so good?" she wondered drowsily.

"Because it's right." He leaned over to kiss her.

"Never meant...to love you back. Didn't want to."

He froze. His hand tightened on her waist as he hovered over her, torn between shocked disbelief and joy. "Haley?"

But she didn't respond because she'd finally drifted off to sleep, and he wondered, as his heart threatened to burst, if she'd even realized she'd spoken out loud.

As he drifted off to sleep, the storm outside their shelter let loose.

# Chapter 13

In the dark, cold cave, Haley stirred from her dreams, gradually becoming aware of an incredible, healing warmth surrounding her. In her half-wakefulness, she smiled and curled back against it.

A band around her chest tightened, and a husky growl sounded in her ear. Her eyes flew open.

She was on the cave floor, spooned up to Cameron's hard, warm body. He had one leg thrown over her, another thigh nestled between her legs. Her back cozied up to his chest. She was using his arm as a pillow. Snuggled between her breasts, holding her possessively against him, was his other hand.

His thumb made lazy circles over her tight and achy nipples. "Good morning."

"It's...not morning yet." She gasped as his teeth sank gently into her neck. A liquid heat seeped through her despite the remarkable cold of their surroundings.

"Mmm. I know." There was a hint of regret in his voice as he rolled back from her. At the loss of his body heat, a chill instantly gripped her. And with that, their circumstances came flooding back to her: the airport, being shot at, running through the woods to make their escape. Making love with Cam.

He'd come for her, even at the risk of his own life. If that didn't define the depth of his feelings for her, she didn't know what did.

"It's time to go," he said.

She rolled onto her back and stared up at his tall, muscular form as he stood, and watched as his wide shoulders moved beneath his shirt, his long legs rippling with strength. He caught her staring and smiled a little wickedly, as if he knew a secret. A *good* secret.

"Unless, of course, you want to delay a bit." Those expressive eyebrows lifted suggestively.

She had to laugh. "We can't." Then her eyes caught the bulge in his jeans that told her he wasn't kidding. Unbelievably, an arrow of longing pierced through her. "Well, maybe we could... But we shouldn't."

Grimacing, he shifted his hips, losing his smile. "No, we shouldn't. But around you, my body rarely pays attention to my brain."

She felt herself blush hotly, and thankful for the relative anonymity of the dark, she sat up. Nothing mattered, she thought, except making sure Cam's family had gotten out safely. She'd do whatever was needed to ensure that, even if it meant giving herself up to Branson.

But one look at Cam's lithe frame above her, poised and unusually intent, told her the terrifying truth: he wouldn't let her go; he'd fight with his very life to save hers. Swallowing hard, humbled to the bone over his love for her, she took his proffered hand and let him pull her up.

She rested her hands lightly on his chest, a little embarrassed to remember the passion he'd dragged from her, the unbelievable emotions he'd coaxed—

The man was grinning.

"What?" she asked warily.

The grin broadened when her eyes narrowed suspiciously. "Nothing."

"It's something," she insisted, stepping back, her hands on her hips. "Do I snore? Did I grow a third eye? *What?*"

He laughed softly and hugged her, twirling her around. "Worse," he whispered. "You talk in your sleep."

"Well, let me have it, then. What did I say?"

"I'm not telling."

The cave was still too dark. All she could see was his vague, annoyingly cocky outline. "Cam."

"You can beg me later. Maybe, just maybe, you can change my mind and get me to tell you. But no promises, darlin'. You're going to have to work damn hard at it."

Before she could demand a better answer, he'd moved to the entrance of the cave, motioning her to follow. She stepped up to him and he pushed her behind his back as he stared out into the predawn woods.

Turning slightly, he whispered, "This is the safest time to go. We'll take the long way around, back to Tex's farmhouse. We'll use the phone there."

"What about your truck?"

He shook his head. "He might be waiting."

She took a deep, involuntary breath. They weren't armed. They'd be helpless to protect themselves. Given Cam's sudden tense expression, he was worried about the same thing. He fastened her jacket, then lifted her chin with his finger, staring into her eyes for a long, intense moment, his gaze drinking in her every feature.

Then he lowered his lips to hers in an incredibly tender kiss that brought a stinging moisture to her eyes. "Let's go," he whispered, stroking her cheek once.

He took her hand and led her down from the cave.

Only minutes later, the eastern sky was streaked with light from the rising sun. Together they jumped down from a high rock. She had absolutely no idea where they were, but beauty surrounded them as the Colorado mountains came awake in their full glory. Tall aspens, brilliant with autumn leaves, were out-lined against a gorgeous sky completely devoid of clouds. The storm must have passed in the night. As Haley straightened and brushed the dirt from her hands, she stilled.

"I hear the creek," she whispered. Her heart tripped. "I thought we were going back a different way."

"We are." He wrapped an arm around her waist and gave her a reassuring squeeze that didn't fool her for a minute. The rigid tension in his body defined every clenched muscle. "We have to cross the water first." He glanced down at her feet, covered in her meager leather flats. Their eyes met. It couldn't have been more than thirty-five degrees outside and she was already cold. When wet, she'd be freezing. With a grim look, he took her hand and they started across.

When they'd made it, he stopped short and looked at her, his head tilted as he listened. Eyes narrowed, he pulled her to a tree and flattened her against it.

"What?"

"Shh." He held her still, and his broad shoulders blocked any view she might have had. The fierce pounding of his heart against her was an unwelcome reminder of their dangerous situation.

The distinct sound of a helicopter's blades filled the air. Cam lifted his head and stared at her. "That's either very good news…"

"Or very bad," she finished, a shiver running through her. Every bone in her body screamed with sudden terror. She knew, she just knew, it was Branson; that he was perfectly capable of flying a helicopter. "Cam, he's looking for us—"

He shoved her back and down behind a clump of trees and then squatted next to her, waiting.

A minute later she forgot to be cold, forgot her discomfort as the chopper came into sight. Cam took one look and stood, grabbing her hand. They started running back through the woods, deeper and deeper until Haley thought her lungs would burst.

"Cam," she gasped, tugging on his hand. He didn't stop. Sharp branches tore at her, rocks dug painfully into her shoes, the air thinned until it hurt to breathe, but still they didn't stop.

The chopper vented the cold morning air, closer now. They entered a ravine and she slowed, unable to keep up the pace, but Cam relentlessly, ruthlessly, dragged her on. Sharp rocks lined the mountain walls that surrounded them on either side as they made their perilous way through the canyon floor. The brilliant morning sun shining down on them made it difficult to see.

They paralleled the now rushing creek, swollen with the recent rains. Twice Haley nearly slipped in, saved by Cam's sheer strength and will, but her feet had gone numb with cold. A rock gouged her ankle painfully, but Cam wouldn't let her stop.

"Ahead!" he yelled back to her, pointing. She glanced up, breathless, and saw that they'd made a circle. The caves where they'd spent the night loomed a hundred yards in front of them.

No helicopter could get in there without crashing in on the narrow rocks. But between the cliffs and where they stood was an unbelievably high rock-face they'd have to climb. They stood looking up at the jagged cliff and Haley felt dread overwhelm her.

"You can do this," Cam urged.

"I don't know." She'd never been athletic. Panic engulfed her and she gripped his hand tightly. "I haven't exactly made mountain climbing a habit."

The helicopter had gained on them, was lowering closer, causing a huge whirlwind. Dust rose from the earth; so did small sticks and rocks, pummeling them cruelly as the craft followed their every move.

Shielding her eyes, Haley looked up and nearly fainted. Between the two narrow ravine walls, the helicopter sank, suspended directly above them. She could see Branson glaring down at her through his windshield as he worked the controls. He smiled grimly and she screamed Cam's name.

They ran as fast as they could through the narrow ravine,

closer to the cliffs far above. Their feet pounded the dirt. Cam pulled so hard, her shoulder ached as she fought to keep up.

Then her ankle caught in a rock, sending a sharp, shooting pain radiating up her leg all the way to her hip. She ignored it, figuring if she slowed, a lot more than her ankle would get hurt.

Cam stopped so abruptly she crashed into him.

"Climb!" he shouted at her, turning to push her ahead of him toward the rocky incline that seemed overwhelmingly high and ungiving.

It was a sheer, straight rock and she had absolutely no experience or way to climb it. "I can't," she cried. "Cam, I can't!"

The helicopter lowered farther still, hovering, choking them with dust. Rocks and sand rained down, blinding them.

"You can." Cam boosted her up and she stretched out an arm, trying to get a hold on the rock above. Climbing behind her, he shouted encouragement, practically lifting her himself; all the while she was pelted with debris from the helicopter's wind.

She couldn't imagine how Branson was keeping it from crashing into the ravine walls. There was barely room for the craft to fit as it hovered directly over them. Trees bent from the powerful gusts the helicopter created and Haley felt as though they were suspended in time, caught in a terrifying wind tunnel.

"A little farther, Haley, come on...you can do it." Cam pushed at her, his urgent voice and scrambling, bloodied hands conveying the message simply enough.

*They were going to die if she didn't hurry.*

Risking a look, she twisted to stare down at Cam. His head was level with her hip, his arms were braced on either side of her legs as he waited for her to go higher. Blood trickled down his temple from where he'd been nicked by a flying rock. Sweat ran in rivulets down his face and neck, and dirt streaked over his clothes. Every muscle strained, quivering as he bore most of her weight as well as his own.

Then she caught sight of the canyon floor so far below, and

the tips of the trees that swayed beneath them. Her vision swam dizzily.

"No!" Cam shouted, with a sharp shake of his head. "Don't look down, Haley! Just keep going."

*Just keep going.* Swallowing a sob, she twisted back to the rock, pulling herself higher. Cam followed, his big strong hands helping her often. The helicopter came even closer.

Her ankle felt like it was on fire. Something sticky and wet clung to her cheek and when she swiped at it, she realized it was blood. Her blood. Her fingers screamed as rock dug into them. They were as scraped and raw as Cam's. She sobbed out his name when she slipped, falling into him.

"Got you." Holding her steady until she regained her footing, he told her over the roar of the engine, "You're doing it, Haley." His arms continued to surround her as his hands lifted her farther. "You're doing fine, just don't stop. Whatever you do, don't give up."

She could almost feel the blades of the chopper dig into her skin as they whipped far too close for comfort. But then her fingers reached for and felt the top of the wall. Relief took a back seat to pain. Struggling, she tried to pull herself up and over, but she couldn't get the leverage she needed.

She cried out with frustration, which turned abruptly to horror.

Branson tilted the helicopter, probably to get a better aim, and through the window she saw him raise a rifle to his shoulder.

*He was going to shoot them down.*

Cam grabbed her, and in an unbelievable burst of strength, he lifted and threw her over the edge, yelling at her to stay down.

"Cam!" she screamed.

In the same instant, the helicopter lurched sideways as Branson momentarily lost control of the craft. Haley saw him struggle to raise the gun back up.

Cam still clung to the side of the cliff.

"Cam!" She scrambled to the very edge with some half-baked idea of yanking him up with her bare hands. "Hurry!"

He was trying. She could see it in every one of his trembling, bulging muscles. Haley reached down for him just as he got one hand to the edge.

Above them, Branson made a fatal miscalculation.

A horrific sound echoed as the blades caught in the sheer rock cliff, only a few feet from where Cam hung tenuously to the side.

The chopper careened wildly into the wall and caught fire, just as Cam flung himself over the top to safety. He didn't pause, but leaped toward Haley and flattened himself out on top of her, shielding her from the rain of fire as the helicopter blew up. Seemingly in slow motion, it fell to the canyon floor, far below.

When it hit, the earth resounded and shook.

Like an earthquake.

Fitting, Haley thought, as her world spun and her vision faded. *Branson had created one last earthquake.*

Haley opened her eyes and blinked. Cam's face hovered above her, streaked with dirt and strained with fear.

"Thank God," he murmured, yanking her hard against him.

The sun had risen fully, but the air still should have been icy cold. Instead, heat from the fiery crash below scorched them and dense smoke rose, making breathing difficult.

"We need help, Haley." He cupped her face and held her slightly away from him. "Are you able to walk?"

Nodding, she tried to look over the side, down into the fire, but he pulled her back.

"Don't look," he said.

"Is he dead?"

Ripping his sleeve off, he pressed it to her cheek, wincing when she jerked back. "Haley, you're bleeding everywhere."

"Is he dead?"

"Hold still a sec!" He applied pressure, frowning when she yelped. "Dammit. You need stitches."

*"Is he dead?"* Haley *had* to know, felt as though she couldn't even take her next breath until she did. "Cam, tell me!"

"No doubt, he's very dead." His voice was very uneven and his fingers shook as he worked on her face.

She sat back, as shock took over. Dead. Branson was finally dead.

"Have to say this for you, Haley. Life hasn't been a nap in the hammock since I met you."

What she'd put him through suddenly stopped her cold. She couldn't bear it. She stood, with some half-baked idea of running and never stopping, but she cried out and nearly collapsed at the sharp pain that speared through her ankle.

Cam hooked a hand around her waist. "Lean on me," he murmured. "Don't put any extra weight on it."

She stared at him. His mouth was moving but she could hardly make out the words. She could, however, make out the haggard lines on his face, the blood seeping from a series of shallow cuts over his bare arms and hands. *Her fault.* A shiver racked her. "I'm fine." But she took one step and would have fallen flat on her face if not for Cam's arms. The pain twisting through her made her feel nauseous.

"*Damn.* Okay, darlin', sit down a sec." Lowering her gently to the ground, he glanced back at the flames leaping in the air from the ravine below. "Tuck your blouse up and over your mouth and nose," he instructed. "Like this." He pulled the neck of his T-shirt up over the bottom half of his face. "It'll help you breathe."

Breathe. She had to breathe. *Branson was dead.* It was like a mantra in her mind. She couldn't believe it.

Cam knelt before her to peel back her pants from her ankle. His strong fingers touched her lightly while his mouth tightened. Already, the ankle—a lovely, mottled shade of blue—had swollen to twice its normal size.

"It's just a sprain," she said, struggling to stand again.

"It's broken."

"Okay. I'll just wait here for you."

"Like hell." Before she could protest, he lifted her up behind him, piggyback-style. He shifted her into a better position, looping his arms around her knees, then started walking away from the smoke and flames.

For a moment, Haley allowed herself to cling, to close her eyes and hug his back, so thankful, so very thankful he was alive. It had been so close. Branson had almost killed him. She opened her eyes and saw Cam's grim profile, saw the blood on his temple from a cut. She knew he must be every bit as exhausted as she, yet he hadn't said a word. Guilt overwhelmed her. She couldn't believe she was letting him carry her when she'd almost gotten him killed.

"Put me down," she said. "I want to try walking again."

He didn't answer, didn't even slow his pace, just cleared his throat from the now fading smoke and kept going.

"Cam."

"You can't walk, Haley."

This wasn't about her ankle and they both knew it. "He can't hurt me anymore."

That stopped him. He looked over his shoulder at her. "That's right. He can't. But why don't I believe that *you* believe that?"

*Because Branson and EVS, and what he almost did to your family, stand between us,* she wanted to cry.

Unable to maintain the soul-searching eye contact, she laid her head against the strong width of his shoulder and sighed.

He continued across the top of the ravine and back into the shelter of the woods. After another minute, his arms, where they were hooked around her legs, squeezed gently. "You okay?"

"Yeah." She had to clear her throat of the thick tears that stuck there. "I'm fine." But she wasn't, and she didn't know if she ever would be again.

They stopped at the stream and he lowered her to a rock. He plopped down beside her to the bed of fallen leaves, his chest rising and falling harshly.

"Leave me here while you go the rest of the way. I'll be fine—"

"No...I'm not leaving you." He turned away and stared into the woods. "He's dead. *Dead,* Haley. Do you understand that?"

"Of course I do. So why won't you leave me behind?" She gulped, suddenly stricken with tears. She shuddered and shook, as shock again gripped her. "D-don't you t-t-trust me to stay and f-f-face the consequences?"

He took one look at her, then sighed as he pulled her close, rocking her. "You've got to stop doubting me, stop doubting yourself. Stop pushing me away."

She wished she could. But if she closed her eyes she could still see the blood of her colleagues, hear the wicked laugh of the man who'd tried to kill her, feel the pain of the man who loved her.

The sound of a helicopter had them both jerking back, startled. Cam shielded his eyes to see, then relaxed. "*Finally.* It's Search and Rescue. They're coming for us."

When the chopper lowered, hovering near them, a familiar blond head popped out and glanced down anxiously. Haley closed her eyes, sagging in relief, even as she continued to shake.

Zach had found them.

# Chapter 14

"**S**he's perfect. Looks just like me." Jason smiled proudly down at the small bundle wrapped in his arms and wiped a suspicious moistness from the corner of his eye. "We should call her Jason, Jr."

Nellie laughed weakly and winked at Zach and Cam. "She may look just like you, honey, but she's got *my* personality. Which means she's an absolute angel."

Zach shook his head. "An angel with a temper, that's for sure. For the last five hours I've been listening to you scream at poor Jas here from down the hall. And that was *after* I'd asked the nurse for cotton for my ears."

But he laughed softly over Jason's shoulder when the baby opened one eye and seemed to glare at him. "See that? Already, she's giving me dirty looks. Just like her mama."

Zach paled a few shades when Jason slipped the baby into his arms, but after a minute he relaxed, even smiled at the serious creature staring up at him. "What's her name?"

"Ally," Nellie said firmly, smiling when the brothers stared at her with their hearts in their eyes. Ally had been their mother's name.

Jason leaned over Nellie for a long, deep kiss. "She's gorgeous, baby. Just like you. Thanks for my little girl."

For once, even Zach seemed moved by the public display of affection.

Cam touched the soft tuft of blond hair on top of little Ally's head and thought he'd never seen a more beautiful miracle. He'd nearly had a heart attack when he'd learned Jason and Nellie had never made it farther than the end of the road before her water had broken. They'd driven straight to the hospital.

By the time Jason had managed to try to reach Zach, he was nowhere to be found. But that was because Zach had stayed at the ranch to make the calls to the police. Branson, who had come to the house when Haley hadn't been at the airport, had knocked Zach out, then left him for dead.

Which had Cam's poor heart leaping again. *Thank God,* he thought, staring at the white bandage across Zach's forehead. *Thank God* his brother had a head harder than stone.

It had been stress that had sent Nellie spiraling into early labor, and Cam knew that if something had happened to her or the baby, Haley would never have forgiven herself. He'd had a bad moment when he'd relived Lorraine's labor and how things had gone so badly, but apparently Nellie had done just fine. She glowed.

Jason, in contrast, looked positively awful. His hair stuck straight up and his eyes were ringed with dark exhaustion. Zach had told Cam that Jason had been a complete wreck during labor, and that every time Nellie so much as winced, Jason turned green. He looked like he'd been to hell and back.

But they had a precious bundle of life to show for it.

Cam knew the small twinge of envy was normal, but when Zach handed him the tiny baby, he, too, had to fight back the burning in his eyes.

She felt so light in his arms, smelled so absolutely sweet. The small mewling sound she made tugged at him, and when she opened her eyes to stare solemnly at him, he smiled at her. "Hello, precious," he whispered. The baby yawned, turned her head to his chest and smacked her lips against his shirt. Despite himself, he chuckled. "No milk there, sugar." Gently, he laid her on Nellie. "Better luck with those," he told the baby, grinning at his sister-in-law.

With an ease that spoke of her readiness to be a mom, Nellie soothed Ally while Cam watched, fascinated and yearning all at the same time. "You really okay, Nel?" he asked her.

Her smile was filled with love and understanding as she reached for his hand. "Yeah. I'm really okay." The amusement faded from her eyes. "Stop worrying. It wasn't your fault. Nor Haley's. It was just my time."

He shook his head and remembered the terrifying moments in the helicopter as Zach had told him what happened, how Nellie had suffered with the long labor. "When I first heard, I thought—" He sighed, knowing it didn't bear repeating. "Never mind what I thought."

Nel pulled him down beside her, placing his hand on the baby's warm body. "You thought the worst. I'm sorry I scared you, Cam. I know what you've been through. But I'm strong as a horse. So's the baby. See?"

Ally made some more smacking noises, wrinkled her little brow in a picture of distress as no one made the move to offer her what she really wanted—sustenance.

She was adorable, absolutely precious.

"She's fine," Nellie said softly. "And perfect."

Cam nodded, not trusting his voice.

"How's Haley?" Nellie asked.

He wished he knew. She'd been so exhausted that she'd fallen asleep right there on the table while getting stitches, sleeping through the casting of her broken ankle. She hadn't even awakened when they'd taken her to a room, or when he'd checked on her to tell her about Nellie and the baby. "Her injuries will heal," he said carefully.

"The doctor said her ankle was a clean break. It shouldn't

give her too much trouble.'' Zach moved in close, laying a hand on Cam's shoulder. ''And her cheek only needed six stitches.''

It wasn't the physical injuries Cam worried about. Those would indeed fade, and rather quickly. But the psychological scars went deep, to the bone. He could see them in her haunted gaze. How long would those take to heal?

Jason sat on the other side of the bed next to Nellie and took his daughter's tiny fist in his fingers. ''You guys looked pretty awful when you were brought in,'' he said to Cam. ''Gave us all gray hairs. You ever going to tell us exactly what happened up there?''

''Branson's dead,'' Cam said flatly, closing his eyes and reliving the sight of the man raising his rifle and aiming it at Haley's head as she scrambled up the rock; seeing all over again the horrifying helicopter crash that had been far too close for comfort. ''That's all that matters.''

Jason nodded soberly. ''Haley's free, as soon as she answers the authorities' questions about Branson.''

Nellie looked at him. ''Make her stay. I want her to stay with us.''

Zach nodded. ''Me, too. Tell her we all want her to stay.''

They all looked expectantly at Cam, their hopes so obvious in their eyes. He had to let out a little laugh despite the heavy ache in his chest. ''I can't ask her.''

Three sets of eyes widened in surprise.

''But you have to,'' Nellie cried.

Jas hugged Nel and the baby close. ''Why won't you?''

''Did you upset her?'' Zach demanded.

''It's not up to me,'' he started weakly. ''She has to *want* to stay.''

''Well, make her *want* to, then,'' Nellie said simply. ''Woo her.''

''Yeah, woo her,'' Jas repeated firmly. Zach nodded in agreement.

Again, Cam had to laugh, but the sad truth was, he had no

reassurances for them, because he had none for himself. Haley had made him no promises.

*But he hadn't made any, either.*

He stilled at that shocking realization. Whether it had been for fear of losing his heart, or the confusion and lies—he didn't know. But he'd never offered her any permanence. He wanted, more than anything, to do that, to make her an entire lifetime of promises. And he wanted her to make some in return.

He smiled, then kissed Nellie and the baby. "I've got to go."

"Good. About time."

"Maybe I'd better come with you," Zach said, rising. "Just to make sure you do it right."

Jason laughed when Cam bared his teeth and snarled. "I think he'd rather do it alone. We'll have to trust him."

Nellie just smiled warmly, her eyes filling. "Tell her we love her, too."

Which brought it all into perspective, Cam thought. They loved Haley, wanted to be her family. He could only squeeze Nellie's hand and hope Haley wanted that also.


Haley woke slowly, and unlike in the cave with Cam wrapped snugly around her, this time she had no lingering sense of warmth and security.

She sat up in the hospital bed, glaring down at the cast on her ankle. A federal agent sat by her bed. He smiled at her when she blinked warily.

"I understand you have quite a story for me," he said.

She nodded, nervous. But she told him everything—from the beginning—wanting to get it over with. When she'd finished, she waited for his disbelief.

Instead, he put away his small recorder and notepad. He stood and smiled gently. "Thank you. You've been great, very helpful." He handed her a card. "Can you keep me informed of your whereabouts in case I have any more questions?"

*Or in case they need to arrest me,* she thought glumly.

"Do you need a lift?"

"I'm...free to go?"

He looked at her strangely. "Of course."

A nurse slipped into the room. "Oh! You're awake." She smiled cheerfully at Haley. "The doctor released you, honey."

Haley forced herself to smile. "Great. Thanks." She waited until both the nurse and the agent had left the room to wilt back against her pillow.

She was free to go.

But where to? She'd lost her taste for geology, at least for the time being. Pushing up from the bed, she reached for her crutches. She'd been working so intensely for so long.... For the first time ever, she felt as though she needed a break.

A vacation.

The thought made her smile sadly. She didn't want a vacation; she wanted to live in a huge, cluttered ranch house with noisy, caring, loving people all around to tease and torment daily. She wanted Colorado and its wide-open skies, glorious mountains...and Cam. She wanted Cam.

But that wasn't meant to be. Not after what she'd put him and his family through.

She hadn't seen him since they'd arrived. She'd fallen asleep and he'd been gone when she'd wakened.

Just as well. It would make it easier to leave.

She tried out the crutches, tentatively moving about the room. It was clumsy and awkward, but manageable. But then she caught sight of her image in the bathroom mirror and cringed. Her hair stuck up over one ear. What little makeup she had left was under her eyes. The nurse had cleaned and bandaged her face, getting most of the blood off, but she looked gray and wan. She turned away, disgusted.

She could remember every agonizing second of their helicopter trip. From what Haley understood, Search and Rescue had searched frantically for them until it had been too dark. Then Zach had spent an uneasy night, divided between pacing at the hospital while Nellie labored, and being terrified for them.

They'd resumed their search at first light.

The helicopter crash and resulting explosion had led them right to Cam and Haley.

She knew the USGS wanted to talk to her. She'd tell them everything she knew—except how to re-create her system.

Pacing, she continued to experiment with the crutches, but soon, too soon, her muscles quivered with fatigue. And her brain hurt from thinking.

She'd never be able to forget how she'd put them all in danger. Zach could have been killed. So could Jason and Nellie, but they'd gotten out safely, thank God. And Cam... She'd nearly lost him, as well. The sight of him hanging onto the cliff by his bloody fingers as the helicopter blew up only a few feet away from him was going to haunt her forever.

On her second awkward circle around the room, Haley saw her purse. Cam had put it on the nightstand for her. That was it, then. She had everything she'd come with and there was nothing to stop her from leaving. Swinging the strap over her shoulder, she moved toward the door, but the purse kept swiveling in front of her thigh and getting caught in the crutches, making her trip.

She didn't want to go.

It hurt that she'd never see Nellie again. Or Jason and Zach. She'd have liked to say goodbye, but she had to go now, before she lost her nerve.

*Liar,* she thought. It would be too hard to say goodbye to the only people who had ever truly cared about her, and the guilt she felt would break her.

The door opened suddenly, and she stopped short.

Cam stood there, holding a fistful of wildflowers and a bag. Her heart tripped at the wonderful, familiar sight of him—the one man who'd stolen her heart, her soul, her love.

But his soft, easy smile faded when he took in the crutches and Haley reaching for the door handle. A huge frown creased his face when he spotted the purse slung over her shoulder. "You shouldn't be up. God, Haley, look at you." He tossed the flowers and the bag onto the chair and reached for her. "You're shaking. You look like you're going to pass out any second."

Backing her gently to the bed, he fretted over her while she sat stiffly, nervously. She hadn't planned on having to see him again, certainly hadn't figured on what it would do to her insides. He had a bandage on his forehead and his golden hair fell across it in a roguish sort of way. Those deep brown eyes looked at her with a mixture of affection, worry and— She slammed her own eyes shut against the onslaught of emotion that he caused.

*She had no right,* she thought as her throat closed up, no right at all to have him look at her with that much heat, that much hunger and love. "You brought me flowers," she said breathlessly.

"And a change of clothes. Why are you up?" he demanded.

He'd cleaned up, donned a fresh shirt. She tried not to notice how nicely it stretched over his shoulders. It was tucked into black jeans that had faded from too many washings, making them soft and snug enough to show off every exceptional inch of his lean hips and long legs.

Impatiently, he set his fists on his hips, bringing them to her attention. The big, gentle hands she'd come to love so much were bandaged. Because of her.

She tried to swallow the lump away, but it couldn't be budged. Damn him. Did he have to stand there looking better than any man had a right to look after the ordeal they'd been through?

"I thought you were sleeping," he accused. "I wouldn't have left if I'd known you'd wake up."

"I *was* sleeping." Couldn't he see how difficult this was for her? "I'm sleeped out, I guess."

"And ready to go," he added softly. His jaw tightened as he looked at her purse, then at the way she gripped her crutches like a lifeline. "My God. That's what you were doing when I came in just now, isn't it?"

Her guilty little start gave her away.

"Haley—"

But whatever he was going to say faded away as three grown-ups, a wheelchair and a baby all struggled to fit through the doorway at the same time.

Cam took one look at Zach, and then Jason pushing Nellie, who held the baby, and groaned audibly, confusing Haley.

"I told you *I'd* handle this," he said to them through his teeth.

Surprised by his rudeness, Haley looked at her extended family with a mixture of bittersweet pain and joy. It seemed that she would have to say goodbye, after all.

Zach squeezed past the wheelchair, coming forward to give Haley a gentle hug. "Are you doing okay?"

Cam muttered something under his breath about meddling family members.

Zach glanced at Cam, then back to Haley's tense face. "Is he being nice enough, Haley? Need me to sue him for you?"

"No, thanks." She felt a little overwhelmed by how much they obviously cared. "He's..." She looked at Cam, who had tipped his head back, studying the ceiling beseechingly, as if waiting for divine intervention. "He's being nice."

Jason scooped the bundle of joy from Nellie's lap and brought her forward to show her off. Peeling back the blanket, he revealed the sleeping infant.

"Oh," Haley whispered, reaching out to run a finger over the soft cheek. The little nose, the closed eyes, the tiny perfect red lips. Had she ever seen anything so lovely? "She's beautiful, Jason, so beautiful."

"Her name is Ally. And she looks just like me." He glanced at Cam's tight face, then grinned at Haley. "You *are* going to take mercy on him, aren't you, Haley?"

"Jas," Cam warned, taking a step toward him. "If you didn't have that baby in your arms—"

"Whoops!" Nellie covered her breasts with her hands. "I think it's time to feed the baby. Jas?"

Her husband frowned, paled. "But the doctor said you wouldn't have milk for two days—"

Ignoring him, Nellie deftly scooted the wheelchair between Cam and Jason, taking Ally back. Smiling easily, she reached for Haley's hand. "Honey, we didn't mean to intrude—"

"Then get out," Cam said, glaring at his brothers.

"But," Nellie continued serenely as if he hadn't spoken at all, "we just wanted to make sure you know how much we love you." Her voice wobbled a bit, her eyes welled. "Oh, Haley, honey, it's meant so much to have you around. I just really want you to believe that. I think of you as my best friend."

Haley's throat closed. Cam spared her a reply.

*"Out,"* he ordered in a gritty voice. "Everyone out." He held open the door, relenting when Nellie wheeled through. Bending, he gave his new niece a kiss on top of her head and squeezed Nellie's shoulder.

"Don't be mad, Cam. I just had to put my two cents in," she whispered.

Zach and Jason said nothing, just glared at Cam. One by one, they filed out, each giving Haley a last look that reminded her of Max when he was waiting to be fed.

*They wanted her to stay.*

The thrill faded quickly enough at the thunderous look on Cam's face as he carefully shut the door.

"They're—so nice," she finished lamely as he moved toward her.

"Yes," he agreed in a deceptively light voice. "They're very nice. And so meddling, too."

"They just wanted..." She trailed off, suddenly not sure what exactly they wanted.

"Yes?" He waited. "They wanted?"

"Me to stay," she whispered.

"That's right, they do. So do I."

At that unexpected admission, she fumbled, and words abruptly deserted her.

Cam had no such problem, and he advanced on her.

"Just a moment ago, when I came here, you were leaving," he accused in that same low, controlled voice with which he'd just dismissed his family. "You were actually going to walk out of here without a word." He shoved hands through his hair and turned slowly around, as if he needed the space. Then he whirled back, hitting her with those eyes. "After all we'd been through, after all we'd talked about, you would have just left?"

She looked down at her hands to avoid the grief in his voice, the agony in his eyes.

"Why, Haley?"

Her ankle throbbed, but it was nothing compared with the excruciating pain in her heart that his simple words caused. "I can't stay, Cam. You know I can't."

"I know nothing of the kind. There's no reason for you to run away. There's nothing to be frightened of anymore."

She lifted her head. "I'm more frightened now than I've ever been."

"Because of me?"

"Because of what you make me feel."

That was clearly beyond his ability to comprehend. "That's nothing to fear. I love you. For some reason, you think that's not possible, that no one could love you. But you're wrong. Nellie loves you, too, and so do my brothers. They don't want you to leave, either."

"But you're a family."

"Yes. And you've never had much of one around, have you? So let *us* be your family. Stay with us.... Marry me."

Her heart stopped.

"You heard me right," he said, nodding, watching her reaction carefully. "Marry me, Haley."

One of her crutches clattered to the floor. Slowly, his eyes holding hers, Cam bent and retrieved it, but he didn't hand it to her.

"My job," she said weakly, in a voice barely audible. "What happened before—"

"Forget what happened." Tossing the crutch across the bed

and out of her reach, he took her wrist in one hand. "As far as your work, do whatever you want, Haley. Work, don't work...I don't care. I want you, and I want you to be happy. With me."

She didn't want to think about what his caressing thumb against her palm did to her pulse. Didn't want to ignite that glimmer of hope in her heart. "I want you to be happy, too, Cam. That's why I'm going."

In a rare burst of temper, Cam snatched the other crutch from her and tossed it the way of the first. It slid noisily from the bed to the floor. "No."

Stepping back from both him and his anger, Haley let out a surprised cry as she remembered her handicap.

Eyes blazing, Cam stopped her fall, pulling her up against his hard, vital body.

"You don't get it, do you?" Tender hands swept over her, holding her close, while his eyes continued to burn. "If you leave me, I'll be as helpless as you are without those crutches." His voice broke, went hoarse as he admitted, "I was so damned lonely before you, Haley. We were *both* hiding out at the Circle C."

Tears filled her eyes and she tried to avert her face, but he tipped up her head, forcing her to stare at him and feel, *see,* each and every emotion. *"I need you,"* he whispered in an achingly husky voice. His hands soothed and coaxed a response she didn't mean to give and her body arched against him.

The glimmer of hope roared into a flame and she threw her arms around him, burying her face in his chest.

"You see?" he whispered triumphantly, spinning her around and around. "You need me, too. That doesn't make you weak, Haley. Or less of a person. Need is good. Love is good. We'll fulfill each other."

"I didn't think you could love me anymore," she managed, cupping his face because she couldn't help but touch him. Her lips hovered a breath from his. "Not after what happened. I felt so guilty."

He shook his head and held her closer. "Don't blame yourself. And never, *ever,* doubt my love for you. Promise me."

She could only nod. For a long moment they clung to each other, but finally she had to say it: "I keep expecting you to change your mind."

He pulled her more firmly to him and bent his head to kiss her neck, her jaw, her face. "I'm never going to do that. *Never.*"

Pleasure made her light-headed. Was it possible? Was it truly possible to be so loved, and to love so much in return? He caught her head in his hands and kissed her deeply enough to have her heart racing. Then he looked at her with an intensity that might have frightened her, except his tone was light and teasing. "You never found out what it was that you said in your sleep last night in the cave."

He kissed her again, before she could say anything, stealing what little breath she had left. His mouth was as firm as his body, and he tasted so good. After a minute, he lifted his head again, waiting—she knew darn well for what. She might have told him right then, but her emotions were raw and she felt dazed, dazzled by what he'd told her, all in one kiss.

And what a kiss it had been. His breath was controlled and deep, but unsteady in a way that told her exactly how affected he was. All she could think was that she no longer had a reason to leave. That he was perfect, and all hers.

Her middle rubbed against him as she leaned back in his embrace to see his expression, and she felt the rigid pressure that brought a gleam of mischief to her eye. "So tell me, now," she whispered with a small smile, her heart beating wildly against her chest. "Tell me what I said. Tell me and maybe...just maybe..." She slid her hips against his, reveling in the hardness she found there. She was rewarded by a muffled groan as he laughed and gripped her tightly.

"You can't distract me that easily." He caught her chin. "You know what I think? I think maybe you know what you said up there on the mountain." He kissed her again, softly this time, his lips barely a whisper against hers. "Don't you?"

The undisguised need in his eyes made her feel like the strongest woman on earth. "I told you what I've been too chicken to admit while awake," she said, turning her face into his hand and kissing his palm. "But awake or asleep, it'll never change." She took the biggest dare of her life. "I love you, Cam. I always will." The words were barely out before he whooped and again spun her around the room.

When her head stopped spinning, she smiled and said, "I want to be with you."

He went still. "Define 'be with.'"

It wasn't easy to explain—not when she'd kept everything inside for so long. "I want to stay in Colorado. And write." She cleared her throat and voiced her new dream. "A book."

His eyes darkened, smoldered. "A romance?"

She blushed, knowing he was thinking of her journal, and where *that* had led them. "No. I have a feeling I have all the romance I need. I mean...I want more than just to stay. I want to be Mrs. Cameron Reeves."

His eyes lit up with happiness, boosting her confidence.

"I want that more than I've wanted anything in my entire life."

His slow grin was wide and gorgeous. "Well, darlin', that makes two of us."

A cheer went up on the other side of the door. Zach's, Jason's and Nellie's voices became clear as they began to congratulate each other. Ally cried.

Cam looked at Haley, laughing. "Wait. It makes six of us."

\* \* \* \* \*

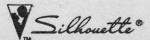

# Take 2 bestselling love stories FREE

## Plus get a FREE surprise gift!

## Special Limited-Time Offer

**Mail to Silhouette Reader Service™**

> P.O. Box 609
> Fort Erie, Ontario
> L2A 5X3

**YES!** Please send me 2 free Silhouette Intimate Moments® novels and my free surprise gift. Then send me 6 brand-new novels every month, which I will receive months before they appear in bookstores. Bill me at the low price of $3.96 each plus 25¢ delivery and GST*. That's the complete price, and a saving of over 10% off the cover prices—quite a bargain! I understand that accepting the books and gift places me under no obligation ever to buy any books. I can always return a shipment and cancel at any time. Even if I never buy another book from Silhouette, the 2 free books and the surprise gift are mine to keep forever.

345 SEN CH7Z

Name _____ (PLEASE PRINT)

Address _____ Apt. No. _____

City _____ Province _____ Postal Code _____

This offer is limited to one order per household and not valid to present Silhouette Intimate Moments® subscribers. *Terms and prices are subject to change without notice.
Canadian residents will be charged applicable provincial taxes and GST.

CIM-98

©1990 Harlequin Enterprises Limited

# COMING NEXT MONTH